BED-STUY IS BURNING

BED-STUY
IS BURNING

A Novel

BRIAN PLATZER

ATRIA BOOKS

New York · London · Toronto · Sydney · New Delhi

ATRIA
BOOKS

An Imprint of Simon & Schuster, Inc.
1230 Avenue of the Americas
New York, NY 10020

First Atria Books hardcover edition July 2017

ATRIA BOOKS and colophon are trademarks of Simon & Schuster, Inc.

For information about special discounts for bulk purchases, please contact Simon & Schuster Special Sales at 1-866-506-1949 or business@simonandschuster.com.

The Simon & Schuster Speakers Bureau can bring authors to your live event. For more information or to book an event, contact the Simon & Schuster Speakers Bureau at 1-866-248-3049 or visit our website at www.simonspeakers.com.

Interior design by Dana Sloan

Manufactured in the United States of America

10 9 8 7 6 5 4 3 2 1

Library of Congress Cataloging-in-Publication Data

Names: Platzer, Brian, author.
Title: Bed-Stuy is burning : a novel / Brian Platzer.
Description: New York : Atria Books, 2017. | Includes bibliographical references and index.
Identifiers: LCCN 2016032068 (print) | LCCN 2016039359 (ebook) | ISBN 9781501146954 (hardcover : alk. paper) | ISBN 9781501146961 (trade pbk. : alk. paper) | ISBN 9781501146978 (eBook)
Subjects: LCSH: Bankers—Fiction. | Neighborhoods—Fiction. | Gentrification—Fiction. | Social conflict—Fiction. | City and town life—Fiction. | Change (Psychology)—Fiction. | Bedford-Stuyvesant (New York, N.Y.)—Fiction. | Psychological fiction.
Classification: LCC PS3616.L389 B43 2017 (print) | LCC PS3616.L389 (ebook) | DDC 813/.6—dc23
LC record available at https://lccn.loc.gov/2016032068

ISBN 978-1-5011-4695-4
ISBN 978-1-5011-4697-8 (ebook)

For Alex

Then they said, "Come, let us build ourselves a city, with a tower that reaches to the heavens, so that we may make a name for ourselves; otherwise we will be scattered over the face of the whole earth."

But the Lord came down to see the city and the tower the people were building. The Lord said, "If as one people speaking the same language they have begun to do this, then nothing they plan to do will be impossible for them. Come, let us go down and confuse their language so they will not understand each other."

—GENESIS 11:4–7

12 YEARS OLD
10 SHOTS

Jason Blau was walking home
carrying a video game
controller

The Police Killed him—
SHOT HIM TEN TIMES

THIS MUST END!
BY ANY MEANS NECESSARY

We will obey no more

MONDAY MORNING WE
STOP FOLLOWING
THEIR RULES

#12yearsold10shots   #bedstuyrising

Part 1: Rosh Hashanah

Chapter 1

Things were good. As good as they'd been in years. Maybe ever. IPhone in hand, Aaron lay in bed and focused the baby monitor app's display in on Simon's little chest rising and falling. Then out, in order to see Simon's hands and feet. They were fiery white blobs against the flat-white crib mattress sheet. The infrared light shone from his son's skin in the next room over. It shone from his baby's face, fingers, and toes. Aaron focused the display in, and the light shined from Simon's nose and cheeks.

"What?"

"What?" Aaron said.

"You were laughing," Amelia said.

"Was I?"

He tried to direct his thoughts away from Simon, though not toward the next day's numbers at work.

Amelia read *People* magazine in bed next to him. On the back of the folded-over page: "Hot MOMMAS! Celebrities are showing off their BABY BUMPS this summer!"

The featured Hot Momma wore pink bikini bottoms and a humongous floppy hat that hid her face. She cradled her pregnant belly with one arm and covered her bare breasts with her other, the hand of which held a giant untouched cupcake. "These

Hot Mommas Are Eating for Two!" read the caption below. Except the Hot Momma hadn't been eating at all. Aaron could see her collarbone and shoulders jutting out of her taut skin. She was suffering, the Hot Momma, and it needed to stop. Someone had to save her. The Hot Momma looked malnourished, starving, obscenely pregnant, and forced to pose with a monstrous strawberry cupcake.

Aaron shook off the thought. He was trying to shake off thoughts like these lately. Thoughts that brought attention to imaginary injustices. Maybe the Hot Momma was blessed with a high metabolism. Which was part of what made her so hot. She was a movie star, Aaron remembered. Maybe she'd devour that cupcake and ten dozen more.

Aaron tried to relax. He was lucky to live on this block—the nicest block in Bed-Stuy—and lucky to be sharing a life with Amelia and Simon, who breathed steadily on the video feed in Aaron's hand. He was lucky to have a baby who looked just like him. Everybody said it. *Well, we know whose baby this is!* Both Aaron and Simon had hardly any neck and tiny ears. Aaron had never been proud of his tiny ears before. They both had little bug noses, too. Amelia said their noses were cute on both of them.

Aaron thought it might be slightly narcissistic to enjoy looking at his boy as much as he did. Before he went to sleep, he pretended to be working on his phone sometimes. But he was gazing at Simon—even though at night the infrared light meant all he could see were gray patches and blindingly white ones. He watched the bright packet that was his son's chest rise and fall. He thought about how funny it was that this little baby was going to grow up with him as a father, with Amelia as a mother.

With these neighbors as neighbors. That this life would be this baby's life. That this baby's father was an investment manager and this baby's mother profiled celebrities for glossy magazines. Aaron reminded himself to breathe. To slow down his breath. Nobody felt relaxed on Sunday evenings.

Chapter 2

You up?" Amelia asked. It was two, three, four in the morning. She wrenched her neck to see the clock: 4:05 according to its spectral red light. Simon was whimpering still—again. It meant he was alive, at least. SIDS was mysterious enough to claim sleeping children in the night, their whimpers signs of life.

"Mm," Aaron said.

"I want to sleep," she said. "But I can't." Lying in bed was the only time Amelia didn't feel as though she was about to fall asleep. She didn't sleep anymore, nor was she ever fully awake.

"I know," he said. "Just try. Rest at least. Resting is something."

"Everything is something," she said.

"Resting is a particular kind of something," he whispered. "A good kind."

Her body was moving through interstellar depths. Everything around her—stars, planets, galaxies—was something. She was something, and Aaron was something, and little Simon was something. And when they all died, they'd still be something—only something different. Death was something. Everything was something. Even the darkness through which she floated was something.

"Dark matter," she murmured.

"What?" Aaron asked.

She'd been sleeping, or not-quite-sleeping. "Simon! Is Simon okay?" she said.

"You're confused. Rest. Try to rest."

"'The only important thing is rest,'" she said. She was quoting Aaron quoting his mother.

He rolled toward her and put a hand on her thigh.

"Hot momma," he said.

She rolled away.

Chapter 3

A few years back, Aaron was still a rabbi, but he already disbelieved. Belief had never been at the core of his rabbinical path. Aaron had wanted to help people through their problems. He had wanted to lead the community. He had wanted to give speeches. He enjoyed analyzing literature, and in this case the Bible would do. Additionally, he was someone people liked talking to. He was reliable. He was a good listener, and he made people feel heard. He was young and bright, and people were proud of him—even people who'd just met him—and he'd spend hours, days if necessary, at temple, their homes or hospitals, sitting with them and listening. He had a way of sitting and listening where he tried to anticipate what someone was going to say next and ask it as a question, like, "And you must have been furious?" so they said, "Yes, exactly!" which made them feel very close to Aaron. It wasn't a pretend feeling. It was real. Kindness, intelligence, sympathy—these were the most important attributes a rabbi could have, Aaron thought.

The problem was that unless you're a psychologist, too, it turns out that the only way you're going to truly help someone as a rabbi is through God. Sure, you can tell them that what mitigates the death of their son is that he'll live on in their memory. But how does that make things better?

In fact, it makes things worse. All that meant, really, was: Don't suffer, because you can spend the rest of your life in pain over your son's sudden death. And when she asked how God could allow such a thing to happen, the only tolerable answer was that God didn't exist. What could another answer be? That God was testing her? How, by murdering her son? That it all fit into a larger plan? How is that helpful? That God was punishing her? That could only lead to more pain. The truth—that life is unfair (or, better yet, a-fair? non-fair?) and she must do her best not to allow her suffering to define her—this had nothing to do with religion at all. This was, as he'd understood it in his undergraduate philosophy class, existentialism. What he believed was that there was no greater meaning, so mankind was responsible for creating his own meaning. But in the position he often found himself—counseling someone in the face of tragedy, telling a woman that it was her responsibility to create meaning from that tragedy—it seemed cruel. This was a moment when God should step in. But God never stepped in. And Aaron didn't know how to. Aaron profoundly felt the lack of a higher power in his inability to ease his congregants' pain. All Aaron had was himself, and that wasn't enough. Aaron began to suffer. He stopped sleeping. He began to feel his congregants' pain as his own.

An itch, a tickle—frustration that grew into impotent ache. His inability to help gnawed at him. It was shameful. People came to Aaron with pain—real pain that caused real tears and ruined lives—and he met them with platitudes.

It will pass.

I know it hurts.

You're not to blame.

He met them with nothing. Even if he wanted to believe in

God, even if he *did* believe in God, Aaron's inability to channel God into lasting comfort for members of his congregation or—especially—for himself was more than shameful. It was intolerable. God hadn't been able to save Aaron's great-grandparents. God hadn't been able to save Aaron's mother. And God wasn't doing much of a job with Aaron. The whole enterprise was an intolerable shame. He stopped being able to bear it.

The reason God never stepped in was because Aaron hadn't been good enough to bring him in. Once Aaron had realized this, he put the realization away. But he couldn't keep it away, and it constantly returned to persecute him.

Even if Aaron could have proven that the sacrifice of that woman's son had been somehow worth it because of what would happen afterward in her life, his unique position as a rabbi in the century after the Holocaust of the Jews made that answer, rational or not, insulting to all those who were murdered and all those who'd lost so many of their loved ones, like Aaron's now-deceased grandmother.

It was all so agonizing and mixed up in Aaron's mind.

That Aaron's great-grandparents—all eight—were taken in the Holocaust had once been another reason Aaron had believed he *should* be a rabbi. In addition to the fact that being a rabbi seemed to match his interests and that, more than anything else, he wanted for himself the particular kind of respect given to kind, hardworking, capable leaders in the community, he felt he owed it to the history of his family to become entrenched in the religion he doubted. *If Adolf Hitler and hordes of Germans murdered so many of my family members because they were a certain thing, I should become that thing even more.* That was what he believed, and, more than believed, that was what he felt down to the core of his being: that he should live his life in a way to redress the horrors that had come before him. And when Aaron graduated at the top of his rabbinical class having already been awarded a prestigious internship, which quickly became a permanent position, at Rohr Shalom, the Upper East Side's most prominent synagogue, he saw his grandmother's beaming eighty-year-old face—her cane propped against her chair—and knew he'd done right.

. . .

That was only six years ago.

His grandmother had since passed away. She died happy because of him. His mother had since passed away. She died in pain from cancer and the chemotherapy and radiation. Aaron lost his congregation to the extent they were ever his, and now he could no longer open a Gideons' Bible in a motel room without feeling disappointment and shame.

The story, more or less:

It was a sure thing. A tip, in passing, from an agent—the father of a boy studying for his bar mitzvah, of all people. A college quarterback was hurt, and the backup didn't know the system. Aaron was going to repay the money to the synagogue. He just needed it over the weekend. He needed it to win one bet. Then he'd pay it back, settle his own debts, and stop the craziness. At this point, Aaron owed a hundred thousand dollars, and his own bank account was empty. His savings were gone. The bookie wouldn't take another bet from him on spec once he owed that much. Aaron needed this bet to settle his accounts. His bookie had been threatening to show up at the synagogue to collect. Aaron didn't believe that he would cut him off like that and lose the cash flow, but there was always a chance.

It had started a year or two earlier. Aaron had gone on a few all-night benders to see if drinking could make his work any easier, but it had only made him feel worse. Like he was getting further from God. Like he was somehow conclusively demonstrating God didn't exist. He was drunk online one night when he clicked on an ad for online poker, and everything changed. He felt good for the first time in years. He felt great. He felt like the first time he'd realized a girl was interested in him. Chance. Risk. And something he could control with a previously untapped inner strength. He won a few dollars that night. And then he gave himself over to a higher power he did believe in. Math. Skill. But mostly sheer luck. He couldn't sleep. But not because of pain or empathy or philosophical uncertainty. Because of excitement. He'd get home at 4 p.m. or 9 p.m. depending on what service he led and go right to the computer, fall asleep at four, five in the morning, and wake up excited to get right back on.

Then Saratoga in the summers. Belmont in the fall. Trips to AC and Mohegan Sun. A bookie in New York. Football season was the best. The worst. Every week betting on the spread. Money lines. Over/unders. Knockout pools. Three-team teasers. He was good at it. It made his professional life tolerable. When he was lying to his congregation or unable to help folks in pain, he thought about the rush to come that evening. In the beginning he won more than he lost. Which, in retrospect, was lucky and disastrous. It was what he imagined God was supposed to feel like—when God answered your prayers. The only time he caught himself praying was at the end of a close game. The irony wasn't lost on him.

So with an empty bank account and inside information, a hundred thousand dollars in debt to a gangster who was going to ruin Aaron's career, he took a risk. He grabbed money where he had access to it. All four rabbis had the synagogue debit card. He put on a suit and his kippah, and at the Citibank around the corner, he transferred fifty thousand dollars into cash. Forty-eight hours later, he had tripled his money. It was the best night of his life. He'd spent it sober, alone, in shorts and a T-shirt watching TV on his couch. The next morning, he paid his debt to the bookie. Returned to the Citibank. Transferred the funds back where they belonged. And first thing Monday morning, the senior rabbi called him into his office and fired him.

The senior rabbi received alerts every time anyone touched the account.

Aaron didn't admit wrongdoing. "The temple funds were never in any danger," he said.

"Wait a minute. You took that money out of the account to gamble?" the senior rabbi asked. "I had no idea."

"It was a sure thing," Aaron said.

The two men stared at each other. Aaron fought a longing to be hugged. The senior rabbi told him to vacate the premises.

. . .

The first therapist Aaron saw afterward asked him if maybe he was punishing himself—if he'd known he'd get caught because of course there'd be a paper trail. Aaron believed now, lying in bed on a Sunday night six years later, the same thing he responded to the therapist then, which was that he honestly didn't think so. He'd needed the money. He'd withdrawn cash a few times from the synagogue's account and it had never been an issue. As much as five grand once, for the annual singles mixer. He had no reason to believe the senior rabbi had been alerted then.

13

He could have taken a leave of absence and traveled, he told the therapist, eventually ending his relationship with his synagogue in a much less painful way. He sincerely didn't believe he'd wanted to get caught.

This was the worst thing that had ever happened to him. This was Aaron's, to use a Christian concept, original sin. Without it, he'd still be a rabbi. Happy or suffering, he had no idea. But he'd still be comforting families when they needed it most. Or he could have retired. Written books or articles. Continued to gamble or stopped. Worked on Wall Street. But not this. It was the worst thing he'd ever done.

Thirty-one years old with no job, no savings, and shame—the polar opposite of the self-satisfaction he'd spent his entire life up to that point accruing. He'd had to stay in New York City because he couldn't leave his father alone with his arthritis, severe sciatica, and isolation, so Aaron found a job at an investment firm. He told the HR representative that he had had a crisis of faith and needed a career change. She asked surprisingly few questions. Between his analytical, moral background and his mind newly trained in running numbers, Aaron did well with his clients and took on new ones quickly. He met Amelia. They made Simon.

• • •

This was the story Aaron told himself most nights before he fell asleep. Or this was the story that prevented him from falling asleep. It was time to sleep. Amelia was asleep with her bedside lamp on and an open *People* magazine between them. Simon would be up in two or three hours. Aaron had work in the morning. Before long, Antoinette would be ringing at the door.

Chapter 4

Love you," Aaron said. It was two minutes or maybe ten minutes later. Four fifteen.

"You, too," Amelia said.

Aaron liked to touch Amelia's shoulders, and she liked to be touched there. He loved her, her skin.

"Mmm," she purred.

That's nice, he thought.

Mmm, she thought.

He crept his hand down her lower back.

"I'm so tired," she heard herself say in the voice of the most tired person in the history of the world. She sounded to herself as though she was suffering—as though she was very, very ill, and very brave to be speaking at all, through the pain. Cholera, ty-phoid fever. She was a pioneer woman crossing the plains in a covered wagon and she was dying. Who would take care of her seven children? Simon, Simon, Simon, Simon, Simon, Simon, and Simon. Aaron might be a respected money manager, but he couldn't take care of—

"Maybe we could . . ." Aaron said. "Just super quick."

She wouldn't make it. The oldest Simon would have to fend for himself and all the other Simons. Would he know what to do to survive on his own? Could he hunt? Did he remember where she'd set the traps? Did he know how to bargain with Indians? Had she raised him right? She'd tried to be a good mother but it was hard. The world was cruel and pressed against you from all sides.

Aaron slid his hand down the side of her body to her hip. He wedged the tip of two or three fingers beneath the band of her underwear.

Amelia lived in Bedford-Stuyvesant, Brooklyn, New York City, and the Indians the white people hadn't killed lived in poverty in glorified ghettos or ran casinos, and her boyfriend was a good man who provided for her and her Simons, and there was only one Simon, and he was in the next room. Did really big Indian reservations have representatives in Congress to fight for them? she wondered. She'd Google it first thing in the morning. The real morning. Exhausted, she lay still.

Aaron rolled away.

He was a good man. She rolled toward him. She should try. For him. To make his life less stressful. To keep him stable. But she couldn't. She was too tired.

"She said that now that I've stopped breast-feeding, it would come back soon," Amelia said. "Give it a few more weeks. For the drive to return."

"I know," Aaron said. "I love you."

"I love you, too," Amelia said.

Amelia and Aaron's passion had never been primarily physical. Not as it had been with Amelia's first husband—her only husband— when everything else had been terrible. Not terrible. Just . . . tiring. Amelia's life had always been tiring. That wasn't true. But tired now, Amelia couldn't remember a time when she hadn't been tired.

Aaron, whom she hadn't married, was more of a husband than Kevin, Amelia's actual husband, had ever been. There was a real connection with Aaron; he needed her, and until the baby at least, she'd always enjoyed sex with Aaron—it had felt like a deeper more urgent kind of communication. And now she loved Aaron very much, and she loved their son very much—if "love" was the word for what one felt toward a baby—and she loved their life very much, if "love" was the word for what one felt toward a life, and they'd chosen a capable baby-sitter—

"You asleep?" Amelia said.

"Yes," he said, unsure.

"Tomorrow we need cash for Antoinette's MetroCard," she said.

"I've got it laid out already on the table," he said. He'd gone to the bank in the afternoon. Taken out $120 for the $116.50 card. What was *Monday Night's* money line? He could wait a day, make the bet, and give her MetroCards for the next two months. But he wouldn't. He wouldn't even think about it. He would do his best not even to think about it.

"Love you," she said.

"Good night," he said. "Love you."

"I'll be here when Antoinette leaves tomorrow," she said. "I'll be working from home."

"Okay, but I should be home, too."

"Good," she said.

"We can make the ravioli," he said.

Chapter 5

"—NYPD's critics object, in particular, to the department's long-standing practice of maintaining order in public spaces. You're listening to New York Public Radio, WNYC 93.9 FM, AM 820. Police Commissioner Bratton continued: 'This practice, widely referred to as 'broken windows' or quality-of-life or order-maintenance policing, asserts that in communities contending with high levels of disruption, maintaining order not only improves the quality of life for residents, it also reduces opportunities for more serious crime. Indeed, the broken-windows metaphor is one of deterioration: a building where a broken window goes unrepaired will soon be subject to far more extensive vandalism—because it sends a message that the building owners (and, by extension, the police) cannot or will not control minor crimes, and thus will be unable to deter more serious ones.' Commissioner Bratton concluded: 'A neighborhood where minor offenses go unchallenged soon becomes a breeding ground for more serious criminal activity and, ultimately, for violen—' "

Amelia's hand found the off button and she swung her feet out of bed. Having just stopped breast-feeding the week before, she wasn't accustomed to stumbling downstairs to the kitchen for Simon's bottle of formula.

Simon. He was in the room next door. He was stirring, cooing, jabbering . . . soon he'd be screaming, and, as the radio hadn't awoken Aaron, Amelia wanted to let Aaron sleep. She'd never thought she'd be the type to look after her men. She liked being awake when Aaron was sleeping and Simon was up but not yet conscious.

She reveled in the potential energy of the day. The neighborhood was brimming with life. Her neighbors, who had been mistreated for years, seemed ready for some kind of reckoning. There'd been protests on the street the day before. Chanting and praying. She wondered what would come of it.

In the kitchen downstairs, in order to mix the formula, she did a little dance, jumping up and down with the eight-ounce bottle. Her own protest against the morning ritual. She tried to jump and kick her feet off to the side and land gracefully again, and she succeeded!

She was a superwoman, she thought. She knocked back a swig of seltzer and felt the burn of bubbles down her throat. The coffee machine had been timed correctly! She drank a quarter cup scalding and black.

A working, mothering, girlfriending, housekeeping superhero! You see—it could be done!

Amelia hadn't experienced any of the postpartum depression she'd read about. She was generally hungry to have the world see her as she saw herself, but this wasn't depression, it was ambition. She wanted to be a success. A writer. A mother. Not a wife, necessarily, but the family woman her own mother had never cared about being. But Amelia also wanted to lean in. Now that Kevin was far behind her, she had so much to give, and she wanted to give it to Simon, to Aaron, and to the world. She wanted to be present for those she loved. She felt she should be important, and being a mother was at least important to one person. It was the most important person in the world to one person.

She remembered her own mother standing over her bed. Amelia must have been ten or eleven.

"Rub my back?" Amelia had mustered the courage to ask.

Her mother was distracted.

"Just for a minute?"

Her mother sighed, and Amelia felt a hand on the covers, but her mother was already out of the room, watching TV or preparing to go out.

Amelia vowed not to ask for affection again.

Now there were moments Amelia empathized with her mother—moments when she resented her son—but those felt normal, and fleeting. Not a product of depression as much as common sense. No one wanted to be out of bed before sunrise mixing formula and water. No one wanted to be exhausted, to clean poop off thighs and her fingers, to smell like sour milk and be cried at and have no time to herself or interest in sex. But more often, she wanted to feel—and did feel deeply—what she suspected her own mother hadn't felt for anyone.

She wanted to write about the emotions of motherhood, about how she still wasn't sure "love" was the right word for what she felt for her son. Simon was so vulnerable, so needy. He needed her so much, but when the object of love couldn't reciprocate love, was the emotion a mother felt "love" or something more than love or less than love or just different? Like why would what one felt for a baby who couldn't talk or do anything at all be the same word for what one felt for a lover or a parent? They were all strong emotions, but calling them the same word wasn't right. The emotion Amelia felt for her mother had something to do with the emotion she felt for Aaron, but those two emotions had almost nothing to do with what she felt for this needy little wormy thing that had come out of her body. She felt toward all three of them powerfully, but to call it all love seemed lazy. Or paltry. Or something. When everyone asked her if she loved Simon more than she'd ever loved anything, the answer wasn't yes. It wasn't exactly no, but it wasn't yes. It was a feeling she was sure a lot of mothers must share, and she wanted to find the right language for it. The French probably said *l'amour de l'enfant.* Or did that mean the love a child felt? No one in the world knew how to talk about what Amelia was feeling.

Now she was back upstairs. Caffeinated. Looking out a window onto the cross street for any signs of protest or disruption, although she knew both were unlikely at this early hour. A twelve-year-old boy had been killed by cops who'd thought he'd had a gun. They had shot him ten times. Yesterday—Sunday—Amelia had considered joining the marches in front of her house, but when she opened her door all the women were wearing dresses and yellow or purple hats, coming right from church, so she wouldn't have belonged. Still, she was on their side and wanted them to know. She joined the Twitter anger with a #12yearsold-10shots tweet of her own. **A child killed because of scared, overaggressive police. Proud of my neighbors for speaking back to power #12yearsold10shots,** she'd written before going to sleep.

But this morning, no one unusual was outside. All she saw were some preteens laughing and eating chips on the way to school. She sat down with Simon in the glider rocking chair, and he was so focused on the bottle that maybe what Amelia's swelling heart felt was exactly and only love.

Her skin thrilled to her baby's. In her lap in the glider, unswaddled and changed, he was just in a tiny puffy diaper. His arms and legs and chest and back were fresh and sticky, not as dirty surfaces are sticky but as elastic ones like taut cellophane can be. His skin was fragrant and delicate like a summer peach or the pages of a new book. Or the pages of an antique book. Or his whole body was like an olive? Or a tongue! He was squirming and then relaxing very quickly and then squirming again. And smiling. And ducking. Like a boxer. Or a duck. Sucking, then refusing the bottle. Maybe because it was formula and not milk from her body. Looking up at her and resisting, resting, squirming again. Until he found and sucked at the bottle in earnest.

Three or four minutes earlier, she'd been groggy and still thinking half thoughts about essays she didn't want to write, but Simon's skin had made her come alive. She was thrilled to be liberated from the filling and emptying of the milk from her breasts. The early light through the stained-glass windows was cream colored as in a church, and Amelia could almost cry with a sharp morning joy.

Simon wasn't the love of her life yet. But the way all he cared about in the world was the bottle—at this moment, he was so trusting. So attentive. And she controlled the bottle. It was like she never knew any living thing could be so attentive until her son's whole body found the formula sucking its way down into his stomach, and nothing else mattered to either of them.

She couldn't wait until he could really hug her back. Until he could love her back! She wasn't sure if there was such thing as nonreciprocal love. That was what she wanted to write about. But somehow his fragility made up for his inability to love. It was hard to believe he had lived inside her longer than he had lived outside her

She couldn't wait until he could talk!

Simon stopped sucking at the formula and quickly lost

interest even though Amelia knew he must still be hungry. His suck wasn't as strong as it was supposed to be, but the doctor said it wasn't weak enough to raise any real concern yet. He was putting on weight on the low side of normal, but still close enough to normal not to be worried.

Aaron called it the "A-word" and made Amelia promise not to say it anymore, though she had only actually said it two or three times. If Simon *were* autistic—Amelia thought, looking at the baby's tiny arms, his hands, each little perfect finger, each fingernail (wasn't it amazing that his nails had grown inside her body?)—she'd want to run from Simon and remember him for the rest of his life as he was right now when he was a six-month-old little baby just like the other little babies.

Chapter 6

Aaron shoveled cereal into his mouth, reviewing Friday's stream on his computer. Amelia felt it was an invasion of Antoinette's privacy, but Aaron didn't care. Simon was currently in the crib down one floor sleeping off his bottle, while Amelia was in the shower. Aaron wanted to spend his twenty minutes before work watching what his son's day had been like the Friday before.

The software allowed Aaron to watch at ten, twenty, or fifty-times the normal speed, so a whole day took from a few minutes to a few hours, and whenever there was a loud noise or something unusual it would automatically slow down. When Antoinette took Simon out to the park or when Simon was sleeping, the system would skip over those parts, but when Antoinette and Simon were working on tummy time—Aaron had placed the mat in front of the hidden-camera clock—Aaron could see how she handled Simon, if she paid close enough attention to him, if she was too aggressive with him, that kind of thing.

And it wasn't just a way to monitor an employee to whom he paid good money. (He paid her in cash. It was a weekly test of his resolve. He'd passed the test, mostly. Paid Antoinette her stack of seven fifties each week, wincing but taking nothing for himself.

He hadn't bet this football season. Or preseason. Nothing since the NBA finals. Handing her that money each week was a sign that he was starting to be in control.) The video also helped him feel closer to his son. Other than over the weekends, he hardly saw Simon, who tended to be napping when Aaron left for the day and was usually down for the night by the time Aaron got home.

Sure, Aaron was watching to make sure Antoinette didn't abuse his baby, but he loved watching Simon's face as he struggled on his stomach for another ten seconds—as his facial expression turned from concentration to tears. Aaron wanted to quit his job sometimes as he watched this lady build his son's muscles, but before too long he was very happy to have a job that gave him something to do other than roll his baby over. The changing diapers and feeding bottles he actually liked—but how did Antoinette manage the boredom of all the time in between?

And of course the surveillance also had something to do with the gambling. If Aaron could live a public life as a rabbi and an internal one so far away from the bimah; if he could ruin his professional life, a life that had taken so many years of preparation, study, and perseverance—he didn't trust a nanny not to lose herself for a moment and shake the shit out of his baby just because she'd had a bad weekend at home and wanted to get some aggression out (and Simon wouldn't stop crying, and the police didn't respect her, and she thought no one was watching). So Aaron made sure to watch.

What Aaron's newest psychologist said was that because Aaron had a secret that fucked up his life, he needed to make sure other people didn't let their secrets fuck up Aaron's life, too. Aaron said that sounded pretty much right.

"Does that sound healthy to you?" the psychologist had asked.

"It sounds sensible to me," Aaron had said.

"So you are okay with constantly monitoring every aspect of your life to ensure that no one allows their inner lives to spill out into yours?"

"I am okay with monitoring the woman who spends all day alone with my son, yes," Aaron had said. He waited for the psychologist to do something with that. From experience, he knew that a rabbi would give people advice, which was grounded in his own interpretation of the Torah and his interpretation of other people's interpretations of the Torah. Aaron had expected the psychologist to do something similar. But, uselessly, he had ended the conversation there.

"Okay," the psychologist had said. "If you've thought it out and you're okay with monitoring her, then that's good," he'd said.

"And you're sure you've got your own life under control now?" the psychologist had said next session. "Or is this monitoring of your son's nanny easier than monitoring yourself?"

"I've been better lately," Aaron had said.

And that was that.

. . .

So far, video of the previous Friday morning had been the same as every day for the last few weeks: the tummy time, the feeding, the disappearance to take naps or walk to the park or around the block. Antoinette was about Aaron's and Amelia's age. Midthirties, probably. A thick build and pretty, with bangs and full, attractive, smiling lips. Antoinette had been hiding herself, though, for the past week or so, under a scarf wrapped around her head. Either way, Aaron trusted her as much as he could have trusted any nanny in just the few months she'd been working for him. These morning computer sessions built his trust. Antoinette had figured out the same tricks Aaron and Amelia had discovered to wiggle the bottle into Simon's mouth, to tease Simon's lips by pulling the nipple out and making Simon lean forward for it.

But then, halfway through Friday's afternoon bottle—and Simon was really drinking well, drinking better and faster than Aaron had ever seen Simon drink from his or Amelia's own arms—Antoinette looked down at Simon so her bangs covered her eyes, and though Simon was still drinking really well, she pulled the bottle from his mouth, and without breaking eye contact, put the bottle down on the side table and lifted Simon up off her lap.

Simon had lately been getting better at eye contact. Amelia worried about things like this—eye contact, neck musculature—so Aaron wanted to grab her out of the shower one floor down and bring her up into the office to watch, but instead he chose to savor the moment alone.

Antoinette—bottle now to her side—lifted Simon up so his dangling feet grazed the top of her thighs. She sang in a sweet, optimistic voice:

Show me your motion
Tra la la la la
Come on show me your motion
Tra la la la la la
Show me your motion
Tra la la la la
You look like a sugar in a plum
Plum plum.

She supported Simon's neck with one hand and took the rest of his weight with the other hand under one of his arms, and she held him there, the two of them looking at each other. First Simon screwed up his face and smooshed his eyes closed and his lips together, but then he relaxed. She smiled, and Simon made a noise, a nice noise, then Antoinette smiled again. And she kind of shook Simon, but up and down, in a playful way.

Simon must have liked it, because even though he had just drunk formula, he let out a little laugh, and Antoinette put the hand that had been supporting Simon's neck around under his armpit, so both hands were now supporting his body and neither supported his neck, and Simon was fine, supporting his own head, and laughing. Aaron's son was laughing. Aaron had never seen Simon laugh or fully support his own neck. This was unbelievable. It was a movie. But it was real, and it was about his son. It was Simon. And Antoinette didn't stop there. Simon was laughing loudly and Antoinette tossed him in the air a little bit, and Simon laughed even more. Aaron had never heard Simon giggle. Whinny, sure, but this was a much older child's laugh and it was sustained. It started like a cartoon evil laugh, a villain's laugh, deep and silly, but as it continued it grew into something even deeper and funnier, coming from a source of real pleasure, as though Antoinette was causing Simon real pleasure.

Aaron panicked.

His son was growing older, months older in the span of a minute in the arms of the nanny on the computer screen. Aaron finished his cereal and he wanted to hide what he'd seen from Amelia. It would upset her. His son, no longer six months old, was a year old, or two. He imagined running these numbers—six months, twelve, twenty-four—into an algorithm that would guarantee exactly who Simon would be when he was Aaron's age. How old were babies when they could hold their own heads up? When they could laugh? He had no idea. But what was he thinking? He did know now. It was on the screen right in front of him. They were six months old. His boy was one of them.

He'd be late for work, and there might be delays—more protests or the cops taking extra precaution. That poor boy and his family. He couldn't even imagine. He'd been watching his own son for nearly a half hour. Simon was resting after his first bottle. Amelia was drying her hair. But next weekend he wanted to make his son laugh like that. Or tonight, even if it was late. He'd wake Simon up. He wanted to be the one to make him feel that good.

Chapter 7

Every morning at 7:00 sharp Antoinette arrived wearing red or purple nurse's scrubs and listening to spiritual music on her iPhone. Seven o'clock sharp meant leaving her home at 6:15 to catch the A train at 6:23.

This morning, the streets were lined with angry flyers taped to trees, lampposts, and metal gates. Antoinette had read on Facebook about Jason Blau, but the cops never bothered her or Teddy. She always made sure Teddy looked respectable. If this boy's death had been an accident, people had the right to be angry, but everyone made mistakes.

She listened to her church's chorus sing "Oh Devil, God shall defeat you!" which would be the soundtrack to Antoinette's own performance the following Sunday. Antoinette was in a period of spiritual transition. She still danced at church every Sunday afternoon. It was the highlight of her week. Listening to that music, and rising up, up above it. But for more than a week now, she'd also worn the hijab. She didn't see it as a contradiction—wearing the hijab and dancing at church. She took it off at church. And the Bible pretty much said that the hijab was right.

Charm is deceitful and beauty is vain, but a woman who fears the Lord is to be praised. This was something Pastor V had talked to her about the day before at prayer dance, and it was something that rang true given the path of her life to this point. That was one reason she had been wearing scrubs for a year now, her hair tied back, with bangs and no lipstick. It was like a secular hijab. Like *don't look at me sexually*. But the hijab was easier. It was what had attracted her to Islam to begin with. One of the many things (the low-ceilinged rooms, the carpet on her toes, how many women welcomed her arrival with no judgment or questions), and why she'd started taking Teddy to mosque services in Clinton Hill on Friday nights. The only makeup she'd owned for years was stage makeup for her prayer dance. Her lips had always gotten her in trouble. She hadn't realized she could look beautiful until she was sixteen. Then at eighteen she was done with all that. But it was only now, approaching thirty, that she understood why it was so important not to look beautiful. Because beauty got in the way of what was important. It got in the way of the spirit. Beauty was vain.

So even if she wanted to make a new friend, that didn't mean she needed to be vain about it. If Jupiter admired her, he would like her under the hijab. He would admire her eyes. If he admired her at all. It had been a couple of months now, his coming over. They had only ever met inside Aaron and Amelia's house. But she had to admit she looked forward to his visits. She had never had a father. She hadn't had a lover since Teddy's father. And she didn't necessarily want either. But she did look forward to his visits. All Jupiter had said so far about the hijab was that it made her eyes pop. She liked that word. Pop!

Antoinette liked walking to work from the Utica subway station, thinking about the day to come, nodding and offering good morning to faces that looked like hers. Unlike where her previous employer had lived in Cobble Hill, this was a neighborhood that felt like a neighborhood even when she could feel the anger in the air chirping alongside the birds. My God, it was a beautiful day. And she liked the trees. They were well taken care of, with signs like "The poop fairy doesn't live here. Scoop your poop." She thought that was funny.

In most places in Brooklyn, and everywhere in Manhattan, people didn't nod and say good morning, but in this area of Bedford-Stuyvesant they did. The black people did, at least, and nine of ten faces were black. Antoinette walked against the crowd. No one else was walking away from the subway station to the houses. Everyone was nodding to her, finding solidarity in their anger. Jaws locked, eyes focused and intense, they looked like they were heading off to battle. As though on an unspoken mission against a common enemy.

After her previous employer moved out to Jersey, Antoinette went on Sittercity.com, and in less then a week, she received three requests for interviews. The first one was with a family in Manhattan, and the second one was with Amelia and Aaron. She'd always wanted to work for a rich family in Manhattan, but during the interview with Aaron and Amelia, she'd seen a tall bookshelf of all types of spiritual books. Half were in Hebrew, and the other half were in English. When Simon took naps, she read. She read holy books and books about holy books. She didn't care that the books were Jewish. Muslims believed Abraham was a prophet, too. Abraham and Jesus both. She looked up words she didn't know on her iPhone and saved them to memorize and test herself later. A lot of the books had strong bindings and others were very thin and bound in twine and cheap paper that was almost the same as pastel-colored construction paper. They were clearly used, not just for show. Antoinette read the books, then put them right back where she found them every time.

It was a problem that Simon couldn't fall asleep without being rocked and that he couldn't stay asleep with any noise in the house. But Antoinette was confident she could cure him of that. They'd only been together three months, and already they were working on tummy time for two minutes straight. Aaron and Amelia had a hidden camera in a clock facing the couch where they set up Antoinette with the Pack 'n Play, but Antoinette didn't mind. Simon was their child. Their son. It was their right to look in on him when they wished. So whenever she held Simon or fed him, sang to him, played with him, read to him, did tummy time or anything like that, she tried to do it in front of the clock so they knew they were getting their money's worth. Anytime she read the Torah or the books about the Torah when Simon was sleeping, she did it away from the clock.

When Teddy went to day care for the first time, she'd made sure to call every few hours and ask to speak to him. He was three and could have told her if things were wrong. That was how she raised him. That was one of the reasons why, at twelve years old, he was one of the youngest dancers ever to be given top-twenty billing at the holiday Sabaatarian Thanksgiving Jubilee. Antoinette had never been so proud as she was on that Wednesday morning last November.

Teddy had needed to practice every afternoon after school, and it was good he had role models at church, except for the one time when Pastor V had gotten all the boys together and asked them to pray for the girls. He told them that some older girls were sinners for getting pregnant. Of course, Antoinette took this personally. She was sure Teddy did, too, because it wasn't a secret that his father had never been around. Antoinette *had been* those girls before she was saved. She had Teddy to prove it. And he was a blessing. Even though Antoinette took him to Pastor V as often as she could, that wasn't the same. But when Pastor V told those boys to pray for those girls, she knew Teddy was praying for her. "I prayed hard, Mom," Teddy said that afternoon. "I closed my eyes and got down on my knees, even though everyone else was sitting in chairs, and I squeezed my hands together as hard as I could."

Antoinette liked getting down on the floor with Simon and saying good morning with her face right up against his. Sometimes she put her face in his lap, which made Simon coo and open his mouth with his little crooked smile. Antoinette, having raised her own boy, liked knowing that, three, six, twelve months down the road, this useless creature Simon would become a walking, babbling, talking little man.

. . .

She rang the doorbell, stashed the earbuds in her pocket. The weather was hot for autumn. She liked autumn. Amelia fumbled with the door.

"Good morning, Antoinette," Amelia said.

"Good morning, good morning, how's our boy, is he sleeping?" Antoinette said. "He sleeping? Has he had his morning bottle? Where is he? Simon? Simon says?"

"Just starting to rouse," Amelia said. "He drank all eight ounces this morning."

"That's good news," Antoinette said. "We're going to have that child walking and talking soon."

"Is Mr. Jupiter going to come by today?" Amelia said.

Antoinette knew that Amelia didn't like him coming by, but she didn't know how to turn him away. And she didn't want to.

"Don't see why he would," Antoinette said.

"That's great," Amelia said. "Come on in. Good morning. How was your weekend?"

Chapter 8

A aron—shaved, brushed, and suited—kissed Amelia on the forehead. Her profile on the funny guy who used to be fat and was now acting in serious movies was due to her editor at *Esquire* the next day, and she sat drinking coffee at her desk in her office on the top floor of their brownstone.

Amelia couldn't help being pretty, and the room was pretty around her. She wore an old gray T-shirt. Her hair looped around her ears. She was sexy without trying. Or maybe Aaron was going crazy. The three things he used their shared desktop computer for these days were watching Antoinette with Simon, fantasy football, and porn.

The top windowpanes behind Amelia were 1890s stained glass, and they all matched one another. Orange teardrops emanated from a central sky-blue whirl surrounded by golden diamonds. Aaron owned those windows. He and Amelia did together. They owned the stained-glass windows and the original woodwork surrounding them. The wood was mahogany, carved to look like columns holding up a frieze, with little torches surrounded by wreaths carved into the corners. Aaron and Amelia owned this woodwork, as they owned the fireplace tiles around the still-functional gas fireplaces, the sconce lighting, the hardwood floors, the built-in closets.

"Have a good day," Amelia said. "Love you. Stay out of trouble."

"Love you," Aaron said, closing the door to the staircase. He descended the mahogany stairs with latticework balustrades, past the bedroom floor to the first floor, where he tiptoed, holding his shoes, toward the kitchen, parlor, and TV room. There, he kissed Simon, who didn't notice him. Simon was poking at Antoinette's nose while Antoinette laughed. Aaron wanted Simon to laugh, but Simon was silent. Drool all over his lips and chin. Aaron wanted to ask Antoinette how she'd made him laugh on Friday, but he wouldn't be able to explain how he knew about that. They were in the TV room, under a mahogany ceiling that framed a skylight of the same stained glass that illuminated Amelia's office.

These windows were all over the two-family house; Aaron, Amelia, and Simon lived in the triplex on top, and they rented out the garden unit below to Daniel and Thela, a strange, quiet couple they'd found on craigslist and that helped offset Aaron and Amelia's mortgage. When the house hit the market, Brownstoner.com wrote it up as one of the nicer houses on the nicest block in Bed-Stuy, and though some commenters responded that they'd have to be paid $1.3 million to step foot in Bed-Stuy, Aaron ran the numbers and thought it was a steal. They both all but emptied their bank accounts—split the down payment evenly, $125,000 each, with money Aaron made advising investors and the near-last of Amelia's inheritance from her grandmother—and Aaron paid a bit more of the mortgage, which wasn't much because of Daniel and Thela's rent. Amelia paid one thousand a month (until her grandmother money ran out in a couple of years, or, better yet, her freelance career took off), and Aaron paid fifteen hundred, all to live in a three-story turn-of-the-twentieth-century museum.

They shared the garden with Daniel and Thela. Daniel was a freaky professor of some kind of New Age social philosophy. How the media affected (or was affected by) philosophy, maybe? He never seemed to leave the house. Thela was a pianist. Jazz? She played late gigs and gave lessons all day in Manhattan and never seemed to be at home. She was Asian and very skinny. They were ghosts. Ideal tenants.

"Thanks so much for looking after him, Antoinette," Aaron said, neither of them looking at each other.

"See you tomorrow morning, Antoinette. Love you, baby," Aaron said to Simon, who poked at Antoinette's nose.

. . .

There were trees on both sides of the street—tall trees, starting to lose their leaves. It was a crisp and cloudless September day; similar skies had framed the World Trade Center. A member of his congregation had worked at Cantor Fitzgerald, and even as late as 2008 Aaron had been shy in the presence of the man's widow and three teenage daughters.

Aaron and Amelia's house was 383 Stuyvesant Avenue. A little café had opened just around the corner on Decatur, and on the way to the subway, women in elegant leather boots sipped tiny paper cups of espresso. Black women in high boots, white women in boots, Asian women—all with their tiny paper cups. Men, too. Stylish black men in trench coats. White men in sweaters, jeans, and sports coats. There had been tension lately between the police and members of the community—men and women of all races staring down police officers on the way into the subway—which would now be exacerbated by what had happened on Saturday. Jason Blau had only been twelve. A large twelve. In seventh grade and on the JV high school football team, Aaron had read, but still only twelve. What a catastrophe for the police, for his family, and for the community.

But that type of thing was, if nauseating, not unheard of for changing neighborhoods. There was still paradise here. And Aaron was in on it. He'd bought the house because it was beautiful and he wanted to spend his life there with Amelia and, one day, children. But he'd already earned 35 percent back on investment in just over a year. Bed-Stuy was the best bet he'd ever made. It was a real risk, and a thrilling one. It took guts to be surrounded by people who didn't look like him, in a neighborhood without the amenities he was accustomed to, but it was worth it. As long as New York City remained desirable—and Manhattan stayed an island without extra available real estate—the only way he could lose was a spike in crime to scare off new gentrifiers.

Across the street from Aaron's row of brownstones were, unusual in central Brooklyn, three large, stand-alone homes. Two could be considered mansions. One was a large church. It was seven thirty, and the church's chimes were ringing. Walking in step with the chimes, away from his pretty girlfriend and his son, who knew how to laugh, Aaron felt like a man. It was a feeling he relished, one he hadn't known if he'd ever feel again. He was a man with a house and a job and a son and what was essentially a wife. On good days, that was enough to feel connected to the world.

He passed 385 Stuyvesant, bought just a few months earlier by a young couple who both earned in the high six figures. The man and woman had met at a historically black college and now worked in finance. She'd gone to Stanford Business. He'd gone to Harvard Law, where he'd apparently traveled in the same circle as a bunch of men and women who would become good friends of Michelle Obama's. Then 387, which belonged to Mr. Jupiter, a forty-year-old single father and electrician.

"You know what kids are doing?" Jupiter had said last Friday.

"What's that?" Aaron said, not wanting to offend him or answer incorrectly. Last time they'd talked, Jupiter had told Aaron to buy new windows before the winter, and Aaron couldn't tell if he was angling for the job.

"Well you know about Breathalyzer tests, right?" Jupiter said.

"You mean so cops can tell how much you've been drinking?"

"Well, kids have been pouring liquor right inside their assholes," Jupiter said. "Cops don't go around smelling down there, and it enters the bloodstream quicker."

Aaron laughed. "That true?" he said.

"I thought you'd get a kick out of that," Jupiter said. "But it's serious. And dangerous. They take their bottles of vodka and pour the whole thing right down into each other's assholes. With funnels! That's what my son's been doing. I caught him at it. Him and his friends. All bent over with their trousers down around their ankles."

Jupiter seemed genuinely concerned.

"Hey," Jupiter said. "Let's grab a beer sometime? Talk about raising these kids."

"I'd like that," Aaron said.

"Pick up women," Jupiter said.

"Come on," Aaron said.

"It'll be good for folks to see us two out together," Jupiter had said.

But they'd left it at that, and today Aaron didn't run into Jupiter. He'd seen Daniel, actually, who'd been sitting by his open front window, reading—or, rather, not reading, just looking, waiting for Aaron, it seemed. With a book on his lap.

"Good morning, Daniel," Aaron said.

"Good morning, landlord," Daniel said.

"Good morning, tenant," Aaron said.

Daniel laughed, but just kept sitting there, in his chair by his window, watching people walk down the street. Daniel was creepy. Could you imagine being married to him? Thela. She was kind of creepy, too.

But Aaron had smiled and waved, and realized that Daniel didn't know anything about him except that he owned a house and had a wife and baby, and he left to go to work in the morning. And one of those things wasn't even true.

Aaron walked the rest of the block and a half to the subway, sauntered down the steps at the Utica station, but slowed at an uneasy silence punctuated by what sounded like an out-of-control substitute teacher yelling at misbehaving children. When Aaron had run Hebrew school as a young rabbi, the subs could never control the kids. The kids misbehaved and the subs ended up shouting.

In the subway station, the workday crowd slowed to watch. Aaron's assessment of the scene was that two kids had already been arrested for jumping the turnstile, another one was in the process of getting arrested for talking back to the cops for arresting his friends, and two more were being stopped and frisked for reasons the cops would say had nothing to do with the first three. Kids were often lined up like this in the morning. This morning, eight cops—the usual six (a mix of white, Asian, black, Hispanic, male, female, fat, thin) plus two Aaron didn't recognize—were holding seven black boys between the ages of thirteen and eighteen in front of the neighborhood on its way to work. But today, the kids didn't seem to be fighting or arguing. And then another boy jumped the turnstile right in front of the handcuffed kids.

"Come here," the Asian police officer said, cuffing the offender.

"I don't accept this—your authority," the kid said.

"Can I help you with something?" a thin white police officer asked Aaron, or maybe he was talking to a fifty-year-old black man in a muscle shirt and suit pants who was just to Aaron's left.

"This shit is fucked up," the man said.

"You want to get closer?" the police officer said.

"What did I do?" the man said. The arrested kids were playfully trying to kick one another. A female cop got between them and was accidentally kicked. She said, "That's assaulting an officer."

The kid said, "Assault these," and turning around, stuck up both middle fingers behind his back. "You going to kill me now, too?"

The kid had skinny arms and was being pushed up against the grated wall that separated the stairs leading down to the trains from the stairs leading up to the street.

"You want to get locked up?" an Asian police officer said to the black man in the muscle shirt.

"Come on, man, I'm going to work," the man said. "But that kid got killed on Saturday, and now this?"

"Then let me do my job, too," the police officer said. "These kids are daring us to lock them up. Jumped the turnstile while looking me in the eye. You're trying to go to work, well this is my work."

The youngest of the kids in handcuffs was listening to the Asian police officer. "Safer to be arrested," the kid said, "than shot up on the streets. Passive motherfucking resistance."

"You don't even know what that means," a black police officer said.

"Fuck this," another one of the kids said. A group of commuters stopped to take pictures and heckle the police.

"Keep walking," the female police officer told everyone.

"Can I help *you?*" the black police officer said, this time definitely to Aaron.

"Do you need to be doing this?" Aaron shouted back. "Treating them like this?"

"Do I need to be keeping your streets safe?"

"Like this?" Aaron said. "I'm a rabbi."

He eyed Aaron's eight-thousand-dollar suit. "I don't care what you do," the officer said. "Keep walking. This lot should be in school. They are purposefully disobeying."

"I have a baby and a wife at home. Almost every day I've got to see this on my way to work. It's not good for the community."

"You hear this guy?" the black police officer said to the skinny police officer. A train was arriving, and most of the onlookers hustled downstairs to meet it. "He's got a baby at home? Policing the streets isn't good for his community? These kids *tried* to get arrested. What do you want me to do? Keep walking or I'll place you under arrest with your friends here."

"Arrest me for what?" Aaron said.

"Fuck you, man," a kid in cuffs said.

"Yeah, that's right. Keep walking, bitch," a different kid taunted Aaron.

"Sit your fucking ass down," the female police officer said.

"Bitch," the kid replied. It turned out, Aaron thought, that this kid was actually a girl.

"Go to work," the female police officer told Aaron.

"Yeah, you go to work," the girl in handcuffs said in Aaron's direction to laughter from the boys in handcuffs. "You go to work, bitch. I'll take care of that wife of yours."

Chapter 9

Amelia should have been profiling Jonah Hill, but she received a Google alert informing her that her piece on Bed-Stuy had just gone live a week earlier than expected, and she was combing over it, terrified she'd written something that might offend her neighbors. She hadn't really been working anyway. She'd been scanning Twitter: tweets like *I wonder what #JasonBlau would have grown up to be if those cops hadn't shot him dead #12yearsold10shots* and *Bereaved black families seem pressured to forgive instantly, or be accused of complicity in civil unrest. #JasonBlau #12yearsold10shots*

She'd read and edited her article a dozen times, but it was always different once it was live, and the shooting compounded her unease. Between celebrity assignments, she'd researched the neighborhood. This was her first attempt at something more significant. It was about her home and where she was raising Simon. She wanted to fit in, and the way she fit in was to understand a place, and she was a journalist, so the way she understood a place was by research and writing. With this article, she was hoping to build a reputation, do more serious work, be taken more seriously. She wanted to earn a voice—a calming voice, one of understanding. She wanted to help put her neighbors' anger in perspective. But

Amelia also wanted to represent her own point of view. When she'd been with Kevin, her writing had been weightless. Meaningless. She'd only written on assignment. There had been a time in her life for Jessica Alba and Adam Sandler, but now she wanted to take the next step. With Kevin, life—and writing—had been about assembling a collection of experiences and clips. Now, with Aaron and Simon, she was establishing something solid. And after years of writing on command, she felt herself in the process of discovering a subject she was truly passionate about. Maybe it was the neighborhood, or maybe it was something about how real people lived. But either way, this article was a step in the right direction.

The New Yorker had been nice enough to respond to her email telling her she'd need to develop a larger portfolio of long-form essays first, which hadn't been a surprise, but *New York* magazine brushed her off with a form rejection. Finally, just to get the two months of work read, she'd sold it for a hundred dollars to Brownstoner.com, a Brooklyn real estate blog.

THE PARADOX OF BED-STUY

By Amelia Lehmann   9 comments

Bedford-Stuyvesant—popularly known as Bed-Stuy—is the largest neighborhood in the most populated borough in New York City. The name is a product of two neighboring, historic communities: Stuyvesant Heights, named for Peter Stuyvesant, the last governor of New Amsterdam; and Bedford, possibly a translation of the Dutch "Bestevaar," meaning "the place where old men meet." The combined neighborhood didn't exist until the 1930s.

Depending on where you were five years ago, you'd have heard Bed-Stuy either touted as the home of Chris Rock, The Notorious

B.I.G., and Jay Z, or pitied as ground zero of police ineptitude. But these days, Bed-Stuy more likely will have been described as the latest in a series of territories claimed—subway station by subway station—by an army of gentrifiers invading from mission control in Manhattan. First it was Park Slope's turn; then Cobble Hill; then Williamsburg, Greenpoint, Fort Greene, and Clinton Hill. Now Bed-Stuy is facing the point of the spear.

Unlike Williamsburg, which boasts a five-minute subway ride to Manhattan, what Bed-Stuy offers is, according to the *New York Times,* "Perhaps the largest collection of intact and largely untouched Victorian architecture in the country," with roughly 8,800 buildings built before 1900. The availability of brownstones at relatively affordable prices in a neighborhood that most people I interviewed consider "just safe enough" is driving what new residents are happy to call "the return of a once glamorous neighborhood," a return that has brought upscale Italian restaurants and hip new bars.

Newcomers to the neighborhood take comfort in the drop in its crime rate as well as the new amenities. One recent purchaser (and president-elect of his block association), David Lipkins, who recently moved to western Bed-Stuy with his wife and daughter, had the figures memorized. "I was just telling my parents," he said. "They always ask me why I paid $1.6 million to live in the ghetto, so I'm always ready to tell them. Murders in Bed-Stuy are down 80 percent in the last ten years. Robberies are down 80 percent." And Mr. Lipkins is correct. However, his precinct's rates of violent and nonviolent crime are still among New York City's worst, with fifteen rapes in the last six months alone, versus only one rape during that time in Park Slope. This is the paradox of Bed-Stuy: that a booming real estate market exists among housing projects.

So how did we get to this New Bed-Stuy—this mixture of gentrification, pride, and lingering crime? The seeds were sown in its unique history.

In 1889, one of New York City's most talented architects, Montrose Morris, designed Brooklyn's first-ever apartment building, The Alhambra. Morris sparked a building bonanza that produced block after block of elegant brownstones for wealthy industrialists and business owners, primarily of northern European decent. These homes were ornamented with intricate and glamorous detail: terra-cotta tiles, carved mahogany doors, parquet flooring, Byzantine columns, Queen Anne embellishments and gables, and grotesqueries of animals and human faces. With all this elegance, these members of the new American bourgeoisie could live like European aristocracy.

But this aristocratic dream was deferred by the racial drama that began to unfold in the first two decades of the twentieth century. African Americans, who'd begun migrating from the South in large numbers, started arriving in Harlem in the 1920s, and rode the famous A Train into Bed-Stuy soon thereafter. The houses were beautiful, the population less dense, and as Harlem filled up and the Great Depression incentivized whites to sell, Bed-Stuy quickly became the next stop for African Americans, earning the nickname "Little Harlem" as early as 1961.

Not surprisingly, once the neighborhood transitioned from northern European to African American, financial institutions stopped approving loans. Real estate agents wanted to scare off the remaining white residents and chop up the single-family brownstones into three- and four-family units to maximize profits and sell high to African Americans, who were willing to live under less glamorous conditions. Housing projects followed.

In 1950, Bed-Stuy was already half African American, but by

1960, African Americans made up 85 percent of the population. It was already denser than Harlem had been in the 1920s when people were leaving it for Bed-Stuy. Half a million residents occupied just over six hundred blocks, making it the second-largest African American community in the country. Bed-Stuy schools had a 70 percent dropout rate, and underemployment was at 30 percent, high for today, but especially hideous back when New York City's overall unemployment rate was under 4 percent. Infant-mortality and delinquency rates were also more than double New York's average.

Then, in 1964, a black teenager was shot by a white policeman in Harlem, and a race riot spread all the way into Bed-Stuy, resulting in the destruction of many African American and Jewish businesses. City government responded with apathy: garbage pickup ceased, the schools stopped attracting top teachers, crime rose. Redlining and the city's misappropriation of tax resources aggravated the problems. Bed-Stuy became such a nightmare that the muckraker Jack Newfield, after visiting with Senator Robert Kennedy, referred to Bed-Stuy in *The Village Voice* as "filled with the surreal imagery of a bad LSD trip."

But from the lowest point in Bed-Stuy history emerged the culture that revived and redefined it. Beyond Biggie Smalls and Chris Rock, many of the children and grandchildren of the very migrants who came up north in the first half of the 20th century were the teachers, dental hygienists, and city workers who owned these buildings and presided over the community. They have now passed the buildings to their children, who have sold to the gentrifiers or held on and become a new successful class of doctors, lawyers, and investment bankers.

In dozens of conversations with middle-aged and elderly men and women who grew up and spent their whole lives on these blocks, I hear the same sentiments time and again: "There's a community here." "We look after each other." "We all raise each other's kids." "We make sure to get into each other's business and keep up on what's going on."

And this pride extends to the buildings. As the *Times* reported, it is exactly because, "In the 20th century, Bedford-Stuyvesant was not an affluent neighborhood, many of its homes were never renovated," so these homes have retained a level of original detail not found even in the city's most well-known brownstone neighborhoods. "Comparing a Bedford-Stuyvesant townhouse to one in, say, the West Village can be like comparing an original piece of art with a print."

However, this positive outlook belies the resentment beneath the surface, and the fact that Bed-Stuy is still a difficult place for most of its inhabitants. Nearly a third of the population was below the poverty line in 2010. And, as one longtime resident who prefers to remain anonymous tells me, "The new folk—they don't care. They don't say anything to us. They drive rents up, make it so people who have lived here forever can't afford to live here no more. They keep the houses nice, which is nice to walk by, I guess. But that's all I get out of it. I don't get anything except my friends have to move out of the neighborhood."

The legacy owners make $1.6 million, while the longtime renters have to move out of the neighborhood where they have spent their entire lives.

That's Bed-Stuy today.

What a pompous ending. No wonder *The New Yorker,* even its website, wouldn't take it. For *The New Yorker,* she would have needed to find a person who embodied the good and bad of gentrification. A real personality. The article would have needed to go beyond the statistics and make the neighborhood make sense.

Or maybe she had explained everything clearly. The neighborhood had started elegant and for wealthy Europeans. Then with the Great Depression, it was abandoned to any African American who would move in. Now, whites were coming back. Money followed, along with the city services that had been absent for decades. So her neighbors were angry. Amelia had implied their anger, she told herself, even if she hadn't stated it directly. She wasn't writing an op-ed here. Still, she had made it pretty clear that it was unfair that it took white people and money to come in for outsiders to notice the problems. Her article might bring some additional attention. And Amelia was proud of it. It was smart. Well researched. By far the best piece she'd ever written. And it was always possible that it would get noticed by someone. Lead to something different. Bigger or better. (Though, even if she couldn't have anticipated Jason Blau, she should have included stop and frisk and broken windows, and how these tactics divided the community.) But either way, it was something for Simon to read in ten or fifteen years, when the neighborhood was mentioned in the same breath as Fort Greene and Park Slope. Something other than what Jonah Hill ate for lunch.

There were already comments:

amandakin   Sept 8, 2014 at 7:06 a.m.
This article has a distinct outside, White Gaze feel to it. Rather unsettling.

And then:

tnt2   Sept 8, 2014 at 7:16 a.m.

Thanks for telling us shit we already know. No mention of Stop and Frisk. No mention of black boys murdered by the police. No mention of *our children going to jail.*

And then:

SewardWasRight   Sept 8, 2014 at 7:19 a.m.

TODAYS THE DAY BITCHES! POLICE V OUR COMMINUTY. POLICY GOING DOWN!

But then:

transworld   Sept 8, 2014 at 7:21 a.m.

Lovely piece. Captured the tensions of the neighborhood excellently. The type of piece we need more of.

And:

bhinsider   Sept 8, 2014 at 7:29 a.m.

Most of Bed-Stuy is still a terrible neighborhood. Sorry, but that is just true. Dont get the hype at all.

brooklyn72   Sept 8, 2014 at 7:32 a.m.

. . . a terrible neighborhood where you can't find a brownstone below $2M

It's beautiful here; people that think like you do haven't been there since the '70s. People used to say Fort Greene was a terrible place only 5 yrs ago and look at it now; homes are selling upward of $4M.

DH   July 8, 2014 at 8:44 a.m.

Bed-Stuy's great, but, trotting out home sale prices—especially when many of those are bought by investment firms to flip—is, forgive me, dumb.

brooklyn72   Sept 8, 2014 at 9:12 a.m.

Dixon is buying at $2M to flip . . . I don't disagree. Investors see value in these brownstones and in the community and they will most likely flip these homes for $3M+ in the next year or so.

And finally:

Hexr   Sep 8, 2014 at 9:25 am

DO OR DIE MOTHER FUCKERSS!!!!!!!!

Amelia, with Simon screaming downstairs, quit Firefox.

It was already time for his first nap. Antoinette would handle that. Amelia locked herself out of the Internet for an hour and focused on Jonah Hill. He'd been boring in person.

She changed her lead: "Jonah Hill is boring in person."

She liked that. *Esquire* might like that.

"Jonah Hill has a distinct outside, white gaze . . ." *Esquire* would not like that.

"Jonah Hill ordered the dressing on the side. He was trying to keep the weight off . . ."

Chapter 10

D aniel looked out the window. He was supposed to be preparing for his class at Pratt, but he could wing it. His students were artists, or pretended to be artists. They wouldn't care. The morning rush to work was starting to slow. The second morning rush. The first was for the real workers, the laborers—the house cleaners and men in boots, all African American. That was at around 6 a.m. Daniel didn't sleep, so that first morning rush was his first event of the day, and when Thela was away he took his coffee to the front window and savored it.

He and Thela had moved here because it was a large apartment for a relatively small price. It was far from where Thela gave lessons in Manhattan; there was no supermarket or chain drugstore nearby; they didn't know anyone in the neighborhood; and Thela's—albeit short—walk home from the subway at night after gigs scared them. But they loved that they had room for a piano in the apartment; they loved that they could barbecue in the garden; they loved the original woodwork and stained-glass windows; and they loved that they'd never run into anyone they knew.

At least Daniel loved that part of it. Daniel had become a loner over the past decade. He didn't like to waste his time with people he didn't know. They were nothing to him. He was too old to care what they thought. What did he need them for? He was done catering to strangers. They could go fuck themselves. So he taught his courses, listened to podcasts, and read at home. He went on long walks and listened to podcasts. He read at home and listened to podcasts and taught his courses. He cleaned his guns. The guns were both legal. He only cleaned them as much as you're supposed to clean guns. He wasn't a lunatic about guns or anything like that. The guns were because of his brother, who had been in the Marines. It was difficult to talk to him about things sometimes, so the free therapist at Pratt suggested Daniel ask his brother something that related to the war but was not about the war itself, because the brothers had such differences of opinions about war. So when they got together once a week, Daniel asked about tactical geography and how to lead men and what it was like organizing and physically moving and feeding men. Those conversations were interesting to Daniel, especially considering his current academic interests concerning how cloud storage and the mobile classroom enabled smoother logistics in rural settings, but discussion died off quickly because Daniel's brother rarely asked Daniel questions about his life.

Although that wasn't strictly true. Daniel's brother asked Daniel a single question such as, "How's teaching?" or "How's Thela?" but he never asked the follow-up question, so conversations at that point a year or so ago regularly went:

"How's Thela?"

"Doing better, actually. She's starting to get regular gigs at this one-percenter's weekly party, and the Brooklyn Phil is interested in bringing her in as this new kind of jazz resident, so she's feeling pretty good professionally, like things are moving in the right direction."

"Good to hear."

Then they'd both take big sips of their beers.

It would be the same about the classes Daniel taught at Pratt and Hunter, and the academic papers he was thinking about writing. This was okay, especially at first, because Daniel wanted to know everything about his brother's life after obsessing about him through three tours to Afghanistan—talking about him incessantly to Thela, to all their mutual friends, to all their former teachers, their family members, strangers who were interested in politics, his therapist at Pratt. Daniel became more social at first, because of his brother, and then less as people stopped wanting to hear Daniel talk about the war.

So now that his brother had been back for two years and was making big money at Morgan Stanley working in mergers and acquisitions, and living in the same city as Daniel, it was difficult not reaping any reward for all his patience and anxiety and emotional investment. Daniel admitted the likelihood that the transition back to civilian life must be trying for his brother, but he wanted some recompense for all those nights, all that worry. His brother was safe and back in New York. Daniel was living all the way out in Bed-Stuy. He was getting paid four grand per semester per course times four classes per semester times two semesters, which—at thirty-two thousand dollars a year minus taxes—was more like twenty six, so those nights out with his brother really had to be the highlight of his week. It wasn't entirely about the money. He just wanted it to be fun. To feel close to him again.

And when Daniel began asking his brother about guns, that

closeness seemed more within reach. His brother opened up. He said he'd carried a standard Beretta M9. He said some marines liked to bitch about its magazine or its stopping power, but the M9 was the pistol he'd learned on, and if he aimed right, he would stop what he was aiming at. Stop it dead in its fucking tracks. Over those half dozen beers he told Daniel more about officers training; about why he told people he joined up in college (as a philosophy major he strongly believed it was unfair to let what was essentially an economic draft contribute to mercenary armed services fighting wars for our entrenched elites); and why he really joined (fucking leading men! the blood and life of it! the experience of real experience! the guns! and, somewhat, his belief that it *was* unfair to let an economic draft contribute to an armed service fighting wars for elites); and Daniel hadn't felt that close to his brother since they'd been boys. Daniel didn't say, even after all those beers, what he wanted to, which was that it had been fucking inconsiderate to put Daniel through hell just for the fun and the guns, because they were finally getting on so well and maybe one man shouldn't slow the rush of his life because another man—even if it is his brother—suffers back home. Also, Daniel never felt physically more slight and tender than when in his brother's company.

But his brother got drunk that night and promised to get the process rolling for Daniel to register a weapon, and since then they'd been meeting at the range and firing until a few months back when, for Daniel's fortieth birthday, his brother bought him a CZ Over/Under twenty-gauge shotgun, and when the weather was nice and Thela had an out-of-town gig, the brothers went up to the Adirondacks, or upstate farther out toward Albany, and shot skeet and trap, and talked about why neither had kids, and about Thela, and Daniel's brother's wife, and bad dreams, and their own aging parents, and all the stuff that can be difficult to talk about when you're face to face across a table drinking beer.

So things were getting better. Daniel still didn't like seeing people other than Thela and his students and, now, when they were shooting, his brother. And he still spent too much time cleaning this CZ O/U. He liked the smell of the oil, was the truth. And he knew Thela worried about him. But the people at the new café down on Marcus Garvey and Decatur seemed to like seeing him on the mornings he went in to buy a scone. And he'd gotten a new Rate My Professor review that was four out of five stars: *Unorothox and a nice guy! Attendance is probably the most important part of your grade.* And he was making progress on his written work.

Daniel had had to tell Thela about the guns because even though the apartment was big for the two of them, it wasn't big enough to hide a pistol and a shotgun. Also, sometimes the place smelled like gun stock finish or oil. Thela said she didn't mind, and sometimes Daniel thought she was lying, and sometimes he thought she liked it, and sometimes he thought she actually did want kids before it was too late, and sometimes he thought she was going to leave him, especially when what she'd said was going to be a one-night trip to perform in Connecticut or Boston or Montreal or somewhere like that ended up lasting three or four days.

Daniel didn't tell Aaron and Amelia about the guns. It didn't seem like the kind of thing a landlord would approve of. Also, one wasn't required to report legal firearms on the premises to a landlord. Also, Daniel thought Aaron was a douche bag. It was nothing Aaron said or did. Aaron was always nice, and whenever the place needed repairs Aaron called the handyman soon enough.

It was something about Aaron's bearing. There was something feral about him. Aaron was exactly the businessman type that Daniel had hoped to avoid in Bed-Stuy. There was something about the way he walked around the neighborhood like he was its king that made Daniel hate Aaron on behalf of the locals. Daniel knew "locals" wasn't the word. They were all locals. They all lived there. But Daniel felt there was something shitty about making all this money and buying a house for two million dollars or whatever it was Aaron spent and then not only being the only white guy on the block but *renting* to the only other white guy. And, yes, Daniel *was* the other white guy. There was just something douchey about Aaron. Amelia was all over the place. Manic and probably not ready to have kids. Daniel was a couple of years older than Amelia and Aaron, and God knows he wasn't ready to have kids. But he liked someone who was so obviously not really in control of her own life. That was something he understood and almost respected about Amelia. But Aaron was just a Wall Street asshole. So he wasn't going to tell him about his guns. Fuck him, is what Daniel thought after having that bullshit conversation in the morning when they called each other "landlord" and "tenant." Fuck that guy, and fuck his tiny ears and his teeny tiny earlobes like kernels of corn sticking out off the bottom of an egg. Fuck that motherfucking one percenter asshole. Fuck him. Fuck him.

Chapter 11

Aaron understood what had happened in the subway station. It happened two or three times a week. Kids jumped the turnstile, so police officers arrested them and their friends. Kids broke the law—minor as those laws may be—and they faced the consequences.

It was a variation on Commissioner Bill Bratton's "broken window" policy. If one window was broken, criminals were more likely to break more windows. Make the minor arrests—fix the broken windows—so the city stayed nice. Nobody messed with a pristine building.

But then a month ago, two kids had been choked to death during routine ticketing for turnstile jumping, and another—this Jason, just a boy—was murdered Saturday night for who knew what reason, and neighbors, including Aaron himself, made the police officers' jobs more difficult. So there were arguments.

But today kids were getting arrested on purpose.

It was in moments like those at the subway station when Aaron most wished he was still a rabbi. Not a Hassid, whom everybody would roll their eyes at and wonder if he ever showered and if he fucked his wife through a quilt of many colors, but a secular, friendly, well-dressed accentless rabbi who could talk to policemen and black people like human beings. The rabbi he used to be. He wouldn't need to rush off to work. Except maybe today, on Rosh Hashanah. But normally, he could take his time and arbitrate their dispute. That girl who looked like a boy, who was yelling after him. He could sit and listen to both sides, and at the very least, the police officers and the kids from the neighborhood would feel as though they'd been heard.

Over dinner the evening before, he and Amelia had fought. Simon had gone down at eight, and they were eating a dinner of bread and salad and cheese. Their New Year's dinner. They were drinking red wine. Aaron always made a contribution over the Days of Awe, and this had been a good year financially for him. He had made $250,000 at Stifler & McDermott. He had essentially broken even with his bookie. Kept to small bets.

"The point," Aaron had said, "is that I'm going to donate twenty percent of two hundred fifty grand this year, which is fifty grand, a lot of money, and I wanted to talk about where you wanted it to go."

Amelia had frozen up. "To Simon," she had said slowly. "I want it to go to Simon. And to us. Not to strangers. Why would you want to give our money to people you've never met?"

The discussion had been primarily about Aaron—his faults and predilections—not about the money. They had talked about his faults as though they were outside him. He couldn't bear discussing a "risk addiction" that didn't exist, and he couldn't admit to a gambling addiction that might. So he said, "Because that's what good people do. Give to charity. I want to help people who are suffering. I want to help them in a way I couldn't as a rabbi. I'm making enough money to actually help people now. And it's not *our* money yet. When you accept my proposal it will become our money. For now, it's my money, and I've had the best year financially—and personally—of my life. So I want to be generous. Otherwise, what the hell am I doing with my life?"

He'd worked it all out, run the numbers, set the rules for himself. Not having the money was better than having it. If he gave away 20 percent, he'd have a better chance of betting zero. If he gave away nothing, he'd bet the 20 percent. Fifty grand was the right amount to bet. He had $130,000 in the bank. So: he could bet fifty and still have eighty to live off. But if he gave away fifty, he couldn't bet another fifty and live off thirty. It wasn't enough. He wouldn't do that to his family. So the way not to bet was to give away fifty thousand dollars.

He'd told her about his problems after the first time they'd made love—"I owed a bookie money, I borrowed, stole from the synagogue to repay him. It was the worst thing I've ever done," her naked chest on his—and she'd forgiven him with a smile that soured into a smirk.

But she'd brought it up again on their following date, and again and again until she'd gone to therapy with him and his psychologist had helped him convince her he wasn't an addict. A gambling addict, at least.

But then he had been forced to start lying to Amelia.

He believed he was giving the money away for her, too. This would pay off for her, too. The benefit of being part of the community. Of protecting himself and enriching the lives of others.

He believed in most of what was he was saying. It wasn't all a cover. Charity *was* good. Noble. Especially given what he was doing for a living. Betting on the right stocks to come in for his clients. He loved the game of it, but he suffered for the lack of . . . if not morality, then at least full-heartedness. There were no real people at work. No real problems. It was just money. Just games. Just the elation and descent of numbers. He wanted to give this money away. Even if he hadn't needed to give away the money, he'd want to. It was the right thing to do. For them and the community.

But no, Amelia had said. "Good people look after their own. It's money that could go to Simon's food and clothes and education. This is what we know happens to you. Seeing how much you can give away before things get dangerous. But life is different now. It is part of the responsibility of having a child. We've discussed this."

Aaron had told this psychologist, an eager-to-help, young PhD in jeans and a blazer, about the unprotected sex he'd had in high school. About speaking in front of crowds and even his serve-and-volley game. With this one Aaron had tried to make it about something other than gambling, so when Amelia had asked to meet him it had been perfect. Now "risk counseling group" was where he'd told Amelia he'd been the couple of times over the past year he'd succumbed and lost an evening to a Wall Street card game.

"We can make more money for Simon," he said. "Simon is just one person. We can feed so many."

"Education is fifty grand a year and Simon might be one person. But he is our child. I want to make sure Simon has what I didn't."

"You had money growing up."

"Not money. Fucking normalcy. Love," Amelia said. She softened, tears gathering in her eyes. "I'm here for you now. Life is stable. Things are okay."

She thought his giving to charity was submitting to his urges, so she was being gentle with him. Her gentleness broke his resolve, made him want to tell her that she was right, he would donate nothing. He tried to open his mouth to say it, but his mouth wouldn't open. He needed to follow his plan. He had set out his course, and he needed to follow it. Give fifty away, save eighty. Bet nothing. He desperately wanted to bet nothing. But still he wanted to tell her she was right. He was confused. Pressure mounted inside his chest and head. If he'd been alone he would have screamed.

"We'll get through it either way," she said. He saw her swallow. "Have you already spent it?" she asked. "Have you lost it already?"

"I'm not gambling anymore," he said.

"Is this part of some play you're going to make?"

He refused to acknowledge the accusation again; instead he tried to maintain a sense of high-spirited possibility: "Of course. Of course it's all still there. That's what I want to talk to you about," he had said. "We can give it to whomever we want. We can give it to soup kitchens in the neighborhood if you want. Or schools. It's actual good! It's actual money that provides actual food for actual hungry people."

Her eyes closed, tried to close further, she was overpowered, and then they opened again. "Fine," she relented, relieved that at least he might be telling the truth that he was under control. "Give it to soup kitchens in the neighborhood. But watch yourself. I'm worried about you. That all of this is just yielding to your worst instincts. I even worry lately," she had said, "about the house. That it was just the most exciting place you could think of living. Maybe we should sell. Take a profit and move someplace healthier for you. For us."

"Really?" he had said. "I can donate to feed people?" He knew she loved the house too much to sell.

"Sure," she had said. "If it will make you happy."

"It's not about making me happy."

"It's not about making you happy? Of course it is! What else could it be about? You've been doing so well. I thought we were doing so well."

Amelia wiped away tears.

He'd thought right then about getting on his knees over dinner and proposing marriage again.

He needed her, and they loved each other. He was trying to be less damaged. He was trying. She'd saved him, he reminded himself on that subway into Manhattan.

Chapter 12

Throwstrikes Lanes

Twisted clown faces. Garish blaring electronic dance music. Long tubes of orange and green fluorescent lights. Aaron downed a double Dewar's at the Throwstrikes bar before joining the group. A girl had just arrived, too. A woman. Pretty—like a precocious girl grown up.

"Finally!" she said. "Let's start a game! Those guys are too serious, and I've been waiting for someone new to show up because I've rented the shoes and I want to try them out!"

"I'm Aaron," he said.

"Pleased to meet you," she said. "I kind of want to drop a ball on my foot just to see if it hurts. That's the point of these things, right? Otherwise why would we need to rent shoes? What year is it? Renting shoes?"

Amelia was wearing a short red summer dress with her bowling shoes.

"I haven't gone bowling since I was a little girl," she said. Her face lit up, as though she was just at that moment remembering all the pleasures of being a little girl. "I went alone with my mom—the only thing I remember our ever having actually done together—and I was beating her the whole time, but she got two strikes at the end and beat me and I cried all the way home. She must have won thirty-five to thirty! I even sat in the backseat because I didn't want to be next to her I was so angry!"

Amelia's two hands were holding Aaron's right hand. She was looking at Aaron, who was suddenly embarrassed to be wearing khaki pants. Though he was initially taken aback by all this storytelling and the intensity with which she looked him in the eye, it was the first time he'd felt warmth and honesty in months. And the way she was dressed took him back in time to a place before losing his job, before rabbinical school, and before the first time he placed a bet (in high school, the Knicks lost, but it was at the buzzer!). He asked her questions about her absent mother, and she asked about his melancholic father, and miraculously, no one else arrived, and the other people already there were all competitive bowlers who wanted to maintain their game of five.

Their knees touched under the table at a cowboy beer bar on St. Mark's Place between Second and Third avenues. They'd ordered a pitcher and Amelia was drunk. "There's so much I want to tell you!" she said. "I don't get it! I've never wanted to tell someone so much before. I feel like I'm running out of time. You seem like you're in no rush, like you're finished doing whatever you wanted to do and now you can just sit here and talk. But then there's also something else about you. I don't know what I'm saying!"

"We have all the time in the world," he said, feeling just the opposite of her appraisal of him. He had to hold himself back from giggling stupidly or jumping up and down in his seat like a little kid. Years later, when Simon was asleep and Aaron and Amelia were exhausted on the couch in the TV room and talking about those first days, they'd agreed that it was like their lives had somehow shifted or recalibrated and made room for the possibility of someone they'd want to tell everything that'd ever happened to them.

They were rubbing knees and holding hands under the table at the cowboy bar. Amelia was struggling to keep herself sitting upright with all that beer in her, so he was surprised when she stood up to leave. They'd already friended each other on Facebook so he wasn't worried about getting back in touch—but it was early for a Saturday, not even eleven, and he was surprised she didn't want the evening to continue. After walking her out, he returned to finish the pitcher of beer and wonder if he could allow himself to put this much hope into a single person. He'd told her he was a financial manager and she'd seemed fine with it. It was a job, she seemed to feel. It wasn't anything more than that.

He found out later that night on Facebook that she was married. He laughed at first, but then he drank. He drank the four beers in his fridge, then he drank the half bottle of whisky he had in the cabinet, and then he opened the good bottle of champagne he was saving for when his father got off enough meds to have a drink or two again. This allowed Aaron to open four separate poker sites and play. He played through the night, through the next day, through the day after that, and he was down eighteen grand when he woke up in the chair three days later. It was a month before he built up the nerve to contact her again.

Chapter 13

Just after Aaron left for work, Mr. Jupiter came over to visit. Antoinette knew it was him, because she feared it was him at the same time she wanted it to be. It couldn't have been more than a half hour after Amelia made it clear she disapproved of his coming over. But Jupiter was Aaron and Amelia's neighbor. How could she turn him away? Even if she had wanted to?

The first time Mr. Jupiter had come over, he'd said he needed to check something on the fuse box. Antoinette kept him outside while she texted Aaron, and Aaron texted back saying to let Mr. Jupiter into the basement, but afterward, when Mr. Jupiter asked to give Simon a kiss on the forehead, she told him no way, her boss didn't say anything about anything other than the basement, and she needed this job.

Things got slightly more complicated when, same time the following Monday, Mr. Jupiter came over with a freshly baked dark chocolate, milk chocolate marshmallow cake, like he could tell that kind of thing was Antoinette's favorite. Antoinette would have preferred dark chocolate all the way through, but anything chocolate was fine by her, and the way he'd asked to kiss baby Simon on the forehead the first time made her think he was okay, so she invited him in and they sat at the dining room table and talked. Mr. Jupiter cut two big pieces of the dark chocolate, milk chocolate marshmallow cake, and Simon sat like a good boy in Antoinette's lap. Antoinette's aunt always said there was no better test of a man's character than how a baby responded to him, and Simon seemed at ease around Mr. Jupiter.

The first time—two months ago—Mr. Jupiter had come over he'd been wearing his work clothes and he'd had soot on his hands, or oil maybe, which was also one of the reasons Antoinette didn't feel bad about refusing to invite him inside, but the second time he'd dressed up nicely with clean jeans and a Brooklyn Nets jersey. He asked her if she liked working for Aaron, and she told him she did so far, though it had only been a couple of months. She told him her last job had gone on years, and the first six months were always difficult to tell. She told him the truth, though even if she'd hated the job she wouldn't have said so. There was always a chance that Mr. Jupiter and Aaron drank together, and when men drank together, they talked about what they knew might be of interest to the other.

That second time, Antoinette asked Mr. Jupiter how long he'd lived in the neighborhood and he said going on fifteen years. Simon was napping in the Pack 'n Play, so they hunched over the dining room table together speaking in whispers. She asked where before that, and he started telling her all about his life, about how he was born in Georgia, but his people down there just didn't want enough for themselves.

Her mother had always said the same for their people in Jamaica, but Mr. Jupiter didn't really listen; instead he just started talking about New York like he was a politician.

"Well, there are two New Yorks," he said.

She asked him what he meant, assuming he meant rich and poor like the mayor liked to say, but Mr. Jupiter meant something else:

"I read that over forty percent of New York City residents were born in another country. Three million foreign-born immigrants live in New York City, more than any other city in the world. More foreign-born immigrants live in New York than there are people in Chicago. And that's not even including people like me who come up from the South. And there are tons of us. Just look around. My family down south—and don't get me wrong, I like to visit when it gets cold up here—they're a bunch of fucking hicks."

He had a funny way of talking where if he began to sound too smart he'd say something at the end of what he was saying to make himself sound ignorant again. "Fuck me up the goat ass," he said.

"Don't talk like that in front of the baby," Antoinette said. "Even if he is sleeping."

"Sorry," he said. "I'm sorry."

"It's okay," Antoinette said.

Antoinette made it a point not to let Teddy talk like this. Teddy was going to grow up smart like Mr. Jupiter, but he wasn't going to feel the need to apologize for it. If he wanted to say something smart, he could just say it without following it up by calling his family a bunch of fucking hicks.

"If you ever need to go anywhere," Mr. Jupiter said, "ever need a break or anything like that, just let me know, and I can watch the baby. I've raised my own boy, you know. And I've got a few guys working for me now. So they can take care of business and I can come over and look out for the baby."

"Thanks," Antoinette said, "but that won't be necessary."

"I just mean if you need to go the bank or the hardware store or anything, or if you need to take your own boy to the doctor. With the hours you work, I know how hard it must be for you. And I've raised my own boy. When I was nineteen, twenty, I had a baby with an island girl like you. The DR. Not Jamaica. I like Jamaicans more. They've got more rhythm, more kindness, usually. But I fell hard for this girl."

"Yeah?" Antoinette said. This story didn't concern her, and she didn't want to encourage him talking too much and asking too many questions, especially if it meant he'd feel it was acceptable to keep on coming over to the house while she was working, but she was interested in what kind of life he lived. She liked that he'd raised a son. He kept on making sure his Nets Jersey was tucked into his jeans. There was something cute about how careful he was with his clothing. And though she'd never trust the baby to someone else when he was supposed to be in her care, it was generous of him to offer.

"I'd been up here living with an uncle and aunt and they wanted to kill me when they found out I got a girl pregnant," he said. "Even though I cared for the girl and I was willing to marry her. Shit. I wanted to marry her. Who'd ever heard of a pregnant girl unwilling to marry the father? I was living in East Brooklyn for a piece. Her parents wanted to kill me, too. Turned out she was seeing another guy the whole time. That was why she wouldn't marry me. Impossible to tell whose boy it was without paternity, and I'm not going to take the test after sixteen years raising him as my own. He's even got my name."

"Jupiter?" Antoinette said.

"Ha! That's a good one. That's a good one! No! I mean, yes, of course, Jupiter. But his name's Derek, too. Like mine. We're both Derek. You can call me that if you'd like."

"I like Jupiter," she said. "It's uncommon."

"Then I do, too. So. So. After nine months of doc appointments and my working my ass off to get us set up in my aunt and uncle's place and promising we're going to move out—no drink, waking up early, no gambling, nothing, and then a year more of hardly seeing either of them—the girl or my baby—because of how much I'm working and putting money away, weekends, everything, she ups and moves back home to the DR one day without saying anything.

"Haven't heard from her since. Been sixteen years." He scraped his plate with his fork. "I used to tell Derek his mom died, but I think he knows the truth by now. There wasn't a funeral or anything like that. He could have asked around and found that out. But he never brought it up with me. I used to spend time fearing that conversation where he'd find out she was living and I'd have to come clean with him, but I think he must know that I know that he knows by now . . ."

By this point the plates were empty. They'd both eaten two large slices and pushed the plates forward toward each other. The story he was telling was too much. It was too much to be true. A mother abandoning her son. *Behold, children are a heritage from the Lord, the fruit of the womb a reward. Like arrows in the hand of a warrior are the children of one's youth.* A father raising a son alone she'd heard of, but a son not knowing that his mother was still alive and a four-hour plane ride away?

"Do you want some milk? A cup of coffee?" Antoinette asked.

"I mean what I said," Jupiter said. "I'm a friend and neighbor, and it's nothing to me taking care of a little boy if you ever need to step out. I promise I no longer need to take revenge on island girls. Ha! I've still got a soft spot for y'all."

That was all on the second visit. Since then, he would come over with cakes, and the two of them would talk. About his ideas. About the city. About how crammed her life was with work and Teddy. It was always his past, his ideas, or her current life. Never about her past or the potential of their life together. But in talking about Teddy with him and spending time the two of them with the baby, she couldn't help but imagine what their life could be like together. Teddy having a man to ask questions. Antoinette having Jupiter nearby all the time. He had this big house two doors down from where she worked. She wasn't really imagining anything for herself, like it actually would happen. But in the same way she was transitioning into Islam, she was easing into these thoughts. She was still going to church where some of the power was wearing off, while starting at the mosque, which was full of possibility, and in six months or so, she'd be a true Muslim. She imagined she might experience a similar kind of new acceptance with Jupiter.

But on this morning, he showed up earlier than he ever had before, and he didn't bring cake initially or show any of the softness or personal vulnerability that Antoinette had liked so much on his previous visits. He wore a clean white T-shirt and cargo pants, stood in the doorway, and then asked to sit. Even when they were seated, he seemed a bit shaken. Like he wasn't as suave as before. Like he needed someone to ground him.

Maybe it was because he had a sense that Amelia had said something disparaging about him earlier that morning.

But when a truck backfired around the block, Jupiter jumped up and put his hand on Antoinette's arm in a nice way that made her feel that although his words might be colder, more barren, his tone not as affectionate as it had been the last time he'd come over, this wasn't due to any change of desire or personal warmth.

He jumped up and said, "I've got to go grab something from my place—be back! I'll be right back. Don't go anywhere. Okay?"

Chapter 14

On the subway between Utica and Nostrand, he could feel the lightness and excitement already start to permeate his brain. He fought it. He didn't want to succumb. He didn't want to let Amelia down. *Let down* was a fake way of saying it to himself. The real way was *lie*. He hated lying to her, even if she'd never find out. Her life was his life, and he was letting her down. He was lying to her. He didn't want to. But it had already been decided. He wasn't the one in control of his body. Of his mind. His pulse wasn't his. It controlled itself. He hated his body when it was like this. And he never felt as good.

The scene at the subway station had merged with the fight over dinner, and he could feel the tension spreading through his legs. And on Rosh Hashanah, he shouldn't need to work. He had too much to think about, to take stock of. Amelia, his baby laughing in a stranger's arms, and now this, the fact that his neighborhood felt like a bomb whose fuse had already been lit. . . . He would take the day for introspection, to refresh himself and start the new year off correctly. Even if he wasn't a rabbi—if he wasn't at synagogue—he could observe the day. He wouldn't go to work!

He started to get what he cringingly referred to once (and the psychologist insisted on forever after embarrassingly repeating back to him) as the "happy feeling." The feeling like he was outside himself and his work and his problems. Like suddenly his desk and computer and meetings didn't matter. The closest he ever felt anything similar to it before that first night on the poker site was during his senior year of high school on the tennis court. When his backhand was as strong and reliable as his forehand and he could place his serve with kick on either side of the box. When he'd choose to serve first because he knew the other guy couldn't touch it. He walked onto the court with an impatience to get the match started because he knew he'd either win or play someone who'd make him work. That was when he felt it first, the "happy feeling." When a popular girl at a summer camp told him that another girl he'd never even heard of liked him—and he could tell she wasn't making fun of him—he felt it again. Then maybe something like it again on the bimah during the couple of years when he'd settled in and felt good leading the congregation in the main synagogue. In front of all the stained-glass windows and hundred-year-old wood and hanging chandeliers, with the senior rabbi sitting behind him, proud. Then he felt it at the cowboy bar. And the first time he saw his son's face. When the generic baby inside Amelia turned into his specific, individual Simon. It was the opposite of anxiety—it was a flow, a loosening in his muscles— an ability to breathe deeply and happily throughout his body. It was about things unfolding as they should because of who he was and in spite of him.

And this was something like how he felt as he exited the subway at Nostrand and walked the block to the LIRR Hempstead line. It was how he felt when he texted his boss to apologize for not confirming earlier that he was going to be late because of Rosh Hashanah services.

An hour later, Aaron sat in section J at the finish line between the box seats below and the restaurant above, twenty grand in one pocket, a racing form in the other, and as focused as he'd been anytime since he'd sat alone in this same section when Amelia was barely in her second trimester.

Chapter 15

The cops had murdered the Blau boy in cold blood Saturday night, so this would be different. Not just the usual letting off of steam. Community organizers had shown up, and gang leaders, too. Jupiter had heard they'd stepped away together to discuss the issue. Jason Blau was a big, imposing, eccentric boy, but his father was the sort of man who was everywhere in Bed-Stuy, the sort of man who made people feel good to be around him. He had a good job running a painting operation and was trying to do better for himself.

Earlier this morning before going over to see Antoinette, Jupiter had been home in front of the oven, baking her a cake. Dark chocolate all the way through. No marshmallows. No milk chocolate. Just flourless dark. Jupiter could tell. Both pieces the last few times, she'd saved the dark chocolate for last. And with some women you didn't know. Maybe they ate what they wanted first. But not Antoinette. She was a savorer. No doubt in his mind. Muslimah or not, she was a sensualist. A hedonist, maybe. Hopefully. He'd get there. Slow and steady in his middle age. But he'd get there. He preheated the oven to 375 degrees and buttered a six-inch round baking pan, then tossed it into the sink and buttered his eight-inch pan instead.

Lined its bottom with a round of parchment paper and buttered that, too.

The cops expected a reaction to Jason's death. Jupiter chopped chocolate into small pieces. More cops had been out yesterday than he'd ever seen. And twice as many as that this morning. Those posters were everywhere: Monday Morning We Stop Following Their Rules. It sounded so goddamn fucking young. But Jupiter envied the sentiment. At the same time, he feared what it would do to his son.

Derek had told him this morning that something was going to go down because half—his boy said half, which meant in reality a couple, but still that was a lot—of his friends had already been arrested in the last twenty-four hours. Jupiter wouldn't be shocked if his boy had had a hand in those posters. In a metal bowl set over a saucepan of barely simmering water, Jupiter melted chocolate with butter, stirring, until perfectly smooth. Derek used to love this cake. It used to be the cake he took to school with him on his birthday. The other kids did cupcakes, but Derek would show up with three cakes for the class that he'd slice himself. Jupiter had always included the cake knife with the dull blade so Derek could cut slices without getting hurt.

Jupiter knew that Derek was angry. Angrier than he'd ever seen him. The neighborhood violence had mixed into the Malcolm X he was reading. If he was reading that at all. Jupiter was the one who'd given him that. Along with W. E. B. Du Bois and the Hardy Boys back in the day. All that good old stuff that Jupiter had read in high school. And a subscription to *Yankees Magazine* before that. Jupiter didn't know if Derek read anymore at all. He used to be glued to books. Jupiter used to have to make him go to sleep, to turn off the lights. Or maybe that was in a movie Jupiter saw—a character that reminded him of Derek. But now Derek was getting into fights. He'd even jumped a white guy for an iPhone, from what Jupiter had heard at the plumbing supply store. Jupiter had given Derek a cold look when he saw the phone in Derek's room, but Jupiter didn't have a full confrontation in him. Things were tenuous enough between them at the moment, and he didn't want to lose Derek completely.

Derek had always defended the police to his slacker friends— "Someone has to do the job," he'd say—but now they were all he could talk about. How the police were just bullies. Bullies in school that grew up to become bullies on the street. *"Stop and frisk is a political tool, victimizing one group of people so another group feels protected. It's humiliating hundreds of thousands of people, for what? In stops, weapons are found less than two percent of the time, and sure they say that's because people don't carry anymore, but everyone knows that's bullshit. Was there any evidence of Jason fucking Blau carrying last night before he was shot ten goddamn times? No. None."*

Jupiter didn't know where his little boy was getting this stuff.

He knew that if the neighborhood's anger was to be expressed it would be directed first against the cops and then against white people.

Everyone knew that the only white-owned house on this block, the nicest block this close to the subway (which was where all the cops hung out), was two doors down from his, and it was where Antoinette spent her days.

And he knew he liked Antoinette.

He removed the bowl from the heat and whisked a lot—but less than Derek liked—of sugar into the chocolate. He added eggs and whisked again. He sifted cocoa powder over the chocolate mixture and whisked again. He turned on the radio to NPR, but they were talking about Syria and Iraq and Afghanistan and Ghana and elephants and Haiti and rights of pregnant women. He poured the chocolate batter into the pan and slid it to the center of the oven. He left it to bake while he went down to the basement for the boards, hammers, and nails. He hammered the boards into the wooden window frames, took his shower, and rang his neighbor's bell.

This was only the tenth or fifteenth time he'd talked with her indoors one-on-one, but he'd been watching her, looking out for her in a nice way, not a creepy way, for almost three months, and he could tell she was a good woman. She was pretty enough, but more important, she was good. Christian or Muslim. She was a single parent like he was. She was originally from out of the city like he was. She liked kids like he did. She was two doors down every day. She liked his baking. And he thought he could tell she liked him.

So needless to say, if some kids knocked on the door hoping to give Aaron or Amelia a hard time today not realizing it'd just be Antoinette there alone with a little white baby, Jupiter wanted to be there to make sure they didn't get any farther than the front door. He couldn't tell this to Antoinette, because she'd tell him he was overstepping, that he was crazy, that she could handle herself. And though she'd probably three-out-of-three be correct, he still didn't feel it'd be right to leave her alone. He didn't want to.

Now, having returned home for just a moment, he was back at 383 in his clean white T-shirt and cargo pants holding the warm, still-breathing cake. Antoinette, having waited at the door, greeted him there, because she didn't want him to ring again and bring Amelia downstairs.

Antoinette wanted for herself whatever Mr. Jupiter was going to bring. He plated the cake for the two of them. It was just off the cooling rack, dusted with coca powder.

Antoinette laughed, and so did Simon, whom she forgot for a moment she'd been carrying in her arms.

Chapter 16

Amelia's computer voiced: "You're back on!" when her Internetless hour was up. But her iPhone had been on her desk the whole time. She'd answered a dozen emails and checked Facebook (babies, Obama), Instagram (food, babies), and Twitter (*#12yearsold10shots* was trending). And Snapchat. She'd done a story on Snapchat for *Marie Claire* and convinced her friends to try it in the process. Now they used it all the time. Messages that disappeared. Teenagers used it for pictures of their nipples, but Amelia and her high school friends, closer to fifty than fifteen years old, Snapchatted pictures of torn seams, of humungous diapers, of their sleeping husbands' asses. Not Amelia. Aaron wouldn't approve.

But that was what had taken her away from Jonah Hill: Amelia's friend Megan's husband, Jesus, had carved out the bottom of an egg carton and put his hairy, purple testicle in among the brown eggs. It was the kind of thing that would have been hilarious at thirteen, pretty funny at eighteen, tired at twenty-five, and at thirty-three?

Amelia wondered what her friends said about her life. Divorced at thirty. Baby out of wedlock. Living in sin with a former rabbi. Hanging out with celebrities and writing articles that had to simultaneously celebrate and mock them. And why was the baby out of wedlock? That was what everybody wanted to know. It was what Aaron wanted to know. And her parents, and her friends. And Aaron's father, who was physically falling apart and addicted to good news from his son. He called every day. He'd even told Aaron that Aaron's happiness was the only thing keeping him alive. He meant it literally.

She couldn't have told her friends about Aaron's addiction without revealing too much. So she answered honestly and evasively about wanting to live like the Europeans. She didn't see any reason to get married. "Because it worked out so well for me the first time?" she said. And deprecatingly with a greater gesture toward self-knowledge and sincerity, "Because it was so embarrassing the first time to put on a dress and parade in front of all my friends and family and say *until death do us part* and then fail at it, or, whatever, admit that I couldn't hack it with Kevin, that even if *we* didn't pay sixty grand and have the biggest party in the world again I just hate the idea of going through the whole lifetime commitment thing." She'd only said something like that to Aaron once, because when she'd said it, he looked at her as though she'd taken the chair beside her and lifted it off the ground and smashed it across his face.

That had been two weeks ago, and of course it had something to do with their not having slept in months or having had sex for about that long, too, but when she'd said it she'd both wanted to take it back and leave it said, because she'd meant it. In the moment, she'd added that she was elated to have a child with Aaron because she loved him and was happier with him than she'd ever been with anyone or imagined she could be with anyone, but 100 percent confidence still seemed an unattainable goal.

"I mean, look at my parents," she'd said.

"Then why would you want to have a child with me?" Aaron had said.

He was crying. He was looking away from her furious and terrified.

Simon had meant everything was stable for him and would be for the rest of his life, Amelia saw, and her one comment about not being able to guarantee a lifetime commitment had taken it all away.

"Because I love you," she said, wanting to give back to him as much as she could. "And I've never loved anyone as much as I love you. I want a family with you. And I want to spend the rest of my life with you. But that's a really long time. People change. As hard as we're going to try. And I don't see the need to swear it in front of a judge or minister or rabbi."

"Or my dad."

"Yes! I'm sorry! Or your father. I can't—neither of us can live our lives to make your father happy."

"But it would make *me* happy."

"I don't want to promise if I can't be one hundred percent absolutely sure that either of us can keep that promise. I can promise that I love you and I feel incredible affection for Simon and I can't see that changing. And more, not only do I love you, but you're the only thing I love. You and Simon are the only thing that matters in my life. Yes, I'm saying that might change. But for now, there's Megan, my mom sort of, and who knows how long she'll live—I'm being as honest as I can—maybe a couple college friends I'm seeing less and less since Simon—and you and Simon. There are probably twenty people in the world I'd care about if they weren't alive tomorrow. I mean it. More like ten, probably. And you are at the top of that list. You and Simon are that list. Why isn't that enough for you? And I don't know if I ever felt that way about Kevin. Which was maybe why I already got the marriage thing wrong once. And since I got it wrong once, I don't want to go through it again. Why do you want to make me?"

Still, Aaron was furious. Or, rather, he was sad, and his sadness made him embarrassed, which made him angry. He didn't hear the loving parts, only that she wouldn't marry him. He was grinding his teeth and clenching his fists. He was a tiny little boy who couldn't have what he wanted. Amelia wanted to give him what he wanted, but she couldn't. She couldn't make her body want to sleep with him, either, which would have solved things in a different way, so she blew him for the first time since Simon was born, and afterward, in a joking voice, he said, "Don't think this makes up for not wanting to marry me," and in a joking voice she said, "Not even a little bit?" and in a joking voice she said, "Maybe a little bit?" and in a serious voice she said, "I love you," and in a serious voice he said, "I love you, too."

. . .

She did love him. That first time she'd met him, she'd felt the potential of it. Then over a month with no contact. She'd tried to forget him. Then a second date talking about how he'd been a rabbi until he could no longer pretend to believe. When they'd finally had sex, he'd told her ten minutes after that he hadn't quit his job as a rabbi. They were at his small apartment. He'd been so attentive to her body. He told her about the stolen money, how he'd needed to steal it. She'd tried to give him the most forgiving smile she could. She'd been married at the time. She was disappointed in him, but she wasn't perfect and couldn't expect perfection. She wanted to help him. No one had been hurt other than him. She'd wanted to help cure him. She'd never been able to help Kevin in any way big or small. He'd never even let her hammer in a nail or make a reservation. Aaron kissed her.

She asked him the next time they were together to tell her about it again. And then again. She wanted to understand it better, but she couldn't. He was just an asshole. A thief. He had his reasons, sure, but he was a thief. Who stole from decent people and could steal again.

He told her the story fifty, a hundred times. They slept together sometimes afterward. It was sick, for a while. She'd ask him to tell her, he'd tell her, and then they'd sleep together. It was a routine. They couldn't get past it, even after Kevin. She liked him so much. More than Kevin. It wasn't fair that the man she liked, really liked, the first, only man she really liked—loved—was rotten like this. She wanted to make him better, to care for him as she'd never been cared for, but she couldn't. She wanted to hear nuances in the story that made it different from how she understood it, but there weren't any.

She tried to stop thinking about it until it consumed her. They stopped seeing each other. Then he showed up at her apartment one night when she was thinking about him, and they slept together in a messy, full-bodied way that was more like how she'd slept with Kevin. She and Aaron started seeing each other again. He apologized. Said he wasn't that man anymore. It was a one-time mistake. He'd been seeing a psychologist. He was getting better, he said. Just look at his life, he said. When she'd been in it, he was getting better. Her, and his new job. Things were good. He didn't gamble anymore. He'd only stolen because of the gambling. And he wanted her in his life more than he wanted anything else, more than Kevin had ever wanted her.

But she couldn't take his word for it. They talked about it sober and drunk. He didn't know how to convince her. She suggested they see his therapist together. She wanted to understand what the problem was from an objective professional.

And it made all the difference.

"A hypocrisy driven by living under untenable circumstances. Being a rabbi in a doctrine he didn't believe in. We don't think gambling is his problem," the psychologist had said. The psychologist had been a warm, young guy.

"No?" she had said.

"That's what I've been telling you," Aaron had said. "Risk taking is the problem that presented as gambling because of how much stress I was under. Because I was in a situation that was rife with hypocrisy. I've always been a risk taker. Since grade school when I ran away from home to live with my mother at the hospital for a week. I didn't tell anyone."

"And now that he's no longer a rabbi, it shouldn't be a problem," the psychologist had said. "We are monitoring it closely, but we feel that the crime was one of context more than character."

"But still," Aaron had said, "the doctor has set me up to see someone, a specialist in risk addiction. I've asked him to, because I felt it was important. For us. The truth is: I am an addict. But not to gambling."

"It was just a product of his environment, what led him to bet? And steal?" Amelia had said.

"Yes," the psychologist had said. "That's what we believe."

"And I can create an environment for him? So he doesn't feel like that again?"

"Not alone, but you two can do it together," the psychologist had said. "Which was why I was so pleased when Aaron said you wanted to come in to talk to me together."

So she could start a new life with him.

And Aaron was wonderful. Wonderful with Simon. He worked hard every day to pay for more than half the mortgage. He loved her. She loved him.

The one time they'd gone to the track together, he hadn't bet more than ten dollars on a race. He had let her choose the horses. He'd been in control.

And before they'd bought this house together, she'd asked him point blank if he had a problem, and he'd sworn he could manage it. What more could he do than swear? The Gambling Anonymous programs were God based, and he disbelieved. He'd been seeing the risk-management therapist.

She was taking care of him. He was on the right track. He clearly had his moments—a basketball game he seemed to care too much about—but nothing out of control. She was putting him in a position to succeed. They were building a life together, even if she wasn't ready to call that life a marriage.

. . .

Amelia heard laughter downstairs. Adult African American laughter. The kind that wasn't meant for the sake of a baby. She heard plates and forks. She was happy for an excuse to get away from Jonah Hill.

"Remember *Superbad*," she'd written, "that 2007 ballad to teenage ineptitude starring Jonah Hill and Michael Cera. Hill was the intensely, caustically funny one. Even so, you probably thought, Brother, you just hit it big; enjoy it while it lasts, because you'll be playing second fiddle for the rest of your career. And for a minute there, it did look like Cera would be the one on first violin."

After Antoinette said Jupiter wouldn't come over, here he was. Less than an hour later. Surely that was grounds for dismissal. Amelia liked Antoinette as much as she could like anyone her son loved more than her, but this was Amelia's home. And workplace. How was she supposed to get work done if Antoinette was downstairs with friends all the time.

Amelia wasn't being fair. Simon was a baby. He loved whoever spent the most time with him and gave him food and held him. On Sunday evening at the end of a weekend, he loved Amelia. On Friday afternoon, he loved Antoinette. Antoinette wasn't to blame. But guests? And Jupiter of all people—one of the few neighbors who still hadn't asked them over.

When Aaron had originally suggested the move, Bed-Stuy seemed too much like something Kevin would propose. An adventure, more than real life. But once she'd met her neighbors and they'd invited her to see their homes, to compare interior details, to eat (the couple next door prepared the most delicious fish tagine and laughingly referred to her and Aaron as "the diversity" on the block), for the first time in her life, Amelia felt part of a neighborhood. She'd grown up in the suburbs, where the other houses were spaced far apart and without children her age. After college, she'd lived in big cities where everyone was anonymous, and then she'd married Kevin, with whom she moved around too often to get to know people. But Bed-Stuy was a fixed community where everyone welcomed her as someone they'd known forever. One of the few owners on the block, however, whom Amelia didn't have a personal connection with was Jupiter. He seemed more interested in Antoinette and fixing fuse boxes than getting to know her family.

Amelia ran her hands down the wooden banister and crossed the front of the parlor. But then she stopped. She saw her baby at the dining room table with this other couple.

"You know Mr. Jupiter from the block," Antoinette said.

"Of course she does," Jupiter said, smiling.

That the couple was black and her baby was white was what first struck Amelia. The racial incongruity of the little white baby with the two dark-skinned adults. She'd dated a black guy in college and liked the way her fingers looked intertwined with his. She liked the way his legs looked intertwined with hers. But now Amelia felt she couldn't let on that she was thinking about race. She looked at her baby, only at her baby, but her mind went back to how she didn't know Jupiter beyond the ridiculous stories Aaron told about him, and there he was in her home two feet from her son. That wonderful smell was chocolate cake. It struck her that Antoinette wasn't wearing a scarf, after all. It was a Muslim scarf. Not a burka. A hijab. A sign of masculine hegemony over the rights of oppressed women all over the world. But she hadn't always worn one. Had she?

"Is everything all right?" Amelia said, getting as close as she could without disturbing the little family they made at the table. That morning she had dressed her boy in a plain white onesie and striped blue-and-white pants. Now he sat with this fake mother and father at his real dining room table.

"Simon can't eat that," Amelia said.

"Of course not," Antoinette said. "He's only got three teeth! I hope it's okay I'm using your plates. I'll clean up after. Mr. Jupiter baked a flourless chocolate cake."

"Aren't you hot in here? If you're going to wear that in the house, don't you want me to turn up the air-conditioning?"

"No. I'm comfortable," Antoinette said.

"I mean. It's just us in here," Amelia said, pointing out herself, the baby, Jupiter. "You don't need to wear that for us."

"It's to show you respect. And modesty. To respect you," Antoinette said. "I want to."

"The cake smells great," Amelia said.

"Have a slice," Jupiter said.

"It's too early," Amelia said.

Simon looked over, but he didn't reach out to her.

Amelia stifled a rising sob. Her body heaved to be closer to her son.

"We were just talking about the weather," Jupiter said. "About how warm it's been. Hot. About how hot it's been for September. It's been the hottest September we can remember."

"It looks nice out today," Amelia said, thinking that she couldn't think of a kind way to make this man leave her home. So as an attempt at useless reverse psychology, "Can I get you something to drink?" she asked Jupiter. "A glass of water or a cup of coffee to wash down the cake?"

"I'd love a cup, if you're pouring. Would you like a cup?" Jupiter asked Antoinette.

"It's okay," Antoinette said, unsure if Jupiter was purposely badgering Amelia or if he didn't understand that she wanted him to leave. Antoinette was worried that the longer Jupiter stayed, the angrier Amelia would be with her. But then there was the problem of the cake. The cake was delicious and they had only each eaten half of a slice, so there was no way he could leave until he had at least finished his slice and wrapped the rest of the cake to take home or she told him to take it home and he insisted that she give the rest to Teddy. Teddy would love this cake.

Amelia didn't know whether to stand or sit or take her son or return to work. Jupiter's T-shirt looked ironed. Was it possible that he ironed his white T-shirts? Or maybe he had a cleaning lady to do that for him. He was a good-looking man. Amelia had interviewed Ben Affleck at a charity golf tournament, and Jupiter looked like an older, overweight, black Ben Affleck. It was in the eyes.

Simon looked up at Antoinette like she was everything in the world to him. He cocked his neck, which a couple of hours earlier had been in Amelia's hands, the two of them alone together. He screwed up his face and then relaxed into a smile. He looked up at Antoinette and smiled. He didn't want anything. Amelia wanted to get him formula, but Simon didn't want formula.

"You were just saying," tired, black Ben Affleck said. Amelia tried to laugh. He was talking to Antoinette, talking past Amelia. "You were just saying that you were going to make yourself a cup. How it was funny what air-conditioning did to your throat. We'd both like a cup, if you don't mind. Antoinette was saying something warm on a warm day sounded good because of the air-conditioning and I was saying that in India, in warm cultures, they drank a lot of tea, because the warm beverage helped them sweat, which cooled them down."

"No problem at all," Amelia said. "But I really should be working, so I hope you won't think me rude if I serve you guys then head on back upstairs." *Hope you won't think me rude* and *head on back upstairs* were both expressions she'd never used before.

She was furious at these people for acting as though her house were their house and her child their child. She turned off the air-conditioning to punish them but quickly turned it on again for Simon. She ate a big scoop of vanilla gelato from the freezer. She poured three stale coffees and put a big scoop of vanilla gelato into hers. She brought theirs out first so they wouldn't see her gelato coffee. They were laughing, pretending Jupiter's finger was a mustache over little baby Simon's upper lip.

Chapter 17

Amelia called Aaron.

"Jupiter is here again, and he won't leave," she said.

"What?" he said. "I'm in a meeting."

"Jupiter is here and he won't leave," she said.

"Did you ask him to leave?" he said.

"No."

"Good," Aaron said. "He's our neighbor. He's a nice guy. And—"

"Now Simon is crying. Do you hear that?"

"Through the phone? I'm in a meeting. Hang on one sec. I'll step outside. Sorry. It's my . . . It's about my son. It'll only be a moment. Okay. I'm here. Ames? I'm here. What can I do?"

Amelia started to cry.

"Ames? Ames? Are you okay?"

"My God. No. I don't know. Yes."

"Do you want me to call Jupiter? Tell him you're not feeling well? That you're not up to company?"

"It's not just him. I don't know." Amelia took a breath. "My Bed-Stuy article came out today and there were all these nasty comments and I don't want to write about Jonah fucking Hill and Simon loves Antoinette more than me even though it's only

Monday and he was just with me all weekend, and this man I don't know is in our house, and my friends suck, and I don't know. I miss you."

"I love you, sugar. Simon is a baby. He likes whoever is holding him. You know that. And we can fire Antoinette tonight. Tomorrow. You'll always be his mom. Antoinette is just our employee. I can ask Jupiter to leave. He is just our neighbor. You don't need to write about Jonah fucking Hill. These are all temporary things. What matters is that we have each other and we have Simon and he has us. Antoinette doesn't matter. Neither does Jupiter. Commenters online don't matter. You'll never meet them. They are pretend people. We're the only people who matter. Okay?"

"Okay," she said.

"I love you. Okay?"

"Okay," she said.

"Okay."

"Okay."

"Okay," he said. "I love you."

"Okay."

Chapter 18

Aaron put his phone on vibrate and slipped it into his jacket pocket.

Belmont Park was perfect. A breeze cut into the heat. There were a few seats between him and the next guy, a weightlifter in his forties wearing basketball shorts, a white T-shirt, and a backward Yankees cap. The guy sat with a newspaper alongside a plastic bag overflowing with oranges.

"Apologies, boss," the guy said. "I got in trouble once for not offering, so I'm just going to say it from the get-go: I'll talk if you want, but I'm not going to share my oranges. Sorry to be rude, but that's that."

"No problem," Aaron said. "Not an oranges guy."

"You missed a helluva first race," the guy said.

Third-generation Polish, was Aaron's guess. Or Czech? Maybe Jewish even and eccentric? But strong. Or Italian? He seemed like a nice guy. A guy who wouldn't ruin the day for Aaron. Might even add to the thrill.

"Yeah?" Aaron said.

"Eighteen-to-one wire-to-wire, stumbled down the stretch for no reason."

"Claiming race," Aaron guessed.

"But still."

"You bet it?" Aaron asked. Aaron didn't like to talk previous bets with strangers, but this guy seemed harmless, and Aaron wanted to know how the track had been racing.

"No."

Starting to flip through the *Daily Racing Form,* Aaron didn't like any horses in the second race. He was focusing on the third. It would be the first decent race that day. Aaron was familiar with some of the trainers and owners at least. He scanned the practice times.

"Fine, fine. My apologies. Have an orange," the guy said, peeling one indelicately. Ripping off small pieces with all his fingers. "Have an orange. My apologies. That's a nice suit. I don't need to be like that. My apologies about before. It's just that some guys come in, and the first thing they say is, 'Can I have an orange?' They even specify. 'Not too many seeds.' Like I don't have a system? Like I just go to the store and buy whatever the fuck oranges my hands go to first? I don't want the ones with too many seeds, either. Seriously, my apologies. My deepest apologies: it would be my pleasure for you eat one of my oranges. I've got extra napkins, if you're worried about your suit. I've got like fifteen oranges here. Good brain food."

"Stop apologizing," Aaron said. "I'm good." Aaron liked this. It felt right. In the mood Aaron was in, this guy was adding to, rather than ruining, the day. There was only one thing that could take him out of the feeling now, and he still had a full race he wasn't going to bet before getting to the race he was.

"Okay, okay," Mr. Oranges said. "My apologies. I won't be pushy." He sat four seats over from Aaron, and the other nearest seat taken was a couple of rows back. Belmont was dead. Citrus wafted over the stands. There was an even-money favorite in the third, but Aaron couldn't figure out why. No reason to overthink it. Aaron liked a race where there was a favorite he could confidently bet against.

The sky was blue, like from a watercolor painting made for a kid's bedroom. Aaron felt like a kid. His knees were jumping. There were a couple of clouds in the sky, as if just to show how blue the sky was. His heart was pumping, but it wasn't nervous energy. It was good energy.

"How's the track running lately?" Aaron said.

"Like a dream."

The two men sat there as though they were best friends. The guy ate four oranges in ten minutes. They smelled clean. Seeds and peels were everywhere.

Aaron narrowed down that third race while the second race ran. He looked up to watch the finish. To listen to the track announcer. To watch the horses pump their muscles. This was one of the reasons the track was so great. On a day like this. To get outside. Be around other people. See strong, beautiful animals. And play. It wasn't like the computer. Or inside watching TV. There was nothing shameful about this.

Some women and a few men were up front cheering, but most of the people there were like Aaron, watching as though casually.

At the very end of the race, he heard, "Come on!" and, "That's it!" scattered throughout, but it was nothing like Saratoga or even the weekends at Belmont with everyone in the stands cheering. Weekday mornings were different. The stands were mostly empty, and among the people there, there was restraint, resignation, camaraderie. Elegance.

Aaron loved it. His knees were bouncing and he didn't even have a horse in the race.

The stands lifted and settled into the time between races.

Aaron had fifteen minutes to place his bet and get back to his seat. Alabaster Arrow, a filly paying seven to one, had never won anything before, but she seemed to have a better pedigree than her competitors, her practice times were improving, the jockey was trustworthy and new to the horse. Aaron just liked what he saw. It felt right. And mostly, Aaron felt right thinking about it. Aaron felt great. He felt better than great. He felt whole. He remembered this morning and seeing Simon laughing at Antoinette's laugh. It didn't bother him that he wasn't getting married. The last time Aaron had been at a track, he didn't have a son, and now he did! He wasn't breaking any oath, really, or even if he was, this was his celebratory trip. His cigar. He hadn't lit a fatherhood cigar. He had a perfect woman and a perfect son. It didn't bother him now that the cops were too aggressive with kids in the subway station or that the kids were too aggressive with him. He had to let all that go. He had to do his job and be a father and put all that behind him. Savor the moment.

"Ten minutes to post," the track announcer said.

"Where you from?" Oranges said when Aaron was back from the betting window, a five-thousand-dollar ticket in hand.

"Brooklyn, you?"

"Rochester," Oranges said. "I couldn't find anyone to like in this one, either. How about you?"

"Alabaster Arrow," Aaron said.

"Really? She's never won anything. Why would she start here? You seeing something I'm not?"

A hot weight flooded Aaron's body, and he couldn't get his breath. He had a sudden vision of himself years earlier, of sprinting down Second Avenue in the high seventies. He had just won five grand after a long losing streak. After losing more than fifty grand in less than a month, he had won five, and he was sprinting down Second Avenue to find his bookie so he could put that five grand down on a basketball game before the second half started. He was on the verge of tears that it would be too late to place what turned out to be a losing over bet on the second half of whatever game that had been. It had been a West Coast game, so this must have been past midnight, and Aaron wouldn't sleep that night before heading, sick, to work in the morning.

Aaron turned away from the guy and his oranges. *It doesn't matter what he thinks. He doesn't know any better than I do.* Aaron forced himself to smile.

"Probably just hope," Aaron said, "We'll see." Everything was darker now. Aaron was going to lose again. He knew it. His phone buzzed inside his jacket pocket.

"You're okay?" his father said when Aaron answered. "You're okay? I was worried." His father's voice strained with false calm.

"I'm fine," Aaron said, shielding himself from Oranges.

"Today is Rosh Hashanah. You know that, sorry," his father said. "I thought it might bother you, but you're okay."

"I'm fine," Aaron said. "I can't talk now, but—"

"I hadn't heard from you today is all," his father said.

A woman down below bought ice cream from a track-side cart.

"I'm going to try to take a walk in the park," his father said, "and I was thinking I could bring Simon if you were comfortable with that?"

"Simon's with his nanny," Aaron said. "An hour commute from you. We'll see you on Sunday."

"Sunday, right, and you *are* okay today?" his father said.

"Dad," Aaron said. "I'm fine. I love you."

"I love you," his father said. And after a breath, "Sometimes it hurts so much. I love you so much, it hurts."

"Love you, too, Dad," Aaron said.

"I know," his father said. "I know you do. You'll pick up when I call tomorrow?"

"Of course," Aaron said.

"Or if I call back today? It's just we hadn't spoken yet today," his father said.

"I know. And you'll see us on Sunday."

"I love you," his father said. Aaron ended the call, silenced his phone, and slid it back into his pocket.

"Where in Brooklyn you from?" Oranges said.

It took Aaron a moment to answer. "Bed-Stuy," he said.

"No, seriously."

"I was being serious," Aaron said.

"You buying to flip?"

"It's a beautiful house," Aaron said, telling himself to be calm. He was okay. His father was okay. They would see him on Sunday. "Eighteen nineties. Original stained-glass and wood and everything."

"It's safe around there? For your wife? You've got a wife and kids?"

"It's safe," Aaron said.

"My apologies. I don't mean to pry, but you're not a majority in the community?"

"Two minutes to post," the track announcer said.

"What?" Aaron said.

"Don't get me wrong. I work with some. Real hardworking, great guys. Really great guys. I'm just asking. Because where I live—it's like my kids—my wife. And I can see, you've got the nice suit. Good job. I can see you're a family man. An upstanding man. Where I live we have a real sense of a community."

"They've taken me and my family in," Aaron said, indignant. "They come over with food. Look after my son. They've been there for years, and they're thrilled to have us on the block. It's safe and clean. I've never felt a part—as much a part of a community as I do with them. I mean, as I do there."

"That sounds nice, then," Oranges said.

"Horses at the gates," the track announcer said.

"Good luck," Oranges said.

"And they're off!" the track announcer said.

Chapter 19

Sara acted like she was tired of people thinking she was a boy and then being surprised when they realized she was a girl, but everyone knew she liked surprising people. Sara was eighteen and looked younger when she woke up in the morning or was just out of the shower, but when she was in her sweatpants and a big hoodie and a baseball cap and sunglasses like she was now, she looked older than eighteen, and she looked like a boy. And it wasn't some accidental thing. She liked the way she looked. The girls she was into liked the way she looked. That was half the point of dressing that way.

And Sara liked getting mad when people didn't know she was a girl. Sara and her last girlfriend had fought. They never really talked about why, but they fought a lot, and they fought in public, and usually it was Sara who threw her girlfriend up against a fence, or down to the sidewalk, or against the lamppost on Fulton and Albany. Her girlfriend was dumb as shit but she looked good. She was skinny but she had a body on her. Even when it was cold outside she showed it off. People liked to stop their car and yell out, "You don't put your hands to a woman like that!" and, "What if someone pushed your mom or your sister?" and with her girlfriend halfway down the block by then,

Sara stood up straight and strong and yelled, "I *am* a woman, you fucking bitch! I am a woman! You want to call the cops? You *call* the fucking cops!" which almost always made that car drive away. Then Sara caught back up to her dumb, pretty girlfriend and apologized and kissed wherever she'd made her hurt, and took her home to either one of their moms' places, and because neither Sara nor her girlfriend had jobs, and both of them had police records and were over eighteen so they weren't allowed back to Boys and Girls High to finish off their degrees, they spent the afternoons getting food or smoking or in bed.

But now it was hot out, Sara was in handcuffs, and she didn't have a girlfriend anymore. Sara had purposely broken the law to get arrested, but now that she was arrested she wasn't sure what was supposed to happen next. She was angry. Everyone sitting on that curb was angry. About Jason—even though she didn't really know the kid, and from what she'd heard, people who did know him didn't like him—and how there was nothing to do about him getting killed. Getting arrested had sounded like a protest, but it was fucking dumb. And now her mom was going to kick her out because she'd been arrested again, this time actually for nothing. She had, along with a couple of assholes, jumped a turnstile. Stopped, frisked, arrested, then marched upstairs to sit in Fulton Park. That was new. And fucking racist as shit. Usually they'd just stop and frisk and maybe arrest you, but the march upstairs had never happened before to her or anyone she knew.

Though now she saw why they'd taken her to the park. Too many people were getting arrested. The police must not know what to do with all of them. There were twenty of them rounded up outside the Utica subway station right by Boys and Girls High. Another thirty or so were being brought to where the twelve of them were. The cops seemed tired of arresting them, but every ten minutes it was like another group of everyone she knew was being rounded up and brought outside Boys and Girls High, which was where she would have liked to get her degree from anyway, if she'd been allowed inside.

Sara and close to fifty others stood around for a while, but it was too hot to keep them all there in cuffs. The cuffs themselves were heating up on her wrists and nearly cutting through. And it was embarrassing, even if they'd done it on purpose. It was all dumb: fare evasion in front of a cop, shoplifting in front of a cop, spitting at a cop, threatening a cop. Sara still knew a lot of the kids up in the classrooms who were looking down at her. She'd been in those classrooms eighteen months earlier. She'd never been a great student, but one time in eighth grade the English teacher had them act out a court scene from *To Kill a Mockingbird*, which was still her favorite book, and she and her friend Stace had done this whole speech about how the slave couldn't have done it because there were no witnesses and no motive, and even though the teacher was going to rule on the other side, he said that because she and Stace did such a convincing job, he ruled on their side instead. He even said that they could be lawyers if they wanted to, and because everyone knew even back then that Stace was going to be some fat-piece-of-shit whore, the teacher must have meant Sara could be the lawyer. That was only four years ago. It made Sara want to cry right there in cuffs on the street.

Above her, the teachers didn't have much control of the kids in the classrooms, so the kids were looking down from the windows or wandering outside the building even though school was in. Some kids were shouting down at everyone in handcuffs on the curb. These were kids Sara had been in classes with, so she asked a black cop if she could go back into Fulton Park because of the shade. The cop told her to pipe down and behave.

Pipe down, he said, like he was a cop from a hundred years ago. Sara could tell he was the type of cop who took the job seriously. Not like the lazy cop or the bully cop. The serious cop was like the bully cop, and sometimes there was crossover between the two types, but the serious cop had more pride and less anger. Like he was fulfilled every day he went to work keeping the streets safe. The bully cop just wanted to be in charge of people. The lazy cop just wanted an easy job. But the serious cop wanted things done right. All the time. The serious cop got mad when things weren't done right. "We were told to keep everyone out here on the sidewalk," he said.

"Why?" Sara said.

"Too many of you," the cop said, "coming from all directions. We don't know how many there's going to be, so we were told to keep you in central locations until this simmers down."

"I bet."

"We're supposed to treat you with respect."

"You remind me of my uncle," Sara said. She didn't like to talk to adults usually, but moments of confrontation brought it out of her, and this cop really did remind her of her mother's brother who lived in Philadelphia and she saw each Christmas.

"We arrest you," he said, "but then we give you clemency, or some of you, those of you without a record. To show we are giving second chances. That we don't want to arrest folks for being upset about a shot kid. This is from all the way on up. Commissioner Bratton. After this kid was killed. A shame, if you ask me. But you have a record. Almost all of you do. That's also what's taking so long. To run all of you through the system. So pipe down and behave. Please. This will all be over with shortly. We'll either let you go or get you processed."

There were more than a hundred people now, kids mostly, in handcuffs lined up on the curb across from the Utica subway station. And there were thirty or forty cops looking after them.

Kids from Boys and Girls High on off-periods or just cutting class gathered around outside the yellow tape the police were stringing up to form wider and wider barriers, and some of the deacons and parishioners from local churches along with all the men who usually played chess in Fulton Park were poking around and asking questions. And the teenage dealers on their trick bikes, and the few friendly homeless. Fulton Park was sometimes closed down for autumn carnivals or a little concert or hip-hop show, so it wasn't unusual for a couple of hundred people to gather around. But typically they were inside the park, not right in front of the school, and typically the people were milling about and not trying to get closer to see who was arrested and why.

With such a large audience, some of the kids who'd been arrested with Sara were chanting.

"Twelve years old ten shots! Twelve years old ten shots!" and "What do we want? Respect! When do we want it? Now!"

They were joined by some of the parishioners of various nearby churches as well as some of the high school kids who chanted with various degrees of sincerity. At first, the chants were jokey, then mocking, making fun of the kids who joined seriously, but as soon as the high school kids saw that these chants bothered the police and that they were making the arrested kids happy—some of them now recognizable as classmates or former classmates—they started chanting loudly and with sincerity.

Kind of dumb, Sara thought, but there were enough of them in cuffs that she could chant whatever she wanted without anyone really singling her out. Like, she would never individually chant, "No justice! No peace!" because it was totally unoriginal and nobody would care listening to it, but now that more than 150 people were chanting it outside of Boys and Girls High and they were being heard by the teachers and assistant principals and people on their way to the subway, it didn't bother her to be chanting it as part of a group.

Some people shifted around and Sara was now sitting next to Derek Jupiter. She knew him because he sold pot sometimes. He was a rich kid who lived in one of the nice brownstones on Stuyvesant and went to one of those charter schools where everyone's posture was important and everyone was called by their last names.

Derek wasn't chanting along with the crowd. He was muttering something about how this was all bullshit. Which it was. But he was really angry. Angry about how only black people got treated like this; how, "There were no cops here ten years ago, five years ago, but now white people move in, gentrify, whatever, then the cops follow. Call it stop and frisk, broken windows, it's the same shit. Arrests follow gentrification!"; how he'd been arrested that morning for asking questions about someone else who'd been arrested on purpose; how he wasn't even poor and he was treated like trash.

And then Derek was telling anyone who'd listen—"383 Stuyvesant, 422 Macon, 371a MacDonaugh, Celestino and Saraghina restaurants, Café George-Andre"—sitting there in handcuffs on the curb listing the homes and business owned by white people in the neighborhood. He was pronouncing all the restaurants and cafés with the correct foreign accents. He'd committed a list to memory—"These are the ones I've staked out, the ones I know for sure; 383 Stuyvesant is right on my block. A black family that rented to black people used to live there. No more—" and he was telling everyone to put these addresses in their phones like it was Halloween and they were the best places to hit up for good candy. Derek turned his head in all directions saying—"383 Stuyvesant, 422 Macon, 371a MacDonaugh, Celestino and Saraghina restaurants, Café George-Andre"—telling friends and strangers that these addresses belonged to outsiders, that it'd be doing our community a favor to rid us of them.

What was strange about the way he was chanting—"383 Stuyvesant, 422 Macon, 371a MacDonaugh, Celestino and Saraghina restaurants, Café George-Andre"—was that there was a rhythm to it, and just like "No justice! No peace!" and "Twelve years old ten shots!" were catchy when everyone said them out loud and together with one beat, Sara started to say "383 Stuyvesant, 422 Macon, 371a MacDonaugh, Celestino and Saraghina restaurants, Café George-Andre" with Derek, without even meaning to.

Sara snapped out of it when the "No justice! No peace!" got loud enough to drown out Derek sitting next to her. There must have been hundreds of chanters, fewer than a quarter of whom were in cuffs. She recognized more than a hundred from school or the neighborhood, and then she felt something on her ear, like rain. She looked up and laughed. Guys she used to hang out with—Damien and TJ and Mike—dripping a Poland Springs bottle down on her. They were trying to offer her some water on a day that kept getting hotter. But then they were trying to pour it on her. She looked up and they motioned to her to open her mouth, but she couldn't tell if it was nice because they knew she was thirsty in the hot street or nasty like they were being sexual. So she gave them the middle finger through the cuffs between her legs and tried to turn around, but her wrists hurt from the cuffs, and a cop came over to her and made her face forward. And Derek Jupiter laughed at them all.

. . .

Maybe a half hour passed under a cloudless blue sky. Sara was sitting, it was hot, she was very thirsty, the cops were standing, sometimes the chanting died down, then it started up again. Cops tried to offer a few arrestees clemency, but now close to five hundred people were looking and shouting in front of the school and in the park. More arrested kids and adults were coming over—even one white kid with dreads—followed by what seemed like everyone from the projects on Chauncey. They all watched or filmed on their phones, and a policeman started cursing because someone spat at him. Or maybe it was just the water that Mike was pouring down on Sara.

Sara tried to stand and the cop pushed her down when suddenly her brother, Andy—who was a great guy with a job at the café at the Barnes & Noble on Eighty-sixth and Lex in Manhattan, where he was supposed to be now—jumped the cop. Andy was carrying the metal baseball bat from when he played ball in high school.

Sara's mom screamed "No!" and Sara didn't know where the two of them had even come from or why Andy wasn't at work, and then all the cops in Brooklyn were on top of Andy banging in his head with their clubs yelling, "He's got a weapon!" and, "Get the bat!" while some of the teachers who were done for the day were shouting, "That's Andy Hall? Is that Andy Hall?" because everyone remembered Sara's brother as if not the best, then definitely one of the most respectful students who had come through Boys and Girls High in years. He'd always been polite to everyone.

High school kids stormed out of the building screaming, and men from the Chauncey projects cut in to defend Andy or try to push the cops back. Sara was on the ground crying, "Momma!" and her mom was yelling, "Andy!" while the kids who didn't know Andy were shouting and throwing bottles and books and rocks, if there were any handy, at the cops, and some of the kids in handcuffs were running away. Derek Jupiter was the first Sara saw who took the opportunity to stand up and escape.

Cops stormed in from all angles with their clubs lashing out at whoever they thought was trying to run. Derek was long gone. Other cops drew their weapons but kept them at their sides. Sirens blared. Three boys from Boys and Girls High bled from their faces. Sara could see it from where she was lying on the pavement, protecting herself but trying to keep a view of her mom and brother to see if they were all right. She couldn't see either. Cops had this one kid, maybe twelve years old, in a choke hold and the kid was waving his arms. There was music blaring, but it didn't make sense. Sara didn't know where it was coming from, and it was reggae from years ago. Someone stepped on Sara's hand by accident, maybe, Sara wasn't sure, but it hurt enough to take her attention away from everything else. Sara touched her wrist and it was already swelling but she couldn't feel any blood. Everyone standing up in cuffs started banging into one another, and then all the kids leaving school joined in the different scuffles like they were at a concert. Upstairs, the students still watching from the classrooms threw water bottles and books, too.

And then chairs and desks, slamming to the concrete, flipping around getting tangled in one another, crashed out from the high windows.

"Take cover!" one cop shouted, and by the time another yelled, "Nigger!" chaos had spread so quickly that there was no logic separating student from teacher and cop and arrestee and Chauncey project residents. The press wasn't there yet, but a scared ring of neighbors were taking photos with their phones.

Sara saw a cop grab a woman so powerfully that her hair rollers fell out. She looked pregnant because of a smock, but Sara thought she was actually just a hairstylist. She definitely wasn't one of the people who threw anything or spit on the cops.

Sara couldn't do anything because of the cuffs. She lost track of her brother, but she could hear her mom screaming, "Andy? Sara?"

"Be careful! Cameras everywhere!" Sara heard a cop yell. Someone smashed Sara's arm again by stomping on it. She held it against her cheek. Sara could see blood on the street, and she heard sirens leave and others approach, and a few gunshots.

Down the street at the dollar store, where the doors were always open to invite people in, students rushed in and then out with armfuls of pillows, pants, and kitchen soap.

Sara could see them from the ground. And then all the cops except a few rushed to the dollar store.

The kids in handcuffs were getting away. Sara hoped Andy was with them, even though she knew he was beaten to the point where that was a dream.

Sara heard another gunshot go off, then a few in a row that sounded like firecrackers. Sara couldn't see her brother or her mother.

. . .

Sara woke up and felt heat coming from the Boys and Girls School and heard an explosion from the direction of the Chauncey projects. She saw her deacon shouting, grabbing at his beard. Teachers were crying and so were some younger girls from the school who were standing by. She must have only been out for a second.

Sometime later, Damien and TJ and Mike were helping her to her feet and Mike held her face in the other direction while Damien fired a bullet at her handcuffs to break them apart. The students burned the school, the dollar store, then the plumbing supply place next door. Everyone knew that store had three million dollars of inventory in a warehouse in East New York.

Sirens and a fire hose. What did the firefighters think they were doing, Sara wondered, but the hose was aimed at a fire. Sara could hear people shooting guns in all directions. She could hear people laughing louder than they were shouting or crying. From the concrete sidewalk, she saw people running with furniture, food, and cases of liquor. Mike ripped a part of his T-shirt off and wrapped it tightly around Sara's arm, which didn't make the pain any better, but it was so nice of Mike to do it that Sara wanted to cry. She looked where her brother had been beaten, and nobody was there anymore, not her brother or mother or Derek or any police. She didn't know why her cell phone wasn't in her pocket, but she asked to borrow Mike's.

"It's not working," he said. Mike had very dark skin and had just been some bullshit kid before, but now had warmth or something about him that made her love him and think about her brother.

Damien posed triumphantly with his gun up in the air, aiming at the looters in the burning school. He admired the shorn handcuffs and flexed his muscles. Sara had never held a gun before but wanted to. She had the image in mind of one of the policemen who'd run in to attack her brother. He was thin, young, and white. He was probably only a few years older than she was, and he wore a blue uniform.

"I didn't think that would work," Damien said to no one. "I didn't think I could shoot through handcuffs. Shit."

"What're you saying?" Mike asked Sara gently.

They all leaned in to listen to her, but maybe they were crazy or all the sirens or yelling down the street or the smoke was making them hear things. She wasn't saying anything.

"What are those, numbers?" Mike was saying.

Sara realized she was actually talking.

"Three eighty three Stuyvesant," she said, "422 Macon, 371a MacDonaugh, Celestino and Saraghina restaurants, Café George-Andre. Three eighty three Stuyvesant . . ."

Chapter 20

Jupiter's phone was blowing up. Texts and calls from his friends telling him that he had to come down to the school; to the Utica subway station just to check it out; that he couldn't miss what was going down; to lock up his home; to get people over to his home to help protect it; to get down to the plumbing supply place to help put out the fire. Everyone was asking for his help providing muscle or reinforcements or advice.

Jupiter sipped his coffee. Took a bite of cake. He hadn't heard anything from his son. That's what worried him. So he excused himself and went out to the front stoop to call his son's cell while Antoinette diapered the baby. He told Antoinette not to worry, but things were hectic at work. That was why he was getting so many calls. Clients. It was a busy season for overworked electrical panels, heading into fall.

Jupiter didn't have anyone other than his son. And his friends. And the people on the block he tried to look after. But friends and folks on the block came and went by the decade—family was what mattered, and his only family was his son, and his son wasn't picking up his phone, so there was no use leaving this house to go after him. Derek had long stopped enabling the Find My Friends app on his phone, so there was no way to track him down. He could be in the middle of it. Jupiter didn't doubt he was.

Jupiter had already taken all the precautions before leaving that morning. He'd locked his doors and windows. Boarded up his downstairs windows before sprinkling the final cocoa powder onto the flourless chocolate cake. His house was even more of a fortress than usual. He texted his son, told him where he'd be. Instructed him not to come home. To go instead to his cousin's place in Brownsville where the nonsense wouldn't reach. Derek had always defended the police, so Jupiter hadn't felt the need to lecture him on respect, permission, submission. He wished he had, now. Jupiter couldn't remember the moment when his curly-haired boy with eyes as big as cherries and a smile that lit up the neighborhood went from being considered adorable and harmless to a menace to society. Jupiter's own father had made it simple: *Yes, sir; sorry, sir; thank you, officer.* No other words should ever come out of your mouth in front of one of them. But Jupiter hadn't wanted to teach his son that lesson.

From the front stoop, Jupiter could hear the streets south by the park, school, and projects loud with shouting and gunfire. Guns must have been pouring out of the projects. All those guns that all those stop-and-frisks had made sure never found their way outside before. Guns that Bloomberg had made it his business to stop coming into New York. They'd always been there. And now they were out in the open. Guns from Virginia and New Mexico. Jupiter heard them in the streets. All it took was an occasion and no fear of the stop-and-frisk brigade.

As a younger man, Jupiter would have wanted to be in the middle of it. Seeing who was where doing what. This would be the most important day in most of their lives. (He heard the crack of gunfire, then silence, then gunfire.) Who took what anger out on what cops, on what kids from the block they'd always hated, and then what, with what weapons, what adrenaline . . . this was going to define some of these kids' lives. Some would get killed. Others would kill. Reputations would be made. Men would spend the rest of their lives in jail because of this one day. And though he couldn't see through trees two blocks down, he saw a half dozen groups of five or six kids each already spreading out doing damage with baseball bats and what looked like shards of broken off traffic signs. They were laughing and ringing doorbells at the nicer houses, throwing bricks through stained-glass windows. They were the cops now. Like that movie: "I am the captain now." They were seeing what homes didn't have bars on the windows. Flat-screens were coming out through doors. Bags of groceries. Computers. Football and basketball jerseys. Car alarms were going off. Trunks smashed to loot. It was difficult to riot on residential streets—the process went slowly—but these kids were giving it their best. They were laughing, pushing each other into tree beds, making each other flinch, seeing what they could get away with. One or two younger kids, maybe ten or eleven years old, were standing lookout, but no cops were coming. The sirens were all on the other side of the park along with the fires and guns.

So at that moment, the place Jupiter most wanted to be was looking after Antoinette. He pocketed his phone, locked up. Back inside he heard sirens and car alarms, but there were often sirens in the neighborhood. Probably because all the windows in the house were closed and the air-conditioning units were going at full blast, the sirens were muted, and there was no smell of smoke. There was no street noise, no gunshots.

"Everything okay?" Antoinette asked.

"You're beautiful," Jupiter said.

"Don't go talking like that," Antoinette said.

"I mean it," Jupiter said. "I know your lady upstairs would prefer I not be here. But I want to be here, because I think you're beautiful."

Jupiter looked at Antoinette in a way that tried to get her to understand he meant what he was saying even though they'd never even touched each other's hand for longer than it took to pass along a plate or cup of coffee.

"Is everything okay at work?" Antoinette said.

"It's chaos," Jupiter said. "But it's okay."

The doorbell rang—

"Don't answer it," Jupiter said.

"What do you mean, 'Don't answer it'? It's part of my job to answer it. It's probably diapers for Simon. We're running out of diapers. Amazon Prime."

"It's dangerous out there."

It rang again—

"Dangerous? Here, take Simon," Antoinette said. "Simon says. He'll be asleep in a few moments anyway. Just finished his bottle. You'll like having a baby sleep in your arms. Oh, what am I talking about? You know what it's like. You remember."

"I'll answer it," Jupiter said. He boosted Simon up so the baby's head was nuzzling against his neck.

"Okay, okay," Antoinette said. "I'll hold on to the baby. You get the door. Give me the baby back. Simon. Simon says. Simon Simon. But go get the door before the UPS man leaves. Simon says. With the amount Aaron and Amelia do Amazon Prime, the UPS man, the Postal Service man—they come all day. And Aaron gets angry when he has to spend a Saturday waiting in line for his packages at the post office."

Jupiter handed Simon to Antoinette.

The doorbell rang again—

Jupiter took a deep breath. He crossed past the fireplace in the small, unfurnished room that all these old homes had between the dining room and the parlor. The fireplaces were all tiled in the same green field tile he had in his place.

Jupiter crossed past the same six-inch angels carved in dark wood above the mirror, and the same ten-inch griffins below. He rarely noticed them in his own house, but it was jarring to see these creatures in someone else's. They were angry. What craftsman decided to carve gargoyles into wood at the base of a mirror inside a row of people's homes? Jupiter had refinished his, but somehow Aaron's looked just as good. Aaron must have paid someone well to do his.

The doorbell rang again, this time alongside a banging on the door.

Jupiter could see through the window in the decorative wooden foyer door and then through the heavy glass and metal front door. He saw four or five black kids in their teens or twenties. One of them had what looked to be a piece of broken-off metal—the type that held up street signs. They seemed like kids he could control. Kids Derek's age.

They pounded on the door and rang the doorbell. One kid lifted a brick over his head and was about to bring it forward against the glass door. Jupiter raised his hands to indicate he was coming and they should calm down. The kid slumped back. Jupiter had the same door on his house. It was elegant but basically bulletproof. In the bad old days, a stray bullet once clipped his door at an angle and only chipped off a nub of glass. He doubted the brick would scratch it. But he didn't want Antoinette scared.

Jupiter put on as wide a smile as his face could accommodate. But why answer it? These doors were tough. They were safe inside. And nothing was less predicable than a pack of teenage boys.

Which was when Amelia came traipsing down the stairs. "I'll get it," she said. "Who is it? Why hasn't anyone answered the door?"

"I got it," Jupiter said.

"Oh, is Antoinette busy? I'll get it," Amelia said. "It's my house."

But then she saw the boys and the brick and the metal pole. She saw Simon asleep past the parlor, past the dining room, in the television room, in Antoinette's arms.

"What's going on?" she said. "Something in the neighborhood? Protests? My Internet's been off. I turned it off. I turned my phone off, too."

"I got it," Jupiter said.

"It's my house," Amelia said.

"Better to leave the door closed I think," Jupiter said.

"I don't want them to break anything," Amelia said. "We're two adults."

"Please," Jupiter said. "Do me a favor and let the kids get bored here and go on to the next house."

"*Please,*" she said, ending the conversation.

She opened the inner wooden decorative door wide, and then she opened the heavy glass and metal door to the street.

Chapter 21

Aaron splashed water in his face in the crummy Belmont bathroom. A five-grand loss was okay. It was the beginning of the day. There were more races ahead of him, and he'd been right about that horse. She had placed. He had bet her to win. But he still had it. First race in, he'd chosen a horse out of nowhere and nearly began the day thirty-five grand richer. Not bad. Could have been worse. Could have bet more. Could have bet Simon's entire college fund, is how Amelia would have put it.

Simon would be napping. Amelia working on Jonah Hill. Aaron washed his disgusting face in this disgusting sink. But that wasn't true. Aaron still felt good. He still had time for a half dozen more races, and he'd win it back no problem. He liked the fifth race a lot. A lot more even than he'd liked the third. And he had nearly won the third. He felt good. He felt strong. Like after working out. Installing the workout room on the office floor had been his current psychologist's idea—one of the ideas, anyway—for something to do when he felt like heading to the track.

Because he liked this feeling too much. He didn't even really feel the shame he was supposed to feel after he lost. When he lost, he just felt ready to go back to work. To earn back the money.

His psychologist said that was because his work *was* just another form of gambling and that he really should quit his job, too. Aaron said he liked his job for the first time in his life. He was good at it. And how many people could say that?

At work they sent around this scene of Arnold Schwarzenegger from the documentary *Pumping Iron*. Arnold must have been twenty-five years old when it was filmed, with long, floppy hair, giant white teeth, and fingers like sausages.

He is sitting on an old oversized comfy armchair that somehow looks very large but is still much too small for Arnold. He is wearing a polo shirt that looks humungous but again, on him, is far too small. It is cream colored with green and red wide horizontal stripes and a thick red collar, and he is sitting in front of a giant, floppy plant.

In his Arnold voice, he says, smiling between each sentence as though he is making one great point after another, "Lifting, pumping . . . It is as satisfying to me as coming is, you know? As having sex with a woman and coming. And so can you believe how much I am in heaven? I am getting the feeling of coming in a gym, I'm getting the feeling of coming at home, I'm getting the feeling of coming backstage when I pump up, when I pose in front of five thousand people, I get the same feeling, so I am coming day and night. I mean, it's terrific. Right? So you know, I am in heaven."

Arnold is so excited about what he is talking about he pauses between each sentence and smiles as though to give the viewer time to compliment his latest best idea. He's a puppy, or a little boy seeking approval, but he's a giant, talking about coming.

At work they laughed about how this man could have been the chief executive of a state of thirty-eight million people, but in the Belmont bathroom, Aaron thought about how this was exactly the man who should lead other men. This giant who felt good all the time. This man who felt good out in front of others. For whom sex and performance and physicality were intermingled. Who was able to talk about sex as though it was as easy as lifting weights. Who was able to lift real weight. Who had sex all the time at home as though it wasn't a big deal. The only time Aaron felt like this was when he'd played tennis as a kid, or was asked out for that girl by her friend, or was with Amelia in the beginning and sometimes still, but mostly when he was at the racetrack. And he was at the racetrack now, so he should try to enjoy it.

The people in his office pretended to watch the clip on YouTube to mock Arnold, but they were attracted to the confident, cuddly, boyish, sexual, charismatic, glowing giant with sausage fingers who worked so hard for his muscles to be stronger than any other man's muscles in the world. Sure, he used steroids, but so did everyone else. He was the biggest, floppiest, friendliest cheater in the world. Usually, Aaron couldn't understand how the two of them could both be men, he and Arnold. But he'd felt a bit like Arnold when he'd first arrived in his Belmont seat.

He dried his face and hands on thin brown paper towels and started back to his row, vowing not to let Oranges ruin his day.

He wasn't betting the fourth, so he took the long walk back. He bought a lemonade and, returning Aaron's change, the vendor said, "Good luck and Godspeed."

Aaron considered allowing himself to ask for God's assistance once—a single time—on one of the races over the course of the rest of the day.

Once, he could turn back to a God who didn't exist.

. . .

Aaron was an atheist. Amelia was an agnostic leaning toward a skeptical faith in something larger than nothing, but she wasn't particularly bothered by whether that something larger was just an extra-animal consciousness or a consciousness infused by a greater spirit that was another word for God. "And furthermore," she said the night they closed on their house on Stuyvesant Avenue and moved in with a mattress, sheets, bread, beer, stereo, and bottle of champagne, "if that consciousness infused by a greater spirit was systematized to be articulated with a vocabulary of Jewish ritual and tradition that worked for my mother and my mother's mother's mothers for hundreds of generations, why not keep it going? Especially when I like lighting Hanukkah candles and eating matzo on Passover."

They were drunk, still high off cementing their winning bid on the house, and they couldn't believe that all this was theirs. "My God!" Amelia kept saying. "My God! We pulled it off! We've done it! My God! My God! My God! Look at this place. Look at what we own!"

Until Aaron finally said, "It isn't God! It's you, it's us!"

And Amelia said, "So tell me. Did you never believe? All those years? I don't believe you! What do you think of that? I think you are so disappointed and embarrassed by what happened that you are a revisionist historian who is now claiming that you never believed. Like after a girl broke up with you, saying you never liked her anyway. You spent all those years studying and working and you never believed in any of it? I don't believe you."

Aaron wanted to argue back, and he wanted to cry with gratitude. Of course he had doubted, but of course he had wanted to believe, and of course he was turning his back against the whole thing now. But still—what was the point of calling him out on it now?

"No," Aaron said. "Never."

"Then how did you spend all those years dedicating your life to it?" Amelia said. "I mean, before it became impossible?"

"I don't think any of them believe," Aaron said, drinking champagne out of the bottle. "I don't think anyone believed. Anyone in my class at rabbinical school. Anyone who came to Torah study. People acted like they did. But come on. You've read the Bible. It's crazy! And after Hitler, it's impossible. After you read enough history and Wiesel and Levi and Delbo and Beer and the rest of them, it's impossible to believe. Maybe before, but not since.

"But as you say, religion has a lot going for it, and being a religious leader is fucking fantastic. You get treated like you know everything. You get respected. You get a decent salary at some places. Everyone is proud of you. And most of all, you're connected to so many people. Sincerely connected to their lives. They want you there. You matter to them in a way you'd never imagine. Belief is an afterthought. Worse than an afterthought. My bet is ninety-five percent of rabbis—of religious leaders in America—are rabbis in spite of the religious parts. They want to be leaders, and politics is fucked. No self-respecting man or woman would be a politician. They want to help people, and cops are assholes, and teaching is too limited. You only have your students for nine months. It's the same thing year after year and no one treats you with any respect. You know how all Jewish boys used to be raised being told they had to become lawyers. Do you think they *believed* in the law? Come on!"

Now Amelia was laughing. Spinning around and looking at what they'd bought. They kissed. They stripped out of their clothing. They listened to Janet Jackson really loud. They danced around their parlor floor and couldn't believe that all the stained glass and wood was theirs.

"Look at this little gremlin guy," Amelia said. "He's ours!" She examined the foot-tall griffins below the grand mirror in the entranceway. He had wings, and each wing was carved into feathers, and each feather was carved with little striations. And there were three of these griffins beneath each of the two grand mirrors. Six little griffin guys! And Aaron and Amelia owned all four floors! "My God!" Amelia said.

"Stop saying 'God'! It isn't God!" Aaron said. He was drunk off the house closing and his nearly naked girlfriend and champagne. "I'm the one who worked eighty-hour weeks. Your grandmother's the one who passed all the money down to us. We made this happen. Not God. Why would there be a God? It doesn't make any sense!"

"I'm grateful for you," Amelia said. "For my father's mother."

"And I'm grateful for you," Aaron said. They kissed and danced. They danced and kissed. "I'm sorry," Aaron said. "I just feel like that part of my life is over. Like it has to be over. Like this house, and you, and if we are able to have a son or daughter and get married and make a life together—like all this is more important than pretending a higher power exists anymore. I just want to live from now on in a life where I don't need to pretend anymore."

"I'm sorry," Amelia said. "I'll stop pretending if you want me to."

"That's not what I'm saying," Aaron said. "Don't use your wounded child voice. You're too smart for that."

"Then let me believe what I fucking want, too," Amelia said, slow dancing to hip-hop. "Or I'll rephrase. I'm going to keep on believing what I believe, okay? I really do believe that humans have tapped into this thing that is extrabiological. And if the word that best approximates that is 'God', than sometimes I'll say 'My God!' Or maybe it's just an expression. But there's a chance that you and I differ a bit on this one, and I think that there might be a power out there that's not just quarks and Darwin, okay?"

"Okay," Aaron said. But it was all fucked up, because although she was being reasonable, it wasn't okay. Aaron really did think that no one believed in God. Or maybe it was okay that some people did but not his life partner—not his future wife and the mother of his eventual children. But he was distracted because they were already kissing now and making Simon.

Chapter 22

"What can I do for you?" Amelia said, standing at the open front metal door.

She'd almost said, "What can I do for you *kids*," but refrained at the very last moment seeing something in the eye of the kid in front that suggested he wouldn't want to be called a kid. He was a she. A girl leading a pack of boys. Thinking of Simon or, at the very least, feeling Simon in the room in Antoinette's arms now that Antoinette, curious, had approached, made Amelia sense her own vulnerability. She shouldn't have opened the door. She saw that now. Jupiter had been right. But at least she hadn't said "kid" or "girl" or "little girl."

The kid was getting excited. Rolling up and down onto the balls of her feet. She had a torn piece of fabric wrapped around the cut sleeve of her hoodie and metal at her wrists. They were handcuffs. Handcuffs were showing at her wrists out from under the sleeves. Maybe it was a fashion thing, but they looked real. They looked like real handcuffs, though the chain was broken. And though her clothes were black and gray so it was hard to tell, they looked stained by blood. It might have been dirt or mud. She was wild-eyed, but the Nets cap pulled down with its wide low brim made that hard to tell, too.

Behind her, one of the boys shouted, "Three eighty three Stuyvesant, motherfucker!"

The girl blinked, then blinked again. Amelia wanted to ask if she was okay—to shoo away the other kids, the three boys, to invite the girl in and give her a piece of cake and a warm bath. To rewrap her bruised arm. To help her. The girl so clearly needed help.

Jupiter told Amelia, "Come back in."

Amelia was looking at the girl's wild eyes, which reminded her of the only thing anyone would have thought of, which was a wounded wild animal, when, like a bull who'd been let loose from a trance by a bull fighter, a big-eared boy who was carrying a broken-off piece of a street sign ran past the girl, past the metal front door, through the foyer, past the decorative wooden door, and, pushing her into the mirror, past Amelia and into the house.

Jupiter stood past Amelia, between the boy and the rest of the house.

Street, stoop, outer metal door, foyer, inner wooden door, Amelia, Jupiter, and then the rest of the house, with Antoinette, Simon, and the yellow warmth of their interior world.

The boy ran at Jupiter.

Jupiter roared and got low like an offensive lineman being charged by a bull. The pole glanced against Jupiter's forehead. He was like a football player tackling a bull that was equipped with a jousting lance. Amelia had done a story on bullfighting once, and she had also done one on the grinning sadist Michael Strahan. Jupiter was an offensive lineman protecting the house, blocking the kid with the lance.

Jupiter must have outweighed the kid by a hundred pounds. He lifted the kid, still holding the metal pole, up in the air and took three powerful lunges forward past Amelia—who flung herself back against the wall—through both doors, then outside the house entirely and drove him into his friend with the brick, and all three fell backward down the stoop.

Simon shrieked. Amelia didn't know Simon could shriek like that, and Antoinette must not have known, either, because Antoinette gasped and mimicked the noise Simon had made. To Amelia, the screams were drops off a roller coaster, a knife into her lungs.

The boy and Jupiter were outside the house, the boy swatting at Jupiter and trying to stand, but Amelia couldn't close the door, because she was scared to get too close to the girl and to the boy with the brick in his hand, and because Jupiter was still outside and she didn't want to leave him there alone.

"I've got a baby in here!" Amelia screamed, but no one was listening to her. The sound of her own voice was impossibly feeble. "I've got a baby in here," she repeated.

Jupiter turned and staggered back toward the house, blood on his forehead from where he'd been struck with the piece of metal. Amelia had been right not to leave him out there alone. There were suddenly five kids out on the stoop, including the one who had fallen down the stairs—who was now staggering to his feet. But a firmer barrier between inside and out seemed to have been established. Both the exterior metal-and-thick-glass door and interior decorative door were open, but none of the other kids tried to enter.

"Old man knocked Damien out!"

Jupiter, still outside, reached for the outer door but was blocked by the boy with the brick. Jupiter stumbled back up into the foyer area, and though he was holding his head, there didn't seem to be much blood. Antoinette ran to him to tend to his cut, but

Amelia said, "Stay back with him," meaning Simon.

Jupiter stood alone by the interior door holding his head. The outer door with the thick glass was still open wide, and a few of the other groups of kids were coming over because of the commotion. One boy was pounding his fist against the heavy concrete plant box. Antoinette seemed to be effectively keeping Simon safe in the dining room. Amelia didn't think to take Simon herself, perhaps because she was closer to the danger. Simon had only screamed once, but there was something unnatural about his face Amelia was seeing or imagining. It was red or frozen. Simon was different from what he had been before that kid had rushed into Jupiter.

Now Jupiter, one hand to his head, started to close the inside door.

His chest heaved. He managed to get the inside door closed, but the outside door was still wide open, and the inside door was primarily decorative. The kids didn't know what to do. They just stood there, looking at Jupiter. (Thinking back, this is the moment Amelia can't figure out. This is what she obsesses over, dwells on, and tries to remember over and over again. She understands or can guess why the kids came to her home. She blames herself for opening the door. The initial moment of violence makes sense with the kids all pumped full of adrenaline seeing the inside of her home with all the stained glass and gargoyles, the champagne and Prada that had to be just around the corner. They were angry at whoever was in front of them, and their momentum carried them forward. And she understands why they, after one of them was hurt, wanted some kind of revenge, but why would Jupiter stand there and start talking to them in that strange avuncular voice? Why did he go on lecturing the kids he'd just been fighting with? And why did they just stand there at first?) He told the kids to go back home. How he was sure they were good kids. With all the blood and adrenaline coursing through Jupiter's body, and with noise from down the block, and with the shouting from the kids, and the crying baby, and disbelief about what they'd all just seen—no one, not even Jupiter, it seemed, was focusing on his words.

The kids were trying to listen at first, but their faces became blurred canvases of confusion. The girl in front rolled up and down on the balls of her feet. Maybe Jupiter was trying to calm them down? Turn them back into children? Maybe they reminded him of his son? But they didn't seem able to listen. The kid with big ears who'd been pushed down the stairs was getting up, and Amelia saw that his hand was mangled from where he'd landed.

Through the thin glass in the decorative inner door, Amelia watched him stuffing his fingers into his left pocket, and they looked as though they were bending in the wrong direction, some of them. It was revolting. But still, he was climbing the steps to join his friends. Which meant Amelia was further away from closing that front door. He was lighter skinned than the others and lanky. He was wearing gray sweatpants and white sneakers. And full of shame for how he'd been thrown down by the old man who was now lecturing them.

Jupiter was saying, "Go on home. You don't want to let this crazy day define the rest of your lives. These are decent people here, and Antoinette here and I were just eating a chocolate cake I made."

The kids on the stoop snickered, but more it seemed because they felt they had to than because they wanted to. Jupiter was no longer holding his head and Amelia could see some blood starting to trickle down. The kid in back with the busted hand and big ears was clearly in pain—he was yelling, "Fuck, my hand, fuck," whimpering—and the girl in front rolling up and down on the balls of her feet was listening to Jupiter, and there were two more kids who looked at Jupiter and at the girl in front and didn't seem to want to be there anymore.

"There's a baby inside," Jupiter continued, "a baby named Simon, and I was just taking a bite of it—the cake—with Antoinette with some coffee."

Amelia didn't understand why, but she saw Antoinette and Jupiter both react as though the situation at this moment, just after Jupiter mentioned the coffee, was about to take a turn for the worse. Simon screamed in Antoinette's arms, which made Amelia doubly clench already-clenched muscles. Jupiter clenched his fist as though the cut on his head hurt more, and Antoinette was slowly retreating as though she'd wanted to go to Jupiter but now knew it was the wrong thing to do.

Antoinette stepped back to where she could still see what was going on, but she and the baby were protected by a column in the unfurnished small room between the parlor and the dining room. Antoinette's fear was clouding up the room. Jupiter was still talking, but he was talking in a way that made less sense. He was sounding desperate, as though he wanted to say as many facts about himself in as short a time as possible: "My boy, my son, he's your age, maybe you know him? Do you know him from the neighborhood? He used to love my cooking but now he doesn't dare to admit it anymore. Ha! Fuck me up the goat ass, right? I know he still does because I cook for myself now and I make extra. Late at night, he comes home. I don't dare call him on it, I just clean the bowls in the morning. You know what I'm saying, right?

I don't see him, but the next morning, two whole lamb shanks have disappeared! Do you know him? Any of you boys know Derek? Derek Jupiter?"

"You're Derek's father? You're Mr. Jupiter?"

"Yes, ma'am, I am!"

Amelia exhaled, realizing she'd been holding her breath all this time. Her shoulder relaxed. She looked to Antoinette, whose eyes were on the kid in back.

That kid, lanky with big ears, with the mangled hand in his left hip pocket, put his right, healthy hand in the front of his heavy sweatpants and took out a pistol. He waved it around in the air and, Amelia thought, accidentally tapped a friend's back; the friend felt the tap and looked back and saw the gun and said, "Damien's got a gun out," which made the others look and get out of Damien's way. Damien stepped up through the space made by his friends.

The girl said, "This is Derek's father," but the boy with the gun said, "I don't know no Derek," and a different boy said, "But Sara does," but the boy with the gun steadied it with his busted left hand and closed his eyes and shot Jupiter through the glass of the decorative inner door. Amelia was watching Damien, so she didn't see what Jupiter looked like then. She didn't see Jupiter's face or whether he saw the gun when it was fired. Damien shot Jupiter twice in the chest and then stepped up toward the interior door where the glass had all been shattered, and he shot Jupiter again twice in the head as though he—Damien—was a killer from a gangster movie. The group of kids—Damien and the girl in-cluded—scattered down the steps to run away.

Chapter 23

Antoinette screamed. She'd lost him. Like that. She'd lost him to some no one. Some nothing. A child. Some no one from the street who didn't know her or him took him away from her. Some child from the street she'd never met before, who'd never met her before or Jupiter before took Jupiter from her. Took Jupiter. Took him. He was gone. Just like that. Oh, Jesus. For trying to do what was right. It couldn't be. It couldn't be. But it had just happened there; there, it was still happening. Her future with him was gone, just like he was. He was there, but he wasn't. He was gone. He was there, but . . . she wailed. She wailed for a moment, and the baby wailed. And she stopped. And the baby kept wailing, which made her wail again. It wasn't right. It wasn't right. Why him? He was the good one. Why him?

She hurried Simon to Amelia to free her own hands for Jupiter. She ran to him, his body, to at least be with him for a little while.

The front door was still open. She didn't want to waste any time going to the door when she could tend to him.

Chapter 24

Amelia fumbled for her cell phone in her back pocket. She held tightly on to Simon, who was silent in a way that made Amelia want him to be shrieking again. No murmurs or gurgles. He was breathing shallow breaths.

"Who-oo's my ba-by," Amelia sang. "You're my ba-by—you're my baby, baby." But Simon breathed shallow and quickly. He breathed fierce, scared breaths. He didn't even screw up his face. His face remained his face at rest. His whole body looked at rest, but his heart was beating wildly. Amelia told herself to calm down. She was projecting her own emotions onto her baby. Objectively he didn't have much color. He was white. He was breathing quickly. He was silent. And that scared her. It didn't mean he understood what had happened. He was reacting to *her* fear. She had to calm herself down for his sake.

Antoinette seemed to be praying over the corpse.

"You're my ba-by—you're my baby, baby."

Antoinette's eyes were asking for a few more moments to be with Jupiter before she would come back to comfort the baby. With her hands covered by death.

"Who-oo's my ba-by," Amelia sang. "You're my baby, baby."

Now Simon coughed, and the coughs became choking coughs,

and Simon started hyperventilating and crying. He cried for a moment like normal, but then his eyes glassed over and he became not-himself. He cried, glassy eyed and blind to what was happening around him. He cried and cried. Amelia held Simon closer to her body, soothing him, pressing him harder into her chest until the chokes became deeper coughs, and the cries loud, and Amelia wanted to cry because of the dead body and because she couldn't do anything to help Jupiter or Simon. She shouldn't have let those boys in. What had she done? She hadn't understood anything. Anything. A half hour went by in this way, but it couldn't have been more than a few minutes. She gathered herself for Simon. Awful, awful. Simon was crying louder and louder, and Amelia couldn't do anything to help him. She soothed him and whispered. She sang to him, but the baby thrashed with his hands at his mother's face. It was the combination of the frustration of not being able to solve the problem—a problem she felt uniquely qualified to solve—and heartbreaking empathy for the little creature in pain that wouldn't end and that she couldn't ease. And her headache from the screaming baby and the dead man, a dead man, a body, Jupiter in the front room and her, paralyzed here, soothing her baby. It was the frustration plus the heartache plus the headache and paralysis that built and built until Simon spat up once, twice—Amelia relieved the pressure holding him against her chest—and Simon vomited, paused, and vomited again. Amelia was covered in a white frothy sour milkshake of regurgitated formula. The vomit was warm, but the air-conditioning was cold, and there was a dead man in her house as Antoinette stood over a corpse whispering who knew what voodoo.

Chapter 25

Antoinette kissed Jupiter on the cheek. She said goodbye to him. She fingered the hijab back around her ears.

She touched his hands, still warm. She touched his face. She closed his eyes. She prayed to Jesus. To Allah. That Jupiter was safe with him. With God. With Allah. They were the same.

She prayed that she herself could continue without him.

And then she looked again at Jupiter. It wasn't fair that he be taken from her before they had real happiness together.

Jupiter had looked at her—over the past few weeks, especially. And still, since she'd worn the hijab.

He had *seen* her.

The hijab had been, in its way, a test for him. A test he'd been passing. To make sure his affection for her had been real. And now who saw her? Babies, children. No one else. No one.

She dragged Jupiter's body farther inside the house in front of the mirror at the entrance to the front parlor. It was heavy, but more than that, she had never touched his body before. She had dreamed of it. She'd wanted to touch his hands with hers.

That the Devil took him from her like that. Fury rose within her. It was unfair.

Antoinette had lived long enough to deserve some kind of

happiness. *Is this because I'm leaving Jesus?* She turned to the Devil. *Well you can't have anyone else. You can't have me. You can't have Teddy, and you can't have Simon. The Devil is going to have to come through me, and I'm not going to let it.*

Antoinette had to bring God into this house. To protect the vulnerable in God. Especially baby Simon. Otherwise, the Devil would claim him as his own. Antoinette was strong. She believed in her own strength.

Chapter 26

But just then Antoinette and Amelia heard another two gun-shots, this time from Daniel and Thela's apartment below.

"Crouch down!" Antoinette yelled in a kind of whisper. "Crouch down with the baby!"

Amelia's hands got numb and cold, and she started to cry, and the baby started to cry again. The vomit was already harden-ing, though Simon had vomited less than a minute earlier and it had never hardened so quickly. It was as though they were living in fast-forwarded time.

Simon didn't understand about being quiet. He yipped and yelped and gasped for breath. Amelia wiped vomit from his face with her vomit-covered shirt.

Antoinette crawled over to Amelia and took Simon. With corpse particles on her hands.

Amelia wiped herself off with a linen blanket from Simon's Pack 'n Play. Tossed the soiled blanket to Antoinette and Simon. Simon's eyes were wide open staring at Antoinette. He was trying to see something deep into her. Amelia saw that. Amelia believed that was true.

Sprinting up the concrete stairs outside was a young, thin body in all black and a black baseball cap, running through the open front door, past the shattered decorative interior door, past Jupiter's body, up the interior wooden stairs and up to the bedroom or office floor. She was running from the gunshots, from the gunshots in the street.

"That was the girl," Amelia said. "That was the girl with them."

There was some banging upstairs, some wild banging and crashing, but then the house settled.

The girl, Amelia was nearly certain, had gone all the way up, past the bedroom floor to the top floor, the office and exercise room floor. There was a lock on that door. The girl had locked herself in Amelia's office. The black girl who'd been with the kids who'd shot Jupiter. Amelia tried to call 911 but couldn't get a signal.

Chapter 27

"I shot him!" Daniel shouted, sprinting up the interior stairs from the downstairs garden unit, banging on the door that connected his apartment to Amelia and Aaron's parlor floor.

Antoinette let him in. They looked at each other uncomprehendingly. They had never formally met before, Daniel and Antoinette. Antoinette had only seen Daniel look at her every morning on her way up the stoop.

Daniel had not expected Antoinette, and Antoinette did not want to let this man with a gun into the house. But after a moment, she stepped aside.

Daniel was shaking. "I think I shot the man who shot Mr. Jupiter. I saw it. I saw the whole thing. Well . . . well I couldn't see anything inside the house. I was watching up through my window."

Chapter 28

The streets were full of teenagers. Hundreds of teenagers were already gathering around the house. Daniel was inside with a pistol, waving it around his head. He had a shotgun in his other hand. His arms were shaking around his bright red hairy face.

Antoinette asked Jesus for forgiveness and Allah for strength. She locked the doors and windows, closed the wooden shutters.

A large group of kids gathered outside. A number of them wore ill-fitting sports jerseys probably stolen from nearby closets. Antoinette didn't know if the other kids guilty of shooting Jupiter were with them, but she didn't see any cops there, so she didn't see why not. If Antoinette had been guilty of shooting someone she would have run home, but she wasn't as young as these kids were, and she wasn't as wild. One of the kids who'd shot Jupiter was shot, outside. Another was upstairs in the office. She didn't know if the girl upstairs was good or evil, so Antoinette tried to keep herself calm, with faith and vigilance.

Amelia sat silent, clutching Simon and a bottle. Her shirt was dry but sour. Simon didn't want to drink. He was shaking. "You have to drink, baby. Nothing can touch us. We have each other," Amelia was saying. She wanted to get Simon's body intact through the next few hours. Her body's job was, as it had been when he was inside her, to protect him. It was scary holding him in the same way it had been scary to be pregnant. She shared his vulnerability. And she bore responsibility.

"The girl's in the house," Amelia said to Daniel and Antoinette. She didn't know whom to say it to. She didn't know what to do. Her eyes darted back and forth between them.

"The girl who was with the boy you shot," Antoinette told Daniel. "She must have been running from the shooting?"

"Get her out of here," Amelia said. "Get her out of my house!"

"I should shoot her, too?" Daniel said.

But then Amelia returned to Simon. "There's nothing we have to worry about, baby boy."

Simon seemed worried. He seemed tense. He felt her tension. She tried to relax. She counted backward in her mind from twenty. She counted backward in her mind from one hundred by sevens. She counted backward in her mind in French. Simon still seemed tense.

"Who-oo's my ba-by," Amelia sang. "You're my ba-by—you're my baby, baby."

She pressed him against her chest, and he didn't seem to like it. He screwed up his face. He wouldn't drink. But he didn't squirm away. She held him against the sour smell of his vomit, and he just remained there, rigid. She counted backward in her mind again. She checked her phone but there were no bars. FaceTime wasn't working. Aaron wasn't responding to texts. She Snapchatted him, but he only checked that occasionally. She Snapchatted Aaron a photo of Jupiter's body on the floor.

Chapter 29

Daniel was in Amelia's kitchen to wash his hands. He always washed his hands after shooting.

Amelia tried to call 911 again but couldn't get a signal. She asked Antoinette and Daniel, but Antoinette didn't have any bars, either, and Daniel wasn't listening. Amelia thought briefly about Skype, but that seemed impossibly complicated on her phone, and the girl was in her office.

What damage could the girl do? Access her email, but that didn't matter, probably. She could steal, but who cared? She was in her home. She was a stranger in her home. A dangerous stranger who was in her home and possibly armed. Whose friend had just been shot. Whose friend had just shot and killed Jupiter.

"Should we just let her stay upstairs?" Amelia said. "Simon won't drink."

"For the moment, yes," Daniel said, with a certainty that thrilled him. "She can't do any harm there. And we're three of us here. And armed."

Daniel put his Beretta M9 into the sink, because the sink was empty and the counter was covered in bottles and containers of baby formula. The gun was black, and the sink was white, which had the effect of making the gun look fake. Daniel was shaking.

He'd just killed a man—a boy—in some combination of self-defense, revenge, and because he thought he'd never have an opportunity like this again.

He'd been in bed when he heard the original scuffle upstairs. He'd been spending more time in bed. He couldn't read as well lately, and he had trouble going out. He lay in bed listening to Dan Carlin's podcast, *Common Sense*. Carlin talked about American and international politics from a leftist perspective that pretended to be independent. There'd been a poll out recently that Daniel thought about while listening to the Dan Carlin podcast: 37 percent of Americans consider themselves politically independent, but as John Dickerson had said on *Slate*'s *Political Gabfest* podcast, the statistic was meaningless. Or, if not meaningless, at least more indicative of voters' odd psychologies than whom they were going to vote for. People who had never voted Democrat in their lives called themselves politically independent. It made them feel more autonomous, more . . . independent. Anyway, Dan Carlin shared most of Daniel's beliefs about how war was a great evil and the government should be more transparent. *Common Sense* was a bit wishy-washy for Daniel's brother, who was more of a Rand Paul libertarian without the isolationist bent.

This episode of *Common Sense* had been boring—Carlin was going on as usual about William Binney and Thomas Drake telling the world about the US government spying on its citizens— so when Daniel heard the commotion upstairs he removed the earbuds and ate a few Altoids and put on his jeans and button-down oxford and opened his window and craned his long, thin torso to see what was going on. He only had to wait a minute or two until Mr. Jupiter came tumbling out with a teenage kid. Daniel liked Mr. Jupiter because once the two of them had been up together past midnight. Jupiter had been waiting up for his son, and Daniel had been waiting up for Thela. Jupiter had brought out a couple of beers and they sat on Aaron's stoop for twenty minutes and talked about politics, but then just sat silently for another hour before Thela got home. They'd agreed that though Obama wasn't keeping his promises, the Republicans were mostly to blame because of their obstructionism. Jupiter was the one who'd used that word, obstructionism.

So when he'd seen Jupiter, hurt from the tumble with the kid, gather himself and retreat back into Aaron's house, Daniel was on high alert. Daniel prided himself on not seeing all these kids as just a sea of black faces on the stoop. He knew which ones were going to school in the morning and which ones hung around on the corner up to no good. He couldn't see inside the house, but he could see all four faces on the stoop. He recognized the three boys as kids from Boys and Girls High, he thought, but the tomboy he didn't know.

When, from his window below the stoop steps, Daniel had seen that kid's pistol bulge in his sweats, he'd gotten his own pistol from his nightstand. And when he'd heard the pistol fire four times, he steadied himself and opened his window. When nothing happened for thirty seconds or so, he retrieved his shotgun from under the bed. And when the kid with the pistol saw Daniel with his shotgun, the kid aimed his pistol again, this time at Daniel. So Daniel shot the kid.

Chapter 30

"I can't get ahold of Aaron," Amelia said. "I can't get ahold of Daddy. Texts aren't going through and he's not answering his email."

That girl was alone upstairs as a mob grew outside. Simon was ignoring the bottle at his lips. His skin was transparent, and he was taking what felt like three breaths per second.

Suddenly, a cry rose through the mob, the cry of a wounded animal. Maybe the boy Daniel shot had died. Maybe the others, in a furious imitation, responded with cries of their own. Soon Amelia felt everyone outside threatening and moaning. Cries of anger hurled up at Amelia's building. Kids were climbing up on cars and on trees to reach at Amelia's windows, so far without luck.

"Where is he?" Amelia said, meaning Aaron.

"I wouldn't want him coming here," Antoinette said.

"Oh my God," Amelia said.

"Everything is locked up?" Daniel said. Daniel's eyes were laying claim to everything in her house. "Secure?"

A man's voice that wasn't Aaron's or even Jupiter's sounded wrong in the house. Jupiter's body lay on its back in the entrance-way toward the stairs. Simon kept looking toward it, or maybe

Amelia was imagining it. But it was all Simon seemed interested in. His neck kept turning toward it when Amelia blocked him from it with her body. Daniel's voice was deeper, louder, than it should have been with his stiff, lanky body, and he held a shotgun in his right hand.

"All the doors and windows on this floor," Antoinette said.

"Everything on my floor," Daniel said. He paced back and forth on the parlor floor looking through the cracks in the wooden shutters deciding whether or not to aim his shotgun. Whether anyone was climbing too close.

Chapter 31

The girl was still upstairs. And Amelia was scared of so many things. She was scared of more in that moment than she'd ever been scared of in her life. She was scared that Aaron was missing, and that he'd never come back . . . that he'd come back and accuse her of mishandling the situation . . . that he'd come back and Simon would be hurt and that it'd be her fault . . . that he was worried about her and had no way to reach her . . . that he'd come back and be hurt by the crowd outside. She was scared that the crowd outside would break into her home and hurt her or Simon. That they'd hurt her home, rape her, kill her, and that it would be her fault . . . that it wouldn't be but it would hurt anyway. That they'd kill her baby . . . kidnap her baby and that it would be her fault. She was scared that the girl upstairs would hurt her or her baby, or that Daniel would hurt the girl and she would be able to prevent it but she would be too selfish to.

"The police won't blame you," Antoinette said. "You had to shoot if he was aiming at you." Antoinette was on a chair she'd pulled up, it seemed to Amelia, to keep Daniel company while he kept watch. Daniel had red hair that sprouted in curls on his face and unkempt coils on his head. Antoinette had taken the baby and was holding him on her knee and bouncing him and cleaning him off with wet wipes while she talked to Daniel. Daniel was deciding whether or not to aim his gun at various windows. Antoinette said, "I've always told my son that there were two types of worry: you could like people who worried about other people, and be careful about people who worried about themselves."

"Mm-hm," Daniel said, as though what Antoinette said applied to the situation. Amelia felt completely alone.

"Teddy!" Antoinette said. From her phone, she emailed her boy to tell him to go directly to church after school and that she might be home late. "It's safe in other neighborhoods, right?"

"You've got bars?" Amelia said. "Oh, never mind. iMessage."

"Of course it is," Daniel said, aiming his shotgun, then lowering it.

"Where is Thela?" Antoinette said.

"Boston," Daniel said.

Antoinette and Daniel had never met before that Amelia knew of, but she could tell that Antoinette liked Daniel. From what Amelia could tell, everyone liked Antoinette, and Antoinette seemed to like everyone. Men, at least. This would have shocked Amelia just a few hours before. Amelia had always considered Antoinette good with the baby but cold. Jupiter's body lay there where they all could see it, but only she and her baby ever looked at it. His shoes were workers' shoes, heavy and worn.

"I'll go lock the bedroom windows in case they try to climb closer," Amelia said. "You have Simon?"

"I've got Simon," Antoinette said. "You're not worried about the young lady up there coming down? You're not worried about going to the bedroom floor alone?"

"Take my pistol," Daniel said, jogging to the kitchen to retrieve it. "The girl upstairs isn't armed as far as I can tell."

Amelia laughed. She laughed now at the impossibility of her taking the pistol in the same way she'd laughed when she'd watched as the second World Trade Center building had fallen.

Chapter 32

Aaron didn't check his phone until just before the fifth race, when he had already placed a bet on the favorite. Five grand to win six. But he was confident, and he'd win back the losses from the previous race and have a grand to spare. And start feeling great again. The feeling alone would be worth it. He felt as if he might be a step closer to understanding himself, which meant understanding the world and his new life. The rest of his life. Maybe his latest psychologist was correct, that these races were Aaron's last connection to his old life. "The wagering brings you back each time," he'd said. "It's your final connection to your life as a rabbi." When the psychologist had suggested this correlation—that without the gambling, he'd no longer have any rabbi in him—Aaron had laughed it off, but the shrink had made Aaron focus on the possibility. The basics of Freud as Aaron understood them were that in order to move beyond one's hang-ups one had to confront them—understand that the reason one was working as a professional gambler on stocks and bonds and then sneaking away from work to bet on horses was not for the winnings but for the connection to a life one used to live. Once one understood that, one could contemplate that previous life, for example, and reminisce, maybe, instead of sneaking away from work. And the gambling might become less desirable. And he could become a consultant. Or an academic.

But for Aaron, it didn't go this way. For him the psychological link between gambling and his previous life legitimated the whole thing. If it had just been about the winnings, Aaron thought as he watched the horses wander toward the gate, he could save the money he made at work and be done with it. Or he could work extra hours and get promoted. Or he could lift weights in his exercise room. But after the psychologist pointed out to Aaron that it was about so much more, Aaron understood that his connection to the gambling and what it provided him had to, in some ways, be respected. That it would be disrespectful of the entire first run of his life to suppress the instincts that led him to the track. That without the track, he wouldn't have the pain of atheism, and he wouldn't have the decade of studying that made him a rabbi to begin with. He'd just be some stockbroker or consultant or academic. Allowing himself the occasional fall was a way for him to dip back into the man he used to be. It was a way to not go totally insane with the lack of spiritual depth in his life. All he was was a fucking money manager. He couldn't endure it without some anchor to what he used to be, and to what all men should still want to be at least a little.

There was another side to the argument, he thought, while leaning on both knees to control their bounce. (His shoes were boots, with stretchy brown fabric on both sides that made them easy to slip on. The leather, the first time he touched it, made him literally gag it was so supple. He'd gagged and paid the nine hundred dollars. They went with all his blue suits.) The argument went: that his brain—the brain that he had trained to become a rabbi—was the brain the investment firm was paying to employ, and that his moral center, his kindness, was the person Amelia had all but committed the rest of her life to. He was the person who would raise his son (and possibly future children, grandchildren) and be a member of the community and dedicate himself to his life moving forward, regardless of his profession, regardless of whether the world saw him as it used to.

It still didn't seem enough. There was something calling him back to the track.

"Who you got in this race?" Aaron, wanting to be cordial, asked the orange eater.

"Looking for anyone but the favorite," Oranges said. "But I like the favorite. I think he outclasses everyone else by a mile."

"I completely agree. Going to try to win back my losses on the third."

"Shit," Oranges said. "I was wrong about that. You were right. Lost by a nose there. You saw something. But hey—you said Bed-Stuy, right?"

"Listen," Aaron said. "Like you said about the oranges at first. I don't want to be rude. I'm just here for the races."

"No. My apologies. Sincerely. I totally get that. I get that. Completely. But have you checked the news. It's going wild around there."

"I mean it," Aaron said. "No offense, I'm just not looking to talk politics."

"No. I mean today. I mean right now. I just saw on my phone I got an alert."

Aaron scrambled to free his phone from his jacket. His phone had been on silent. He saw the *CNN* and *Times* news alerts first: *Riots in Bed-Stuy. Police report neighborhood chaos in central Brooklyn.* Aaron saw he had emails and voice mails and tried to call Amelia, but he couldn't get through, not even to voice mail.

He bolted out of his seat. The quickest path was up to the landing then down, out of the track. He saw his future self ten paces ahead, down the escalator, bounding to the train or a taxi if one was idling.

He flinched. The gun had gone off. The horses were running. They were around the first turn, his horse in the lead. He saw it or heard it or just badly wanted it to be true. *Ahead at the rail!* Aaron had taken twenty steps up to the exit, two at a time. And now he took another ten, one at a time. His neck clenched with fear. Anticipation. His horse was in the lead. He stopped. Snuck a look at his phone. At the track—all the excitement and movement. All that life coming around the second turn. He took another half step towards the exit. He—

Chapter 33

Amelia could breathe now that Simon wasn't in her arms. It was wonderful to be free of him. She could do anything now that she wasn't responsible for her baby. Now that she wasn't gasping for breath along with him. Separated from her baby, she was herself again. Amelia heard ambulances but didn't see them. Or maybe she heard cop cars. Did ambulances and cop cars have the same sirens? She should know. As a journalist, she should know. Amelia looked down from the third-floor window—her bedroom window—through cracks in the shutters, and she didn't see fire trucks or ambulances or police cars. She heard them but didn't see them. She heard them but was listening to the floor above her. Amelia was in her bedroom one flight up from her son, Antoinette, and Daniel. She was listening for signs that the girl, one flight above, was making noise in the office. Amelia was holding the gun knowing she wouldn't use it.

Peeking through the cracks in the bedroom shutters, she saw a crowd of faces down on the street. At least five hundred faces. She saw the dead body by the stoop, with two women tending to it. A third making her way over with what looked like a pack of clean T-shirts. Was it to make some kind of statement that they were leaving the body there? How was Aaron going to get in? Her guess was that at first he would try to sneak through without being noticed. Then he would reason, negotiate. Then take some kind of crazy risk and become violent. She'd never seen him violent. But she'd felt it in him. She'd never realized that until now. But she'd felt it. She'd known it. It was part of what attracted her to him, his capacity to turn anger into work, into something active.

Amelia had met Aaron at a birthday party for her cousin's best friend, Ari. She had been looking forward to going but then nobody had wanted to bowl with her. When Aaron showed up she'd felt a need to take care of him. She'd never felt maternal toward anyone or anything before, and that instinct to care for or about someone so strongly had driven her straight out of her marriage and into this new life.

She'd always told Kevin she didn't want to have kids. She was having too much fun with him alone. She liked to travel. She liked to write. She even wrote a much-commented-on piece about it for Slate.com:

I used to feel like the sole female in existence for whom babies weren't the end all and be all, but hundreds of like-minded women emailed me after hearing me discuss my happy childlessness on the radio. Celebrities like Cameron Diaz, Chelsea Handler, and Helen Mirren have talked openly about choosing not to have children. Jon Hamm has also made it clear that he isn't interested in fatherhood—but no one judges him, because he's a man.

Even as a young girl, when I fantasized about my adult life, children weren't in the picture. Some females—some people—simply aren't wired that way. And I'm part of a rapidly growing subset of American women. According to a recent Pew study, one in five of us survives fertility without having given birth, which is a 200 per-cent increase from 1974. And half of the women who filled out the same survey answered that it "makes no difference" whether a woman becomes a mother. The numbers are even higher across Europe. With seven billion people already on the planet, unless I desperately wanted a son or daughter, why would I make myself— or the world—care for another life?

And without kids, she could live anywhere. She and Kevin could take off and spend a year anywhere—they'd just gotten back from France three weeks before that bowling party—and kids wouldn't allow that. With kids, they'd have to think about money and stability. Amelia had grown up without stability, and it hadn't been fair. She didn't want to subject her children to the same slack mothering she'd received. And Kevin had never seen stability as worthwhile.

Kevin worked in the restaurant business. Just as she could write anywhere, he could manage a restaurant anywhere. He had contacts in Bordeaux, and so they lived in a vineyard for a month. He learned about vintages, she wrote an article for *Wine Spectator*.

Whom she fantasized about sleeping with: the owner of the vineyard, the workers in the vineyard, the chef at the vineyard, the server of food, the cleaner-up of food, the baker in town, the teenagers who hung around looking for work. Whom she slept with: her husband. She liked waking up with the white, useless curtains letting the sun into their room.

It was a strange autumn month in Bordeaux in the middle of a strange year. Whenever she reminded herself that she was living in France, she felt a rush of pleasure and loneliness that reminded her of being a teenager. Days were interminable and important.

Meals were gluttonous and difficult. She felt lonely when she was with Kevin, but when she took long solitary walks in the afternoon she felt excited to be married to him and living this life. They drank a lot. It was very different from what she'd expected marriage to be like. She'd expected to be busy during the day and tired at night but warmed by her husband. But as a teenager, then college student, then single twenty-something, then married woman, she'd never met the man who fulfilled that gnawing, wombish childhood fantasy. She was lonely with her husband in the exact same way she had been lonely with her mother.

Until Kevin said he didn't want to go to her cousin's friend's bowling party, so Amelia dressed up as she used to when she was single and in her midtwenties, new to New York, living with a roommate in Williamsburg, freelancing and bartending. She wore the dress she used to wear when she wanted to have a night out that was different from the usual night out. Kevin saw her in the dress, said, "What, no lipstick and earrings, too?" so she put on the whole outfit, and then when there was no one to bowl with she felt she'd deserved what she'd gotten: a lonely night as a married woman dressed up like she was still a teenager. She'd go home and read a magazine next to her husband in bed.

And then Aaron. When she saw him, he looked like an *Alice in Wonderland* version of her high school history teacher all shrunken down and younger, except that wasn't right at all, it was just that they were all older. He was probably the same age her high school history teacher had been back then. And she'd loved her high school history teacher. Aaron wore the same polo shirt and the same khaki pants. They started bowling. They talked about their parents, and when Aaron told her that his father relied on him through chronic pain and that his mother was dead, it took everything Amelia had inside her not to break down crying and hug Aaron right there in front of Ari and all his asshole bowling friends. She kept on thinking the entire night that the whole thing was just to get back at Kevin—that Aaron was so soft where Kevin was hard, or so eager for contact where Kevin was repellant of it. But when they went to a bar afterward and Aaron built up to telling her his biggest secret in the world and that secret was that he was a successful financial consultant, again Amelia had to physically fight the urge to break down crying and hug Aaron in the middle of the bar.

That moment after they'd slept together for the first time. Aaron told her about the stolen money. She was crushed. Before he'd told her, it had been a fantasy. Everything she'd wanted from Kevin, Aaron was offering her. Now she had to decide. But she couldn't. She would have to give Aaron up right after giving up Kevin. It was too much loss. She wouldn't do it. She wanted to save her own life. And Aaron's. She wanted to care for him in a way she'd never cared for anyone. To give him what she'd never received from anyone. And, mostly, she wanted to create something *with* Aaron. Her life with Kevin had been playacting at the life she'd thought she'd wanted when she actually wanted roots and purpose and a home. She was willing to risk being bored if that meant no longer being lonely.

The immediate tenderness Amelia felt for Simon—the reason she was so prepared for it was because she felt that same tenderness for Aaron.

And when she learned more about Aaron—that he'd been the valedictorian of his high school class; that even before his father's physical pain, even when Aaron was little, his father had insisted on constant check-ins, evaluations, and assessments; that every day for Aaron was a fight with a destructive part of himself—the tenderness she felt for him was not only a new component of love that she'd never before experienced, it was itself a new kind of love.

And somewhere along the line she realized she could, in addition to expanding this love, make more of it. She could have a child, a child with Aaron—Aaron's child—and manufacture this love.

She'd been marking time while with Kevin—relishing the loneliness to trick herself into craving him in a certain way that turned her on and approximated what she'd always thought of as love. Now she'd found not necessarily a permanent enduring passion, but something that broke her brain and chest open and made itself so much more important than Kevin had ever been. There were problems with Aaron. Of course there were. They stemmed from that destructive part of him, from a lack of sexual compatibility sometimes, from Aaron's lack of professional fulfillment, and, relatedly, from Aaron's comparing himself to what he imagined Kevin must have been like. If Amelia was honest with herself, the latter was an issue for her, too. She caught herself comparing Aaron in certain moments to Kevin—Kevin's willingness to just drop life and go. Kevin's flash of charisma when charisma was what was needed. His sudden warmth or inspired idea. But these were what had made him unbearable at the end. Life had been unpredictable with Kevin in a way that depleted rather than energized her. Selfish and consequently unsatisfying. Or, paradoxically, Amelia was infused by a greater selfishness now. She wanted more for her life. To mean more, matter more. To take care of people and hope she might be cared for. The selfishness Kevin brought out in Amelia had been too small. It had been about sex and food and fun.

So Kevin was gone. And replaced by Aaron. And childlessness was gone. And replaced by Simon. And France was gone. And replaced by Bed-Stuy. And all of this was at risk now as Amelia made sure the gun's safety was on, as she fortified herself for the stairs up to the office. This was her family and her house and she wasn't going to let some teenage girl scare her away from it.

Chapter 34

From the one time he'd been locked out a few weeks after moving in, Aaron knew his house was impenetrable. Maybe he could jump the side fence from Bainbridge into Jupiter's yard, and Jupiter could let him in through the back, then he could cross over from Jupiter's roof to his neighbors' then his own? Or he could just jump the fence in the first yard off Stuyvesant and keep jumping fences and take the back stairs up into the TV room? Unless kids had found that way in, in which case he hoped it would be locked. If Amelia hadn't thought of it, Antoinette would.

Running to the train, he discovered his phone didn't work and email wouldn't load, but Twitter did refresh once, which was enough for him to learn that the riots had started at the Boys and Girls School two blocks from his house. He still couldn't do anything for another twenty minutes until his stop, and since he hadn't had a chance to use his one prayer at the racetrack, he prayed.

And it felt different. Immediately. He didn't feel the usual blockage. He didn't feel the futility and the anger. The plaque. The tension and worthlessness that had to be gambled away. He closed his eyes. His body was empty. Thoughts were water filling him up from inside. His fingertips seemed accessible from his lungs. For the first time since . . . for the first time in his adult life. He didn't remember being a child. Simon was the child now. Something could be accomplished now. He could go home. He could help. Maybe as a rabbi he hadn't been able to help a woman who'd lost her son. The son had already been taken. But his son! Aaron's son! He was on his way!

The problem hadn't been the lack of God—whether God existed or not. It had been God's—and Aaron's—failure to act. To sit there and watch suffering. But now—soon—Aaron could act.

And the thought of having prayed for money—for sports—it sickened him. The thought of gambling sickened him. Lying to Amelia sickened him. He sickened himself. How happy he'd permitted himself to be, alone without his family, repulsed him. It was a sickness. Having stayed even those extra moments at the track—he did need help. Actual help.

He begged for forgiveness. He begged himself for forgiveness, but that wasn't enough.

He started to cry. He was in a middle seat of a three-seat bench squeezed between two women—one white, one Hispanic—who ignored him. He was on the local C train, three stops away from his Utica stop.

He was thankful for the second chance at life that Amelia had given him. He was thankful for Amelia's willingness not only to see the best in people but to help them. She was there for Simon. She was there for him. She knew he was weak. And she was there for him in spite of his weakness. Sometimes, he thought, because of it.

He was proud of her lately. Proud that she wrote the article about the neighborhood. He would read it tonight. This was serious work. Not like the celebrity stuff. But now he was being patronizing. He focused again on the prayer. He was grateful to be part of what Amelia cared so much about. Not since his parents had someone cared about him as she did. Especially someone so picky about what and whom she cared about. He was grateful for his neighbors and his neighborhood. He was grateful for his time as a rabbi, short though it might have been.

If you give me my son and girlfriend back whole and healthy, I will do anything—everything—I can, Adonai. I will rededicate my life to you. Even if it's just as a congregant, I will turn back to you. Forgive me for abandoning you. I'll try to believe.

Aaron thought about instances in the Bible where humans bartered with God. Sodom and Gomorrah where Abraham bargained God down to just a few good people—if God could find just a few good people (down from, what was it, fifty?) he'd save the city—and still Abraham and God couldn't find them. God had been willing to strike a deal. So this is when Aaron begged.

Save Amelia. And save Simon. And save me. Get us three through this. And if you do, so shall I consecrate my son to you, Adonai. Please, Adonai. Don't let our blood be spilled. Amen.

The train was stopping and going, and then stopping again. He was still at least ten minutes from Utica, where he had no idea what to expect.

Chapter 35

D aniel was the man of the house until Aaron returned. Maybe even after Aaron returned? He loaded the cartridge into the shotgun. He asked if Antoinette knew how to use it. Antoinette told him she wouldn't take a life. Daniel tried to call his brother, but cell signals seemed to be down for good and there was no landline. They turned on CNN and saw police in riot gear with what looked like full military equipment: tanks and camouflage and what appeared to be a missile launcher but was probably some kind of tear gas dispenser.

These military units surrounded the Marcy Projects, which had turned into a war zone. Wolf Blitzer was interviewing Jay Z, who'd grown up there, and as Jay Z was talking, residents of the tower were holding up posters that showed Jay Z with his hand up as though in solidarity with the protesters. Jay Z cut the interview short. He'd been asking for a cease-fire.

Tanks surrounded the Marcy Projects. One of its buildings was on fire.

Wolf Blitzer said the Marcy Projects, "Consist of twenty-seven, six-story buildings on 28.49 acres and contain 1,705 apartments housing about 4,286 residents, many of whom appear to be barricaded in their units throwing projectiles and shooting at the police in riot gear below. Though the incidents started farther east, anger spread west, and these Marcy Projects seem to be the focus of the city's attention. Over to . . ." a reporter interviewing a representative from the city government asking residents to think of the children.

"Whatever your grievances, I'm sure they can be met. Please, please think of the children in these buildings. They will accidentally be put in harm's way."

"Is that a threat?" Wolf Blitzer said. Somehow, Wolf Blitzer was able to jump in and ask the city representative questions, too.

"What? God, no," the woman said. "God no. What's going on is awful. We have to stop the citizens of this great city—the greatest city—from harming one another. We have to contain the situation. We have to put out fires. We'll work with them afterward, but police have to shoot back if they're being shot at—for self-protection purposes—and there are innocents and children in these situations."

"Are you threatening them?" Wolf Blitzer said.

"I'm not threatening anyone," the city representative said. "I'm just a spokesman. What are we supposed to do?"

Daniel said, "We have enough rations. We have two guns. And one of them is a CZ Over/Under twenty gauge. There are bars on the windows. We're barricaded in here safely until the police come our way. Amelia's on her way to take care of that girl."

"I don't think so," Antoinette said.

Chapter 36

Amelia stood in the stairway, halfway between the third floor—the bedroom floor—and the fourth floor, which housed the office and exercise room. The office was big and bright, with stained-glass windows and a large wooden desk, bookshelves, and a rug from her trip to Turkey with Kevin. The exercise room was smaller, on the other side of the office through a simple white door. It was a small white room, which they had once both used, but since the baby only Aaron did. Amelia guessed that the girl was sitting at the desk. Amelia guessed that after jumping up and down in despair and stupidity at running back into the house alone, the girl sat and cried in Amelia's desk chair. Where Amelia had sat just a few hours before, when everything had been fine. When Amelia had been reading comments on her article about the neighborhood. An article that now, just a few hours after it went live, was either entirely useless or exactly the sort of thing that could get her on every cable news channel tomorrow. She could be an expert on Bed-Stuy. If anyone would allow a white person to represent the neighborhood. She'd have to be the third guest on a panel of three. She'd have to be the academic, or the gentrifier. She'd have to be the kindhearted white gentrifier who was trying to understand her angry black neighbors. She'd have to be yelled at by an angry young black man and she could choose whether to take it and apologize or explain that the angry young man wasn't actually angry at her but at cultural trends. Or she could explain that as angry as the angry young man was, his father or grandfather would have had a right to be even angrier. She'd turn down those interview requests, she thought. No, she wouldn't. She'd take advantage of the opportunity. She'd tell the world what a hero Jupiter had been.

Halfway up the stairs, Amelia leaned in to listen. She couldn't hear anything. Knowing she was about to see someone, she smelled her shirt. She'd mostly been able to wipe the vomit away. And it was only baby vomit, which wasn't so bad. But still, she smelled of sweat and baby vomit. She looped her hair behind her ears with her left hand. She was shaking. She gripped the pistol with her right hand and the wooden banister with her left. The girl, from what Amelia thought she saw, was between fourteen and seventeen years old, between 80 and 120 pounds. Amelia gripped the gun in her right hand. She was a righty. She'd shot a rifle before. She and Kevin had in Germany. With his German friends from college. Or Cologne. That was his joke. No one knew if Kevin had met these guys in college or while taking a summer cooking course in Cologne. Not even Amelia.

But she'd never shot a pistol before. Once, she'd held a pistol with the safety on and pointed it at Kevin's chest as what had been maybe, possibly, not entirely, an empty threat, when she'd found out that he was maybe, possibly, sleeping with someone else. He'd denied it. She still wasn't sure. Kevin never said. How could she be sure? She'd wanted it to be true. She still did. She wanted Kevin to be the one who had ruined her marriage. It meant this relationship—whatever it was—with Aaron had more hope. Would last. If Kevin had been the rotten one, then there was no reason to think she and Aaron wouldn't last forever in spite of Aaron's problems. And where had that gun come from? She'd gone from guilt for seeing Aaron regularly at Aaron's tiny apartment to fury over Sandra from the restaurant whom Kevin might or might not have been sleeping with in the same way Amelia was *actually* sleeping with Aaron. She went from guilt to fury to stumbling onto a heavy black plastic case in the suitcase they never used under the bed but now Amelia was considering using if she was going to run off to Aaron's house. She'd been considering telling Kevin about Aaron, she'd been preparing by looking for luggage, she'd checked the suitcase they never used under the bed, and found a heavy black case inside, opened it with his three-digit code for everything, and found a pistol. Then Aaron had come home all happy, too happy, from a dinner with Saaaaaandra. Not Aaron. Kevin. Kevin had come home from dinner with Saaaaaaaaaaaaaaaaaandra, the sommelier at the new place where Kevin was working in Greenpoint, and Amelia took the gun out, checked to make sure the safety was on, and Kevin jumped her, threw the gun on the ground, and they slept together. Liquor on his hot breath. His teeth against hers.

It was the last time they'd had sex like that or sex at all. She went to Aaron's place later that night, told him about the gun, not about the sex, asked to hear the story about the gambling, the money, but never found out why the gun was there or how long it had been in the suitcase or whether Kevin had slept with Sandra or if she—Amelia—was the one who'd wrecked their marriage. If she was the one who couldn't stay married, if the broken marriage was her fault and not her fun-loving, gun-toting,

Sandra-sexing husband's. Was it legal? Registered? Was it to protect her? She never knew. It never came up in the divorce. Because Aaron never came up. Or Sandra the Sommelier. It was all amicable. They didn't have any children or shared assets to fight over.

Now she had this house. She had Simon. She had an entire life.

Amelia was crying. She couldn't do it. She couldn't go up there with a gun and threaten to shoot or actually shoot another woman or, God forbid, a girl.

She began the climb from the landing between the third and fourth floors. She was shaking so her vision was slightly blurry, and she held on to the gun to stabilize herself, but that was ineffective, so she held on to the railing. She heard a male voice, which filled her with joy until she realized it wasn't Aaron's.

"Leave me alone," Amelia said to Daniel. "I'm okay."

She didn't want Daniel coming upstairs and shooting this girl. Not in her house. There had been enough violence already. She didn't want Aaron to come home and find Jupiter's body downstairs and the girl still upstairs. She didn't want him to be in a position where he had to make another mistake and start life over again, again. She would handle it. She trusted herself more than she trusted him. She wanted to control this. She wanted to be in control of the violence if there had to be violence. This was where she was going to raise her son. She trusted her own instincts more than Daniel's. She wasn't sure if it was gender based, but she knew she was the right one to talk to this girl, and though she wanted more than anything else in the world for Aaron to be safe and home, she was still the one to talk to this girl. Daniel she had no patience for. *He had shot a teenage boy, even if that boy had killed a man!*

It was impossible that she was having real thoughts about shooting and killing. It was impossible that she was holding a gun. Then she thought that her skepticism confirmed she was correct in sending Daniel away. He wouldn't be skeptical. He would be aggressive. *He would want to prove himself again and again and again.* That was the difference between men and women. Men constantly needed to prove themselves. Needed to display themselves to the world, for an opportunity to bask in the world's approval. Not her. She needed to know that what was done was done right. She wanted to look after her own. Herself. Her son. Her home. Her family. She was the right one to come upstairs and send this girl away. That was the most important thing. Simon was downstairs and in danger.

But she heard a male voice again, and she wasn't certain it was coming from downstairs, though it definitely wasn't coming from upstairs. She sat to listen. As long as she was between her baby downstairs and the girl upstairs, she was protecting her baby. The gun was in her hand. She heard the voice of a father, so it had to be her father because it wasn't Aaron's voice. Her father was dead, though, his voice available only on a video recording—Amelia three or four years old on a powerboat, her father holding the camcorder asking Amelia if she liked the flags on the bridges they were passing—and this voice wasn't his. This voice was allowing her to sit, though, and relax. It was comforting, and it was telling her the truth. She was at ease for the first time since Jupiter was shot. She wouldn't have disagreed if someone had told her the voice was in her head. Of course it was in her head if it wasn't coming from another person. Of course it wasn't her father. Her father had been dead for thirty years almost. So it was God—if that was the word for consciousness. Or why not just God, actually?

She wasn't wearing a watch, and she didn't look at her phone, because time wasn't at issue. She felt weightless but immovable. She sat on the steps and listened as God or her subconscious told her, on those stairs, that the house she was sitting in was her house purchased with money that had been in her family for generations and that generations of her family would come to live there.

God is here, and I didn't know it, Amelia thought, and she was afraid, and she said out loud, "This is a house of God."

The stairs shined bright above her. The sun filtered through the skylight in thick kaleidoscopic beams, through clouds of dust that teased Amelia to reach out and unsettle them with her fingertips.

"My child," he said.

"My child," she said.

She stood slowly and climbed to just outside the door to the office. The door was thick wood. Mahogany, she guessed. She didn't know what kind of wood it was. She didn't know anything.

"Hello?" she said.

No response.

She knocked.

Then louder, "Hello?" Amelia repeated.

She listened for sobs.

Nothing.

Hello?

She tried the door, which she was sure would be locked, but it wasn't.

Chapter 37

Near Kingston Throop, crowds began to talk.

"I knew it was coming. I had a friend who lives near there, who lives near that area of Ralph, and she's always talking like people aren't as nice to each other as they used to be."

"Uh-huh. First thing happens is white folks move in to the nice houses, then cops move in to protect the white folks, rents go up, way up, then things change, get worse for those people who been living in the neighborhood for—"

"Well that's why did you see those pictures online?"

"I saw them."

"Fire from Marcy all the way across."

"Your family okay?"

"That's what I'm going to find out, maybe join in some of the—"

"I know what you mean."

"But be careful."

"Stan'll protect me, and I know who to stay away from, what corners to let alone."

"I wonder how long the subway's gonna run, or if we'll skip Utica at least."

"Well like I said, I'm getting off after Utica. I'll get off at Ralph, walk toward north. Where you going?"

"All the way to Broadway Junction."

"Okay, then, you be safe."

"Nice to meet you. Holler at Stan for me."

"You be safe."

"You, too."

Aaron wore his suit with the tie still knotted neat against his throat; he wasn't crying anymore. "You hear that?" a black man in a suit asked him. He'd taken the seat of the white woman.

"I live right in the middle of it with my wife and baby. They're there. Right off the Utica stop. This train better let off there," Aaron said.

"Shit, man." And then to the women who were talking: "You ladies hear that? This guy says he lives right in the middle of it and police won't help his wife and baby, so you two watch what you're saying."

"We're sorry."

"Yeah, we're sorry."

"What am I going to do?" Aaron said. "They're looting. The neighborhood's on fire according to the news."

"Be polite. Ask them nicely," one of the ladies said.

"Okay," Aaron said, fortified. He believed in what the lady had said.

But then a group of ten black teenagers got on the subway at Kingston Throop, clearly heading to the same place Aaron was. They were quiet, excited. They were jumping up and down a little bit. They were as eager as Aaron was to get to their stop. There were a dozen of them, not ten. They stood even though there were seats available. They were quiet even though they were sixteen or seventeen years old. It was difficult, riding this last stop knowing that he and these kids were going to the same place—maybe the same house. He couldn't say anything to them. Nobody said anything more to Aaron. He focused on his house, each room, on what he could do when he got there.

The kids were respectful but powerful as a group. One took out candy. He was wearing dark blue jeans and a polo shirt buttoned all the way up. Aaron thought about Arnold Schwarzenegger and laughed. The kid saw him laugh, and both Aaron and the kid looked down, then up, then at a family a few seats away from Aaron that had nothing to do with the riots.

A grandmother, mother, and children, Aaron guessed. Hispanic. The children were both girls. Maybe six years old. Aaron had a good sense of ages from when he'd run the tots program at the synagogue. One girl looked normal. Like a regular little girl Aaron wouldn't have noticed. She wore shorts, a T-shirt, and a pink hooded sweatshirt. Her hair was braided sloppily, and she drank a can of Sprite with a straw. She wore white sandals covered by pony stickers that were dirty from the street. But the other girl was horrible, and she was what Aaron thought the kid with the buttoned-up polo shirt was looking at.

This girl was fat in way that made it seem she was proud to be fat. She was years before puberty, but she carried herself in a conceited, almost sexualized way. Aaron knew many people who would say she was asking to be slapped. She wore tight white pants and a shirt that said Shopping Is My Cardio, and she waved around a long, thin, multicolored woven lollipop that she'd suck on and wave closer and closer to her mother and grandmother's faces until even for those passengers who were on their way to the riot it became difficult not to stare. This fat six-year-old sucked on the long, sticky lollipop, waved it so it stuck to the window of the subway car, wrenched it off the window where it had stuck, sucked on it some more, and swung it around closer and closer to her grandmother's face as though she was daring her grandmother to tell her to stop. But her grandmother and mother ignored her, talking in Spanish about whatever they were talking about.

When the lollipop grazed the grandmother's nose, the black man on the train who'd been talking to Aaron straightened up. The two women who were talking about the riot gasped. The dozen black kids who'd been sharing the candy were transfixed by this point. Aaron was no longer angry with the girl. When he'd thought he was the only one who saw her behavior, it irritated him, but the more people who joined the audience, the less Aaron cared—the more he felt it wasn't their concern. The more he wanted to get home.

The fat girl licked the lollipop. Rolls of her stomach fell over her shorts. She put the lollipop down next to her, on the plastic subway seat. Her sister reached for it, and the fat girl slapped her sister's hand. She pushed her sister, so some of the Sprite spilled. The fat girl grabbed the can of Sprite and threw the straw on the ground and drank the Sprite until it was finished. She handed it back to her sister upside down so some of the sticky last drops got all over the girl's pink sweatshirt, at which point the fat girl lifted up her own T-shirt exposing her fat belly and rubbed her belly making the "mmm, that's so delicious" motion. Her sister started to breathe quickly in a pre-crying hyperventilating way, and the mother was watching the whole thing, but she didn't say anything. Neither did the grandmother. The fat girl picked up the lollipop off the subway seat, licked it, and smacked the grandmother in the face with it. The grandmother remained placid.

"I know you are not going to let her keep acting like this!"

screamed the black woman who'd said Stan would protect her. "I know you are not going to let her treat you with this kind of . . . does anyone speak Spanish here? Does anyone, can anyone translate? Can anyone tell these *mamacitas* that in this country we do not let our children treat us with this kind of disrespect? We whup their asses if they treat us like this. That's why she's growing all fat like that. That's why they have no self-respect, eating lollipops that have been resting where people put their asses."

The black man sitting next to Aaron signaled as though he was about to say something, maybe interrupting, but the woman got louder. "Excuse me—no, it's my time to talk. Excuse me, but I've seen enough. Can anyone tell these people what I'm saying?"

"I do!" one of the dozen black kids on the way to the riot said. "I speak a little."

"Well tell those women that in this country we do not let our little ones treat us with this kind of disrespect."

He translated in a rudimentary Spanish that even Aaron could tell was very basic. The kid's friends were laughing, and the grandmother and the mother were laughing along with the kids.

"What is she laughing at?" the woman yelled at the translator. "Are they laughing at me?"

"I don't know, lady," the translator said, laughing himself now, along with his friends who were making fun of his Spanish.

"They're laughing," the woman yelled, "but they're raising this diabetes fat-ass little girl who hit her own grandmother in public, and she's laughing at me. She better show some fucking respect, coming to this country and laughing at me when I'm trying to help her raise her fucking kids and she's just sitting there like she—and what are you looking at?" the woman said to Aaron.

"Me?" Aaron said.

"Yes, you."

"I just think we should let people raise their families however they want to," Aaron said.

"Do you?" the woman said.

"We don't know anything about them," Aaron said. "We don't know if the girl's dad died this week. We don't know if he got deported. We don't know if they're coming back from a funeral. We shouldn't be so angry," Aaron said.

"Well fuck you, you righteous asshole," the woman said. "I hope your fucking house burns to the ground."

Chapter 38

Police Commissioner Bill Bratton drove down to the Utica station in his black car. His second and third in command were trying to control the Marcy Projects. But Bratton believed in starting at the beginning and tracing the situation forward. A dozen black cars and patrol cars followed him from Manhattan. Vision Zero meant the mayor wanted zero traffic deaths that year, and a car in which Bratton had been a passenger was caught on camera speeding down Atlantic Avenue twenty miles an hour over the limit, so to end the discussion Bratton said he'd drive himself. He'd been on the streets in Boston for a decade before he had a driver, and now, after spending ten years chauffeured around LA, he was happy to be behind the wheel again.

When they reached the Utica station and the Boys and Girls High School an hour after the riots had started, and, Bratton guessed, forty minutes after they'd dispersed, he saw crowds to the north. He was carrying a gun again, and he felt for it at his hip. His wife liked it. Sweet Rikki. His fourth wife. She'd love him no matter what. But the people wouldn't. These riots would be his legacy. The riots and how he handled them. He had a bullhorn in the car. He'd find rioters and police officers, and talk directly to them. He'd be George W. Bush after 9/11.

But even then he'd have to talk afterward about if broken-window policing led to this. If choke holds led to this. If stop, question, and frisk led to this. For the rest of his life. It was already too late. Dead black men led to this. He knew that. Now this fucking shot kid. And the two kids before him. That was all on him, too. Not the stop-and-frisk, but his promise to deescalate and the escalation that followed.

Still, if he just got there, wherever "there" was. To the root of the problem. He could solve it. He always had before. He wasn't going to be mayor. There was nothing left to become, nothing more to achieve. But he had his reputation to protect. And the city's. Their legacies were intertwined. And he was the only one able to keep the darkness of the 1970s at bay.

Utica looked like a hurricane had hit it. Police barricades on their sides, a woodchip pile spread all over the paths, and blood, police tape, black soot, plastic bags, desks and chairs, baseball caps, ripped clothing. It looked like Mogadishu. Bratton had visited Mogadishu in the 1990s to see how police were failing to cope with violence there. Now the LA commissioner and commissioners from Boston and Tel Aviv would visit New York to study his failure.

He panicked at all the time wasting, sped up, felt the engine behind him, realized, with a bitter thrill, that if he drove himself into a lamppost at eighty miles per hour—he was at fifty miles per hour now and could easily accelerate further—he'd be a municipal cowboy hero. His would be the story people discovered the day after the story. Instead of the villain, he'd be a fallen soldier. Jimmy O'Neill was ready to take over. The next chapter in Bratton's legacy would still be written. A stray bullet would be good, too. An assassination, even better. He'd led a good, full life . . . but he wouldn't crumble. He was stronger than that. He was the backbone of this city. New Yorkers needed him. That was why they'd brought him back. The city couldn't survive without him. Jimmy could wait his turn.

But Bratton didn't know which direction to head. He saw the edge of a crowd gathering up on Stuyvesant Avenue. He heard bullets firing to the east, away from Marcy, deeper into Bed-Stuy and East New York; and sirens from fire alarms and fire trucks blared to the south in Crown Heights.

He had his windows open and his two-way radio on. His deputy was in his passenger seat and his personal security sat in back. All this was against protocol, but it was how he liked it. After Vietnam, after Boston, after New York, after LA, after Bratton Technologies and Altegrity and Kroll and NBC and The Bratton Group and Crest and London and Homeland Security Advisory Council and now New York again, Bill Bratton had little interest in protocol. He had little fear of danger.

I'm Bill Bratton, he thought. He'd made the speech ten thousand times at ten thousand ten-thousand-dollar dinners. I have little time for protocol. I use Comstat. We agreed to be held accountable for what we did. We set a goal for 10 percent crimes solved within ten days. We got 15 percent. Then we set a goal for 15 percent. We got 18 percent. We set a goal, and we asked to be held accountable. Every time there's a homicide, my BlackBerry goes off. Because I'm in charge. If I'm in the bathroom, if I'm in Israel, I get notice. And then we respond to that data. We put cops on the dots. We react to data. What is the best medicine? Think of it from the medical perspective. We do some tests. Medical tests. We rapidly respond. We stabilize you. Effective tactics. First the trauma specialist arrives. Then the heart specialist. Then pulmonary.

Then follow up visits. I'm Bill Bratton. I'm taking a medical approach to dealing with crime. It used to be we'd gather stats twice a year to send them off to the federal government. Now it's every day. It used to be a million times a year you'd dial 911 and we wouldn't come, like a doctor giving you placebos instead of real medicine. Now we anticipate the problem.

The first time he was in New York City, he worked his way up from the chief of the New York City Transit Police in 1990. In 1991, due to his politicking, the Transit Police gained national accreditation, which meant a transition from being the head of a pretend security staff to a real municipal subpolice. This occurred nearly the same month as the Crown Heights riots that killed two people and jailed more, and that eventually lost the mayor the city, contributing to exactly the kind of racial and religious hatred that New York had spent the past twenty years recovering from.

Bratton's legacy was a broken-window policy that tried to calm those tensions. He thought about what could happen if the violence spread south on Kingston Avenue and got the Orthodox mixed up with it as well as the blacks. So far it was just the blacks who were angry, and though this was a real problem and Obama was going to get involved, this fit in with what was going on with Ferguson, and after Trayvon Martin, and with Oscar Grant in Oakland, and Manuel Diaz in Anaheim, and Kimani Gray right here in Brooklyn. Kimani Gray. The only publicly identified eyewitness in that killing by two New York City police officers stood by her claim that Gray was empty-handed when he was gunned down, and now she was saying that one of the cops involved threatened her life. Now add Jason Blau to the list.

No wonder there were riots. Kimani Gray was before Bratton,

but what did these rioting kids know? Kimani Gray was news, but the type of news that didn't get the police commissioner noticed, not like riots that involved confrontations of different races. He had to keep the blacks from the Jews. He had to make sure the Orthodox knew he was watching out for them, that he remembered 1991.

So he made his decision. He turned his cavalcade south into Crown Heights and with it, the attention of the New York City Police Department. Three quarters were focused on the Marcy Projects. Bratton turned his attention toward Crown Heights. The death count, as reported by 911 calls at least, had to be in the dozens. And most cell towers were down. Half were down to free up the emergency airways. Half that should have been working were jammed with calls. He accelerated and turned south. Crown Heights was still where Jews and blacks lived together, and now gentrifiers were too close for comfort. It was where people were still shot more often than in Bed-Stuy. He wanted to be there, now. A half-hour ago. It felt too late.

Two boys dead a month before, and then Saturday night in Bed-Stuy. Jason Blau was twelve years old. The officers' fuckup. Both of them. After thirty million extra in the budget for training to avoid exactly this.

Bratton had gone to Mogadishu three years after Black Hawk Down. He'd seen that things were still completely fucked. He saw a leg bone on a pool table. How fucked up? The people laughed, told him it was a dog bone and they put it there to scare him. He didn't get scared so they all drank beer. It wasn't a dog bone. It was a human bone. Bratton was fucking sure of it. To this day, he knew that the bone on the pool table had been a human leg bone.

He had told riot police to head to the larger housing projects, fire departments to get to Brooklyn in anticipation; every cop was now on duty and on the way to the danger zones. The housing projects. The major avenues. The big box stores. The schools were let out. He was on his fourth marriage. Not because the job was more important. That was what he told his friends. They all told him to prioritize family. Four wives, and David. And from him, John and Nicolas. John and Nicolas still fought over plastic toy fire trucks. They were eight and six years old, and they'd live their life hearing about their grandfather who couldn't save New York. Prioritize family! When a city is on fire? A city is always on fire! And Bill Bratton is there to put it out.

And Bill Bratton is there to—

"Sir?" someone said.

There would be stories about missed 911 calls. About cops shot. He'd be blamed. He accelerated harder.

"Sir?"

Not New York the first time. Not LA. *This* would be his legacy. Stop and frisk. Broken windows.

"Steady, sir."

He'd been doing everything right. He would get there quickly, wherever "there" was, and solve this problem himself. He just had to go faster, get there himself, assess the situation, and act.

"Slow the car, sir." He would listen to the people. Put himself on the dot. The city needed him!

"Commissioner Bratton?"

These people rioted because they wanted more than they had. This was their opportunity to get more for themselves and destroy possessions of others. Well he'd give them everything he had. He just needed to get there.

"Commissioner Bratton!"

He skidded to a screech of the tires. The car spun, slid, and stopped. They'd come close to hitting a traffic sign, scraped a few parked cars, fencing, got caught on a hydrant. Bratton exited the car. He felt for his gun. Grabbed the bullhorn. Started running. Felt like he was thirty years old again. With his deputy and security detail, he squeezed into the backseat of the car behind his.

"Go south!" he shouted. "Go! Go! Go!"

Chapter 39

T here is no God but God and Muhammad is his messenger. Antoinette asked for a message from Muhammad. She asked for a sign. She said, "There is no God but God and Muhammad is his messenger," and she thought *There is no God but God and Muhammad is his messenger* so she was Muslim. That's what she was told made someone Muslim, and she believed it. She prayed as many times a day as she could, and she gave to charity on the subway. She would fast during the next Ramadan, and once she got enough money together she'd go to Mecca. She was becoming Muslim while she was still Christian, and then when she was fully Muslim, she'd let Christianity go. She was ready to go to the next level.

Church bells rang at 2 p.m. The back door down to the garden had originally been left open, but she'd bolted that, and then, maybe because she'd been watching so much zombie stuff lately— *World War Z,* with Brad Pitt, and then the *Walking Dead* through her ex-employer's Netflix account (they'd given her the password) through a Nintendo Wii that her mother had sent her for Christmas from Chicago for the fitness game—Antoinette covered all the windows and doors first with shades and shutters, but then she left the baby in the Pack 'n Play with Daniel and put up blankets and cardboard from Amazon and Fresh Direct delivery boxes as well.

Upstairs tearing boxes apart in Aaron and Amelia's bedroom, Antoinette caught a glimpse of herself in the fireplace mantel mirror. Seeing herself like that made her laugh. Tearing boxes, wearing a hijab. The first time she'd worn it, she'd thought she looked like a suicide bomber, but not since. Not since Jupiter had complimented her. She choked at the memory, which she already felt joining those in Jamaica and her childhood in New York—those she didn't permit herself the pleasure and pain of revisiting too often. She had liked the feeling of moving forward. Just hours earlier, Jupiter himself had been part of the forward momentum. She had a deep desire to go to the body—his body was there, right downstairs—but she had work to do, she told herself. She had to block the windows. Antoinette tried not to give into him, the tears, the submission to self-pity. She was still moving forward to Islam. Jupiter had approved of that.

Antoinette focused on her conversion. She'd chosen her mosque—all the way in Clinton Hill—because it had nothing to do with terrorism. Because it was famous for condemning Boko Haram and Islamic State for being sinners. Under the hijab, the way it framed her face, Antoinette had an even nicer smile. That's what Jupiter had told her.

She'd always been a quiet girl with a nice smile who did well at school. She had a better memory than everyone else—for birthdays and things people said and tricks to do in math and places in geography and now verses from the Bible. She had come to the States to live with her aunt in New York. Her mom was in Chicago, and though it was never clear why Chicago wasn't a place for Antoinette, it didn't matter much because she'd always been close with her aunt, who complimented her smile, had more money than her mom, bought Antoinette clothing, and made her take school very seriously.

Antoinette came over in 1990 as a six-year-old, and by 1995 her Jamaican accent was gone. The public school she went to in Flatbush was bad in terms of the education she received, but it wasn't dangerous, and all her friends were Jamaican or from other Caribbean countries, and when she got a little older they started being from African countries like Nigeria or Kenya. Antoinette always did well in school because school was easy if you went to class and listened to the teacher. She never understood why the other kids made a big fuss about school. The facts were interesting and it was fun to try to learn the tricks that the math teacher taught.

In 1998, she was fourteen, and her best friend was a girl named Afafa who went by Afa, and their best friend was a boy from Haiti named Billy. The three of them did well at school and didn't get involved in most of the stuff that their friends did, but they also didn't get jobs. Jobs seemed so awful to the three of them. Antoinette would have been willing, but Afa said that nothing was worse than smelling of fry grease, so Billy quit his job, and the thought of the two of them hanging around all day without her made Antoinette hysterical with envy. The one day she worked at the sneaker store, she had to go to the small bathroom at the pizza place next door to throw up.

Billy didn't play sports, and Afa and Antoinette didn't have boyfriends in spite of Antoinette's nice smile and Afa's ass. People joked that they must be doing threesomes, but it wasn't like that. They told stories and compared what they remembered about the countries they came from, which was mostly just what they saw on trips home over the summer: the food, like which rice was better, and the different ways of drinking Coke, from the bottle or plastic bags. Of course the bottle was better, so they made fun of Afa, which made Antoinette feel good. Afa and Billy lived with their parents and Antoinette lived with her aunt. They didn't drink alcohol. It was innocent.

One time they talked about white people.

"Do you know any white people?" Afa asked.

"Miss Tevelson," Antoinette said.

"Teachers don't count," Afa said. She was the smartest of the three of them and had the biggest ass and sometimes talked to the other two like she was their teacher. Afa was the smartest person Antoinette had ever met.

"My father's boss. A few white people live in my building and they're nice," Billy said. He was shaped like a string bean. "And a few cops, but I don't know them. And when I went to camp one summer there was the head of the camp."

"I don't know any white people!" Afa said.

"I guess me either!" Billy said.

"We're sixteen fucking years old and we don't know any white people," Afa said.

"How about your neighbors?" Antoinette said to Billy. "You said one minute ago that you knew your neighbors." She was starting not to like it that Afa was in charge of conversations among the three of them. They were in Afa's room like they always were, sitting in front of her fish tank. Afa kept beautiful African fish because her father knew the owner of the pet store. One time, Afa's father brought home a turtle as big as the dining room table, but they didn't know what to do with it, so they just brought it back to the store, but not before Afa scratched "A+B+A" into the shell.

"But how well do I really know my neighbors?" Billy said. "And I only met my father's boss two times!"

"Don't tell him what to do," Afa told Antoinette.

"Don't tell me what to do," Antoinette told Afa. "Us, I mean."

"Why are you always belittling us?" Afa told Antoinette. "You think you're better than us."

"Me?" Antoinette said. "I do?" Antoinette looked to Billy.

But Billy looked down, whether in agreement with Afa or not to get involved, Antoinette didn't know.

Afa smirked in Antoinette's direction. It had been unspoken between Afa and Antoinette that Billy was out of bounds. That Antoinette would ruin everything if she tried to be Billy's girlfriend. He was very tall and very black and very smart and very nice and very shy and very clumsy and not at all funny, and he was awkward around adults, and he would have probably made a bad boyfriend anyway. She was so angry to be called belittling like that. And they were getting too old to hang out the three of them together all the time. So Antoinette went to a party that night and dressed up as sexy as she could and went over to a group of kids and was as friendly as possible and became one of their girlfriends and was pregnant within a month.

When she thought about that time in her life later on, it was that conversation about white people she remembered. The drinking and drugs she did after wiped other stuff away. Pot, mostly, but other stuff, too. Cocaine a few times. The real reason she didn't have an abortion was because she didn't want to tell anyone she was pregnant and she didn't know where to get one on her own. It was too late when her aunt noticed. Her mom flew in from Chicago. Afa and Billy dated for seven years after that.

Antoinette wanted to be clean once she knew she was keeping

the child. Not get clean, only. Be clean. So being saved wasn't a hard decision. It was what her mother and aunt wanted for her, and without Afa and Billy who looked down on her first because of the pregnancy and drugs and then because of the religion, it gave Antoinette new friends. She wanted to strip all that dirt off her. She wanted to cleanse herself of all that liquor and those drugs. Jesus was the cleanest thing there was. Clean clothes. No drugs. Clean friends. Clean songs. Forgiveness. No drinking. No parties that felt dangerous. No judgment, after she came clean. After she was saved. She got a tiny place of her own and took in other children whom she could raise along with her boy, Teddy. Only people's kids from the neighborhood, so she couldn't charge much at first, but she could charge enough for an apartment of her own. And she was only eighteen. So that was it. Monday through Friday with her Teddy and three or four other babies and toddlers from the neighborhood. Then Saturday in church. And Sunday was prayer dance. She never graduated high school, but she got her equivalency—that wasn't difficult. And after a few years running the center on the down low out of her house, she paid the fifty dollars to Sittercity.com as a specialist in multiples who had run a day care and received all sorts of job offers immediately. This was once Teddy could start preschool.

But it wasn't enough for her. Being saved once. The baptism and the new set of friends. It had been almost a decade, and the shine of it, the fresh new glaze, had worn off, so now she needed to take another, deeper religious step this time without a white skinny Jesus staring down at her constantly demanding her forgiveness.

.   .   .

They were throwing bricks now, and windows were cracking. There were bars on the downstairs windows, not the upstairs ones where Antoinette was, in Aaron and Amelia's bedroom, and if Antoinette guessed right, it was only so long until they started to climb higher up the trees. What Antoinette knew about this type of situation came half from zombie TV and half from what she heard from friends back in Jamaica in 2010 when Dudus Coke barricaded Hannah Town with trashed cars and barbed wire. Antoinette had long since been in New York, but she'd followed it very closely. She was nannying by then. Dudus Coke spun trucks on their sides and dared the cops to enter. Dudus Coke lasted hours, but then again he had all sorts of weapons and trucks to spin on their sides, and he was the head of the Shower Posse that killed thousands of people and now he was in jail for life. Antoinette's great-aunt had loved the man. Still did. Said Dudus Coke's people gave her ten US dollars every couple of months. He set up community centers to help the children.

But Dudus Coke was offering what the government in Jamaica couldn't. America was different. There were already medical centers in Brooklyn. They weren't pristine, but it wasn't as bad here as people claimed. They didn't know any different. She had good work with a fine boss. And when her boy got sick, he got good medicine. In Jamaica, the clinic only had what it had. Here the Rite Aid had whatever the doctor said you needed.

Antoinette looked down at all the brown faces, and it kind of looked like Hannah Town, and it kind of looked like *The Walking Dead,* but mostly all those faces gawking up looked like what earth was supposed to look like before the coming.

Before the rapture. The swarming locusts of black people surrounding a house with their hands rising high, and what confused her was that sometimes these people were the remnant, the ecstatic welcoming Jesus. But at other times they were the dead souls acknowledging their death and understanding that they'd be left behind. Some of them were begging whoever was inside for one more chance, others were cursing those they knew would never let them in. Sometimes they were the good souls rising to heaven, the good black people who'd lived hard, good lives. And other times the people she pictured with their hands upraised shouting and tearing down other people's lives were the evil ones who lived dirty, lowly, drug-filled, violent lives that poisoned the lives of good people.

But your dead will live; their bodies will rise. You who dwell in the dust, wake up and shout for joy. Your dew is like the dew of the morning; the earth will give birth to her dead. Go, my people, enter your rooms and shut the doors behind you; hide yourselves for a little while until his wrath has passed by. See, the Lord is coming out of his dwelling to punish the people of the earth for their sins. The earth will disclose the bloodshed upon her; she will conceal her slain no longer.

Sometimes those with their hands upraised were raising their hands up to God in praise and gratitude, and other times they were sinners experiencing the first of their damnation.

All Antoinette had were the shutters, cardboard, a white boy executioner in the basement, Amelia who was as scared as Antoinette was, and Jesus Christ, who might or might not have abandoned her for her plans to abandon him for Islam.

"Do you want me with you?" Antoinette called up the stairs to Amelia. "I will help you fight where you need help."

"I'm doing this," Amelia called back. "I can do this, too."

A brick came through the window glass—Antoinette jumped—which cracked and splintered the wooden shutter in Aaron and

Amelia's bedroom window and popped out the cardboard where Antoinette had just taped it up. So she doubled the cardboard and quadrupled the tape. She went downstairs to prepare herself for battle. She would fortify God's side against any fallen angel that might come for her or for the baby in her care.

Chapter 40

The subway stopped at Utica. It was just after two o'clock. Aaron was scared there'd be gangs waiting to ambush him when the subway stopped. He was scared the subway wouldn't stop. He was scared his life would be like an action movie from now on. He had tried to stretch. Between Kingston Throop and Utica he had tried to stretch his arms and legs as though he was about to play tennis, but he'd tried to do so covertly, as though there had been a gentleman's agreement between the gang of black teenagers and himself that they were going to play twelve-on-one mixed doubles and no one was going to stretch because that'd be cheating, but Aaron, because he knew twelve-on-one tennis wasn't fair, and because the outcome of the match would determine the life and death of his family, needed to stretch, so he stretched, though if he was seen stretching, what might happen? He'd be embarrassed? They might stretch, too? They might beat him to death?

Chest to the sliding doors—half to get out quickly and half to turn his back on the lady who'd told him she hoped his house burned to the ground—Aaron, relieved that the subway stopped at Utica, took the steps up to the street two, three at a time. He was prepared to maneuver through crowds, beg police help by the entrance—even in times of relative stop-and-frisk normalcy there were always cops around the mouths of the Utica subway entrance—and ask for an armed pathway to his house, and then for an armed pathway out for his wife and son. But there were no cops there. No one was there. No cops, no kids. There was trash, blood, some police tape, a broken police barricade, wood chips, some trampled autumn bushes the parks department had planted a week before, and signs of chaos—shattered glass, beat-up chained-up bicycles, torn clothing, broken chairs and desks, and the remains of an upturned ices cart.

But no people. Then people emerged—the few who followed him off the train—and their whining and despair. But Aaron wasn't paying attention to them. He wandered up toward his house, found his arms stretching across his chest. The dozen black kids passed him—paid him no notice on the way to his own house. He sped up, heard chanting before he could understand what they were chanting. He heard sirens from fire alarms and fire trucks blaring to the south, but all his plans to jump fences and to use his keys to his neighbor's house to climb up on roofs and then down into his own now seemed insane. Seeing the hundreds of men, women, and teenagers surrounding his home shouting and chanting made him want to slow down, want to be part of the crowd. They didn't seem violent, though some kids, Aaron could now see, were hoping to push things in that direction.

Aaron was a block away from the edge of the mob. They were chanting, "No justice! No peace!" What did that have to do with his house? It didn't make any sense. Others were smashing up specifically Aaron's front stoop and taking chunks of concrete (long ago painted to look like brownstone) and throwing them at the parlor windows. Why his house? Aaron thought. It must be a racial thing. Projectiles were bouncing off the black iron bars, some smashing the glass windows, but people themselves weren't attacking the house, maybe because of the iron bars. Aaron became light-headed. He became dizzy. He started praying. He was trying to communicate mentally with his wife and son.

"What's going on here?" he asked a young woman, twenty, maybe, with a friendly face.

"White people, no offense," she said, looking at Aaron. "White motherfuckers in there killed a kid. Took out a gun and killed a kid. There's his body there," she said.

There was a body, Aaron saw. It was the body of a boy. There was space around it—enough space so people could see it by crouching down or standing up on tippy toes. Women were tending to it, and his T-shirt was covered in blood.

"Why is he just lying there on the street?" Aaron asked. "His body? The boy?"

"Ambulances aren't coming," the woman said.

"There are no guns in that house," Aaron said.

"What?"

"There aren't any guns in there."

"How do you know?"

"Because that's my house," Aaron said.

"What do you mean your house?" The woman spoke English the way Aaron did. Her clothes were like Amelia's.

"I own that house. I live there. My wife and baby are inside. That's my house."

The woman looked at Aaron in his suit. Her face hardened. But then it softened again. Her face betrayed a failed attempt at shutting Aaron out.

"This guy lives there," the woman said. "It's this guy's house!"

Chapter 41

Antoinette had rejoined Daniel on the first floor along with the baby, who needed to be fed and put down for a nap. She'd left the baby in the Pack 'n Play. And he lay there, not screaming, not sleeping. He just lay there on his back, breathing quickly. Antoinette sighed. She felt her moment coming. Where she would have to take Simon's side against a representative of sin. The Islamic word for sin was *haram*. Antoinette liked that. Liked that it was in the name Boko Haram. Liked thinking of herself as fighting sin, fighting *haram*.

Simon could sense the evil mounting around him. He could feel the devil in this house. "He didn't make one sound?" she asked Daniel.

"No. Just like this. He's keeping watch. He's going to be a man one day."

"Nothing good about lying there like that on his back," Antoinette said. She sat down in the TV room with a warmed bottle from the microwave and tried to feed him and then let him lie against her chest. But he wouldn't eat. His lips didn't move. The bottle's nipple just dripped into his uninterested mouth.

Daniel wasn't sure what she was doing, because whether the

baby slept or ate wasn't important. They had to either help Amelia upstairs or find a way out for themselves and the baby. But really there was no rush. The bars on the windows and doors would hold. Daniel was confident now. The mob seemed to be throwing chunks of cement at the windows with decreasing frequency. The windows were shattered. It was hot inside. Maybe that was what was wrong with the baby. But no one was getting inside. Soon the police would arrive. There were still kids up front throwing rocks at the windows. But the people behind those kids didn't know what they were doing there. Last time Daniel had checked through cracks in the cardboard, they looked some combination of angry and apologetic. Like they could be angry at the house, but not the people in it, until they reminded themselves of the dead boy and the possibility that Daniel was the killer. Daniel *was* the killer. But the crowd would disperse. Or Daniel and Antoinette and Amelia could wait the crowd out.

He should help Amelia, but he wasn't doing so. He was staying down here with Antoinette and the baby. He was in charge down *here,* and it was where he wanted to be anyway, and he had just killed someone.

Daniel looked over at Antoinette and Simon in the TV room. He had turned the TV off. There was nothing more vulnerable than a woman with a baby on her chest. He didn't want to leave them, but his presence there meant there was no one in the parlor overlooking the street.

"Calm down," Antoinette said. "Daniel? We need you to be calm."

"I am calm," Daniel said.

"You're scaring the baby," Antoinette said. "He's not eating."

"I'm sorry," Daniel said.

When all this was over, he'd take Thela and they'd leave. If it wasn't too late, he'd apologize to Thela and tell her she was right. That lately he'd been all fucked up in the head. Spending days in bed. Eating beans and rice. His skin needed vegetables. People's skin needed vegetables. Otherwise you look British. He'd figured that out himself when he was ten and it had stuck with him. He had turned into a man waiting for death. He didn't want to wait for death. He wanted to embrace life. He'd have to go on trial. But he'd be acquitted. He'd tell the truth. The kid had a gun, and Daniel's guns were registered legally, and the kid had pointed his gun at Daniel after shooting and killing Jupiter—there must be ten bullets in Jupiter—and Daniel had only fired twice. It wouldn't be like Eric Garner and Michael Brown because he wasn't a cop. He was just some guy who'd had a gun pointed at him. He wasn't a cop, and that kid had killed someone. This situation had nothing to do with those situations.

Had he pointed his gun at the kid, first? No one would ever know.

"Just have a seat," Antoinette said. "Put the gun down, Daniel. It's not doing anyone any good you holding it like that."

Daniel complied.

He and Thela would get out of Brooklyn. He hated Brooklyn. He hated New York, but he really hated Brooklyn. He would get out of academia. He wasn't even in academia. He had a part-time job at a second-rate art school, and he wasn't even teaching art. He was only working a couple of hours a week. He'd always resented that Thela thought he was lazy, even though she never called him lazy. But he *was* lazy. He worked a couple of hours a week and that was all he did. He was barely employed. He was barely married. He complained about how little money he made, but the truth was that his brother worked three or four times more than he did, and the work his brother did was probably ten times more strenuous. Four times ten was forty, so if Daniel made twenty grand a year, forty times twenty thousand was eight hundred grand, which was probably what his brother would be making soon if he wasn't already, and which was totally fair. He had to forget about his brother. He hated his brother. His brother didn't give a shit about Daniel. Except to worry about how much money Daniel was making. It would have been better if his brother had died. No, that was too much. But now Daniel had killed someone, too. Daniel had killed someone, too! Now they were even. Everything was different now! They could meet on even footing. Daniel had a story. Daniel had the experience. And he hadn't done it the artificial way where he ran away to the Middle East and terrified everyone he knew on purpose. "Look at me! I'm going to go do Something Extraordinary! Something for Our Country!" Daniel's brother did some EPCOT Center version of experience where you prepare yourself and you go for some set amount of time and then you come back with what it was like. Daniel had just done the real thing. He was living his life prepared. Daniel had been ready for the moment, and when the moment came he seized it. Daniel took another man's life because he was ready, because he was Daniel, and now he was going to apologize to his wife for being a shitty husband. He would leave his brother and this disgusting city and start over.

"Sit down," Antoinette said. "And put the gun down."

"I'm sorry," Daniel said.

"You're getting excited again," Antoinette said.

"I'm sorry," Daniel said.

"Just have a seat for one minute and try to stay sat."

Brooklyn—Bed-Stuy especially—was horrible. Bed-Stuy was the worst. Daniel didn't mean for black people. Bed-Stuy was fine for black people. Bed-Stuy was the worst for white people. Bed-Stuy was for white people who wanted to live in Brooklyn but didn't want to own up to the fact that they wanted to live in Brooklyn. Of course Daniel wasn't thinking about the poor black people who lived there because they couldn't afford to live anywhere else. He wasn't thinking about the middle-class black people who grew up there or had maybe rented there and then had made some money and then bought in Bed-Stuy because it was the neighborhood they knew, and their friends were there, or their family, too, and in the late eighties and nineties they could buy a house for cheap and look after their people. He wasn't even talking about the gentrifying blacks, the first round of gentrifiers who wanted to buy up the nice brownstones on the blocks where other black people lived because they wanted to make a good investment and live in up-and-coming black neighborhoods and be the kings and queens. Daniel had to hand it to these investment bankers and lawyers and hedge-funders who went to Ivy League schools or historically black colleges and then wanted to come back and rule their little worlds. That made sense. They were the conquering heroes back from making it good in white America, so of course they wanted to find a black enclave to retreat to and settle their families down where they didn't always need to look over their shoulders and wonder if they could let their proverbial (and sometimes literal) hair down.

But why? Why? What, what, what was wrong with people like Aaron and Amelia? People who made real money and could live anywhere but instead wanted to push their way into other people's communities that were just on the cusp of being pleasant? It was offensive for a million reasons. For one, it wasn't even nice yet! Celestino, the one decent restaurant, had just closed! Cobble Hill was actually nice! If Daniel and Thela could have afforded to rent in Cobble Hill, they never in a million years would have lived in Bed-Stuy where black kids got conspicuously harassed by cops every morning in the subway station and there was no Duane Reade within a million blocks. Fort Greene was actually nice! Park Slope was actually nice! Williamsburg and Greenpoint were expensive shitholes, but Clinton Hill, if you were looking to spend a few bucks less than Fort Greene—that was much nicer than around here! But this? The garbage didn't get picked up, and there might be a fucking race riot any fucking day.

Also, who the fuck did these white Wall Street assholes think they were, buying up one of the nicer homes in a community that had been all black and suffering and oppressed for seventy-five years? It just seemed so douchey. White people kept the neighborhood poor and crappy for three quarters of a century, and then as soon as black people worked to make it a more pleasant place to live, this white couple came in and bought the nice house? Granted, it wasn't like Aaron and Amelia were the individuals who'd been oppressing the people in this neighborhood, and granted, the people they'd bought the place from made out well, and the house itself was beautiful, and Aaron and Amelia had the money and therefore shouldn't be forbidden from living in any house they wanted in any neighborhood in any city, but come on! They had to walk into the definitive historical district in the blackest neighborhood in the country and buy *the* house on *the* block? And then not even rent to black people? Fuck them! It just seemed like such a piece-of-shit move.

Antoinette sang to Simon:

There's a brown girl in the ring
Tra la la la la
There's a brown girl in the ring
Tra la la la la la
Brown girl in the ring
Tra la la la la
She looks like a sugar in a plum
Plum plum

Daniel liked what people called "hipster" Brooklyn when he could afford it. Hipster, he thought, was a word like "hick" that was derogatory. People tended not to realize that no one would ever apply it to oneself. But still, Daniel liked cured meats and local chocolates. He liked soft shirts and IPAs and long-form journalism and quirky artistic girls like his wife. Or, he once had liked these things. Now, he mostly slept and drank coffee and listened to podcasts. Which was hipsterish, too, in its way. The problem with Brooklyn was it turned people into either money-spending, restaurant-dwelling hipsters or alcoholics or shut-ins. Of those three, of course he chose shut-in. Who wouldn't? There were no normal people in Brooklyn. Either people did drugs all the time, or they were terrible artists. Or everything about them was hideously precious. The only normal people were the impoverished majority and the ultrarich one percenters, because the former didn't mind eating off-brand Doritos and fried takeout for dinner, and the latter didn't mind spending thirty-eight dollars an entrée. So of course the former was storming the homes of the latter. And of course Daniel had stopped leaving his apartment. And of course Thela was cheating on him with another man or Mother Nature or jazz music, or whatever it was she'd been doing.

Antoinette sang:

Show me your motion
Tra la la la la
Come on show me your motion
Tra la la la la la
Show me your motion
Tra la la la la
She looks like a sugar in a plum
Plum plum

However this ended, Daniel would apologize to Thela and tell her he wanted it to be not like it was once but like other people lived. In other, more normal places. Where people could live without being so extreme. He would be someone she might look forward to spending time with again. He'd try to relax. Get rid of the guns. Cut back on caffeine. They might have a son. Make love again, at least. He might make money. He had skills. He could run an office— a dental office in New Jersey. Or they could start a tutoring and music-lessons company together in California. Or he could become a paralegal in Colorado. They might have a life together. A real life. He was ready to be a real, regular, responsible man.

Antoinette was slowing down and whispering now:

Skip across the ocean
Tra la la la la
Skip across the ocean

Tra la la la la la
Skip across the ocean
Tra la la la la
You look like a sugar in a plum
Plum plum

Simon was fast asleep on Antoinette's chest, and Daniel was standing, holding a shotgun, when he heard a pistol fire upstairs.

Chapter 42

Minutes before, Amelia had stepped into what had been her office. She held the pistol with her left hand and undid the safety with the middle and index fingers of her right. The gun felt heavy, as though in psychological proportion with her ability to shoot it. Like the gun was heavy, but its physical weight would be nothing compared to the weight of pulling its trigger. There were two bookshelves in the office still up on the opposite wall from the doorway, and some books remained on them, but most were scattered all over the floor. Amelia pressed slightly against the trigger and it felt unmovable, but then she thought maybe a touch more pressure might make the thing go off. The rug was twisted up on itself and covered in books, and one bookshelf was overturned and splintered: the bookshelf that Amelia had shipped east from her grandmother's storage unit after her death.

There was no sign of the girl, but Amelia wasn't surprised. When she'd found the door unlocked, Amelia sensed the girl would be in the exercise room. So Amelia took her time. The glider rocking chair was in three pieces next to the smashed stained-glass windows, windows that had lasted the previous 120 years. The glider had been used to pitch over the bookshelf and break the stained glass. The glass was wrenched out toward the garden below. The panes were shattered, and those not shattered were cantilevered open, so wind whipped into the room. One-hundred-twenty-year-old shattered stained glass was beautiful. It was sharp and reflecting the sun. The computer's screen was cracked, too. The desk was undamaged as far as she could tell, but all the photos that had been on the wall were cracked, the bookshelves were destroyed, the computer screen was cracked, the stained glass was destroyed, the—Amelia laughed! Her laughter erupted from below her stomach and burst out her throat. She stopped herself because the girl could hear her—Amelia could always hear Aaron grunt when she was writing and he was working out—but what did she care if the girl could hear her? She had a gun, and this was her home, and the girl was closed in a room with no windows and only one door, and Amelia was willing to shoot her.

But that's not why Amelia was laughing. She wasn't laughing at the destruction. She was laughing at its lack of significance. Books were on the floor. A binding or two had ripped. But she hadn't looked at any of those books for years, except the couple she'd just read and most likely wouldn't ever read again. Aaron's money could buy a new bookshelf. Aaron had more than she did. She had fifty-seven thousand dollars in her bank account, and she guessed Aaron had three times that. She wasn't rich, but she had more money than most people did. Even without Aaron and without landing some big nonfiction book, she had enough to replace a few pieces of furniture and to maintain her independence for a couple of years. And generations of her family would come to live in this house.

A new bookshelf wouldn't be her grandmother's bookshelf,

but Amelia had loved her grandmother, not her grandmother's furniture. Stained-glass windows could be fixed, or replaced with new windows, stained glass or better insulated. Aaron was about to give fifty thousand dollars away to charity. A replacement for the gambling. As long as Aaron couldn't be trusted with his money, she couldn't marry him. Gambling, risk, whatever he wanted to call it. As long as he kept threatening to give money away. Now he could use that money he was going to give away to provide work for American glass artisans. Amelia laughed loudly and gripped her gun. Pointed it toward the white door that led into the exercise room.

"I've got a gun, and you're trespassing and dangerous," Amelia said. "With stand-your-ground-laws and that you were with those kids who just shot my neighbor and now what you've done to my office, I could shoot you right now. Do you hear me? I could shoot you right now, and I don't give a shit. No one would think twice. I've got my baby downstairs. Come on out, and I'll let you out of my house alive. We'll walk downstairs and you can leave. But get the fuck out of my house."

Amelia had begun by yelling and then she was talking in a brusque way, but now she was laughing again. She was proud of herself. She knew her rights. She was doing the right thing, taking care of her family. She was taking care of her family and herself. Nothing substantial had been lost. Yet. She had Simon still, and Aaron, and that was what mattered. Her stained glass didn't matter. Her grandmother had died years ago. Aaron and Simon were the only things that mattered, and neither of them were lost.

There was mumbling from the exercise room.

Amelia moved closer.

"Speak up," Amelia said. She had to get very close to the white door to hear the girl, and something about pressing her face against the crack near the door handle made all the adrenaline that had invigorated her threats run out of her. She heard her own breath. She sat on the floor and looked at the mess and remembered that Aaron was probably on his way home. Probably in a taxi or the subway, if the subways were running.

"I can't," the girl said. "I can't go outside."

"Sure you can," Amelia said, her resolve melting along with the girl's voice. The girl's voice was meek and trying hard to be steady. It was exactly what Amelia feared her own voice sounded like.

"Like you said, I was with those kids who killed Mr. Jupiter," the girl said.

And then they both waited for the other one to talk.

The white door, painted just the year before, was already dirty and cracking. The girl said, "I knew Derek from the block. I can't go home because of the police. And if Derek finds out what happened, he'll fucking kill me, so right now this room with you is the safest place I've got."

"What's your name?" Amelia said. "I'm Amelia."

"Sara."

"Your real name," Amelia said.

"My name is Sara."

"How old are you?" Amelia said.

"Eighteen."

That was older than Amelia had expected. Amelia had expected the girl to say fifteen, or sixteen, maybe. But eighteen was different. This was an adult that Amelia was holding hostage, which was preferable, she reasoned.

"Why did you come here?" Amelia said, feeling the wind whip into the open room. "At first, I mean."

"Because Derek Jupiter said to. He said to come here. He said that nice people used to live here and you drove them out. He said that it was time to take the neighborhood back. Shit, I don't know. What are you going to do to me?"

"Do to you? What am I going to do to you? What was your idea coming here? To do what?" Amelia said. "Why did *you* come here? What does that mean, take back the neighborhood?" Amelia was losing track of exactly what she was saying, but she could feel herself falling into a normal pattern. It was the pattern she used as an interviewer. All of a sudden, through the white door, she was conducting an interview. She wanted to know more about Sara. Mr. Jupiter's *son* had told her to come here? That made the story tragic. So did the girl's eyes, from what she remembered. She was smart. Circle back to "you drove them out," Amelia reminded herself.

"I don't know," Sara said.

"I've got a gun," Amelia said, to shake herself out of the rhythm. But part of her wanted to retract that last statement. She could interview Sara. But she would have to interview Sara at gunpoint. Sara was an individual who embodied the repercussions of gentrification. She could write it as a first-person account of a woman whose friend was just killed by Sara's friend. No one else had a story like this one.

"I know that," Sara said. "You keep on saying you've got a fucking gun. I know you have a fucking gun. Fuck! Is Damien dead?"

"I'm saying do you want to come out? Even though I've got a gun and will have to point it at you? You don't have to leave. Yet. We can sit in the same room."

"Not yet," Sara said. "Is Damien dead? You say you have to point a gun at me. You just killed my fucking friend! You're a total psycho."

"I don't know. Your friend? The one who killed Mr. Jupiter? Is that Damien?" Amelia said, confused. "I have a child."

"What do you mean, you don't know?" Sara said. "He's dead or not. Everyone has a child. You think I care about your child?"

Sara started jumping up and down. The room was white inside. Where Sara was. Sara looked around for nonwhite parts. And black parts, like the machines and weights, didn't count. There was a brown towel on the barbell rack. White walls. White floor matting. These people were crazy rich. Like that Shabba Ranks video. Like every hip-hop video. The workout machines were black. A weight machine, weight bench, a stairs machine, and a treadmill. She was sitting on the weight bench now, with her head in her hands. The door didn't lock, but Sara was confident that Amelia wouldn't open the door. Something about how Amelia kept asking her if she wanted to come out. That made it seem she wouldn't come in. But Sara wasn't sure, so now she held a bench-pressing bar with no weights on it. The bar was metal, but a different metal from the handcuff metal that was still on her wrists. Her wrists were sore from that metal. The weight-lifting metal was shinier. She held it down at one end like a baseball bat. Now Sara was jumping up and down holding the heavy metal bar.

"What are you doing in there?" Amelia said. "Are you all right?"

"Is Damien dead?" Sara said through the door.

"Mr. Jupiter is," Amelia said, "but I don't know anything about Damien except, if he was the guy who shot Mr. Jupiter, that he's a murderer who deserves it. Why did you come here? You're friends with Jupiter's son? What were you hoping to accomplish?"

"Accomplish?" Sara said. "Fuck you. I don't owe you an explanation. What were you hoping to accomplish moving to a neighborhood where everyone hates you?"

"I've got the gun and you're in my house and you killed my neighbor," Amelia said.

"Your neighbor? Fuck you," Sara said. "That's Derek's dad."

"And there's no lock on that door," Amelia said. "You killed him. You killed his dad."

"Then come at me," Sara said. "You want at me, come at me."

"Sorry," Amelia said. "Calm down. I'm sorry. I have a child. Let's both calm down."

Amelia heard what she thought was jumping up and down from inside the exercise room. She heard metal scrape metal. A roar in the street downstairs made Amelia want to go to Simon, but also she was happy not to be with Simon. She would be told if something happened to Simon. Simon was safe with Antoinette. Every minute she wasn't told about Simon was another minute Simon was safe. She didn't want to think about Simon in danger. She wanted to do her job.

"Tell me about yourself," Amelia said.

"What?" Sara said.

"Let's tell each other about ourselves. My name is Amelia. My boyfriend's name is Aaron. Our son is Simon."

"You're not married?"

"No. Are you?"

"Me? Shit no. Why aren't you? Rich white lady with a kid," Sara said.

"That's a good question, Sara," Amelia said.

"Don't talk to me like that," Sara said.

"I wasn't," Amelia said. "Do you want me to answer the question or not?"

"What question?" Sara said.

"About why I'm not married," Amelia said.

"Fuck you," Sara said.

Amelia reminded herself of the goal here. To get the girl out of her house as quickly as possible. Or at least that's what it had been. Now it was to make the best of a bad situation. Amelia had a gun. It was heavy, but nothing she couldn't manage. Now she was alone, without her baby on the same floor. The room around her had been trashed by the girl she was talking to. Daniel and Antoinette could take care of downstairs without her as well as they could with her. They also had a gun.

"Tell me again why you can't leave," Amelia said.

"Because." Sara had stifled a sob earlier, but now her voice was calmer. "Because the police beat my brother. And as far as I know my mother, too. And I was with those guys who killed Mr. Jupiter. I can't show myself right now on the street. Because of the police and because of Derek. I've told you that twice now. What. The fuck. Are you going to do with me?"

"But why did you come here originally?"

"Because the cops beat my brother. Derek Jupiter told me about your place, and I wanted to fuck, I wanted to fuck the place up. So we did."

"Why did the cops beat your brother?"

"Because they're cops. That's what they do. Fuck you. My arm's all fucked up," Sara said.

"Come out and let me take a look at it," Amelia said.

"If you put down the gun," Sara said.

"No," Amelia said.

"How are you going to help my arm with a gun in your hand?" Sara said.

"Come out and let's try," Amelia said.

Sara grunted her assent.

"I'll take a step back," Amelia said.

The door opened, Sara joined Amelia in the office, and Amelia got her first close look at Sara face-to-face and alone. She wore black Reebok sneakers with gray laces, black sweatpants that were badly stained with dirt and blood, an oversized black hooded sweatshirt torn at the forearm, a black Nets baseball cap with a flat brim, and her hood up over the cap. Her braids teased down around both sides of her neck and she had pretty, large brown eyes. She held the rod of the bench press bar like a baseball bat; metal gleamed at her wrists.

I have God here with me, Amelia thought.

"What are you looking at me like that for?" Sara said.

"Why are you holding that?" Amelia said.

The sun gleamed off the cracked computer screen.

"Why are you holding that?" Sara said, nodding to the gun.

"I'm scared of you," Amelia said.

"Yeah?" Sara said.

Sara flinched toward Amelia with the metal rod.

Amelia pulled the trigger of the pistol.

The gun recoiled and nearly knocked Amelia over.

Sara dropped the metal rod.

Amelia had missed Sara by a foot, high.

The bullet struck and disappeared into the painted white wall.

Sara cowered back.

Amelia picked up the metal rod.

"The fuck!" Sara said.

"I'll aim better next time," Amelia said, stifling a sob.

Then full-on crying. Tears and mucus slid down Amelia's face.

Amelia hadn't wanted to do that, hadn't planned to do that. It was horrible. She'd tried to kill this girl.

But it hadn't been a mistake. Amelia had wanted to pull the trigger.

She'd seen that metal rod start to come around toward her.

She'd seen Sara's big eyes.

Sara had been starting to take a swing at her, and Amelia had closed her own eyes and shot, and thank God she had missed.

Amelia's arms were heaving up and down still, holding the pistol facing Sara in case she had to shoot again. Amelia picked up the metal rod from where Sarah had dropped it and pressed it between her left arm and her body.

"Sit down," Amelia said, pointing to the overturned desk chair.

Sara positioned the desk chair upright and she sat. This was an admission in Amelia's mind that Amelia had done right in trying to kill Sara.

Amelia heard someone bounding up the steps.

"Leave us alone!" Amelia said. "We're okay! It was a warning shot! Don't come in here, Daniel! Don't come in!"

Amelia caught her breath, trained the gun on Sara, more confident with the trigger now, and with the weight of the thing. Amelia was calm. And very tired. Like in spite of the adrenaline she could fall asleep right there standing. Shooting the gun and reacting to having shot it made her calmer than she'd been since hearing Jupiter laughing with Antoinette downstairs much earlier that morning.

"What are you going to do to me?" Sara said.

"Nothing," Amelia said. "You can do whatever you want. This isn't the movies. You can leave and go wherever you want. Or if you want to stay here, you can come and have something to drink. We're normal people."

Amelia was breathing crazily now. She could tell. Giving this little speech on how normal she was made her feel crazy.

"Uh-huh," Sara said. Her baseball cap was now lower over her eyes than it had been before, and she was sitting on the chair, legs spread wide like a man.

"Really," Amelia said. She tried to laugh. "I know I'm holding these two weapons. And that's unusual. But this is an unusual situation. You really can do what you want. I want you to leave because I don't know you, is all."

"You think I want to be here," Sara said.

"You nearly hit me with a metal bat," Amelia said.

"Would you rather have the gun or that metal rod?" Sara said.

"Why are you here?"

"You keep asking me that," Sara said. "And I keep telling you the answer. Your house is the one that deserves being picked on. We don't care about you. You don't care about us. You chose this place to live thinking there wouldn't be any consequences. Shit. You think people are just going to welcome you like they're thrilled you moved in? What's wrong with you people?"

"That nice family we drove out of our house," Amelia said. "You were talking about Briceson and Mary. The family who sold? They *were* nice. We paid them $1.3 million. They bought a nice house out in Jersey."

"Good for them," Sara said. "I'm talking about the rest of us."

"What are you talking about? What do you want, Sara?"

Sara looked around the broken room and seemed to think about the question.

"A thousand dollars," Sara said.

"What?"

"If you give me a thousand dollars, I'll leave."

"I have a gun on you. I showed you I'd shoot."

"Ten thousand dollars," Sara said. "If you give me ten thousand dollars, I'll leave."

"I'll just make you leave."

"Twenty thousand dollars," Sara said. "Or shoot me. I don't have shit to live for now anyway. If you can give Mary and whoever he was a million dollars to leave, you can give me twenty thousand dollars."

"Get out of my house," Amelia said.

"Give me the money," Sara said, "and I'll go. Fifty thousand dollars. Final fucking offer. Or shoot me. Or drag my body down and throw me out in front of that crowd and see what fucking happens."

Amelia pointed the gun at Sara.

"Shoot me and deal with it for the rest of your life," Sara said. "I don't give a shit. You think I care? Or let the niggas down there see you throw a black girl into the street. Or give me my fifty thousand dollars and let me go like you say you would."

Chapter 43

Most of the crowd—it had to be at least six hundred people—greeted Aaron with respect. Some of the teenage boys and girls were strangely comfortable perched in the trees, tossing around a Gatorade bottle. Down near Aaron, there were some guys wearing beat-up white sneakers with no laces. Others wore mismatched tops and bottoms of tracksuits. Some fat women wore tight T-shirts, and others had been at the original fight, Aaron figured, and they were beat up themselves or wore clothes that had been shredded or torn. But this was nothing like the scenes that he'd been expecting from the *60 Minutes* reports on Tahrir Square where the crowds were full of Arab men, and the moment the cameras went dark they groped at the pretty South African reporter's clothes, tearing away her shirt and pants, raping her, and leaving her for dead. That's what he thought when he thought riots. These men and women nodded to Aaron. Aaron recognized one guy in a Melo jersey from the deli. They lined up outside his house, gave him room to walk. They cleared a pathway toward his house. They were all black. There was some shoving, but other people held back the shovers.

There were actually two crowds: the back half focused on Aaron, and the front half focused on the house, and as Aaron made his way toward the house, those two crowds reconverged with their attention on Aaron, who now stood on his own front stoop. He wanted to enter the house, but he felt as though they were waiting for him to say something in exchange for the safe passage they'd proffered to his front door. The young woman with the friendly face was no longer there. Aaron looked but couldn't find her. He had minders, though. Two men—one larger, one his size—up on the stoop with him. And whereas moments before, Aaron had been thinking about nothing other than getting to his family, now he wasn't so sure. The individual faces that made up the crowd all looked at him as though he owed them something. He saw the dead boy off to the side—had one of these people killed him?—saw three women tending to the boy's corpse, saw the two men who seemed to be threatening to enter alongside him if he opened the door.

He patted his pocket to feel for the key, and the two men pressed closer toward him. He couldn't see anyone inside. But he saw the shattered interior door and felt something inside himself liquefy. He was sure Amelia was okay. And Simon. He would know if they weren't. He was sure Amelia and Simon were okay. And Antoinette was with them, too, taking care of them.

He had to say something to calm the crowd enough to allow him inside alone. To let them let him go so he could be sure his family was safe.

"May I go inside?" he asked.

The two men looked at each other. They didn't know. The larger one looked at the smaller one. No one was in charge.

"I'm going to go inside," Aaron said. "You two stay out here."

"You're going to stay out here," the smaller one told Aaron loudly. The front dozen or so people cheered the man's confidence, and the larger man grabbed Aaron's arm.

"My friends," Aaron began. "My friends. Is that what you want? I don't know what I've done to deserve you preventing me from my seeing my wife and son. But I've got my baby inside, and I don't know what you want.

"But listen to me, and tell this man to let me go, to give me some room." Both men stepped away. There was shushing in the crowd. The six hundred people leaned forward to hear Aaron speak.

"My neighbors," Aaron amplified his voice. He had not used this voice for a few years, but it returned naturally to him. Even if he'd wanted to turn and flee into his house, now it was too late. "I have only lived here for a year, but this is my home, and I appreciate your leading me here to my wife and baby boy inside. I don't know what you're planning to do, but whatever it is, it's been done. You've scared them, I'm sure."

"They shot and killed this boy!" a single voice shouted from somewhere in the crowd.

It was obvious to Aaron that the crowd didn't know what it wanted to do. It seemed hesitant to go from throwing stones to actually dragging bodies outside and beating them.

"I don't know what you think happened," Aaron said, "but there's no gun inside this house!"

"Well there's a gun here," said a kid near the dead boy's body. He pointed the gun at Aaron.

"Be careful, son," Aaron said.

"Who you calling 'son'?" a voice yelled out from the crowd.

"Please, someone take that gun from that young man," Aaron said, but no one did. "Okay then, that's fine, if there was an accident, as there clearly was, maybe you deserve retribution. And maybe I'm the one who needs to pay it. Keep the gun trained on me. But listen. Listen to me. If that gun gets everyone to listen, then that's okay."

Aaron stood on his stoop. The two men who'd been up there with him had stepped down with the rest of the crowd. Now everyone listened. The boy with the gun kept it pointed at Aaron.

Chapter 44

Antoinette saw herself across a table set with white linen. The cloth her mother used in Chicago. Teddy drank cold milk, and a masculine presence called from the kitchen. A masculine presence. She was toying with herself. She just didn't want to acknowledge it. Jupiter was in his kitchen. She was at his table, set with her mother's tablecloth. Teddy was humming a song that Jupiter had taught him. An old-fashioned song Antoinette didn't know. *Ba-daba-da-ba* . . .

She sat at a table set with proper silverware, and Jupiter leaned over to serve chicken and rice with three different vegetables and freshly baked bread. He'd prepared and plated the vegetables in the kitchen. In the kitchen, he'd wiped the edges of the plates clean so as not to stain the tablecloth.

She lay in bed with him at night, her head on his chest, his hand at the small of her back. They were small in her bed in his house, Teddy sleeping in the room next door, maybe Jupiter's boy sleeping down the hall. Jupiter smelled of Teddy's father, of Billy, and of chocolate cake.

She heard a gunshot upstairs. Snapped her focus back on the baby.

"Seek, baby Simon, seek the Lord," Antoinette said. "While

he may be found. Now is the time. We must act now. Call upon him while he is near. Let the wicked forsake his way, for you are not wicked. And the unrighteous man—let him forsake his thoughts: and let him return unto the Lord, baby Simon. The Lord will have mercy upon him; and to our God, for he will abundantly pardon.

"You hear me, Simon Simon?"

Nothing. No response. And that gunshot.

Simon lay back, halfway to becoming a corpse.

Antoinette dropped him alone in the Pack 'n Play, but Simon didn't react. Antoinette went to Aaron's bookshelf and took down the oldest, largest books. The books she'd been scared to disturb since she'd started the job. The ones she'd most wanted to take down from the shelf. They looked like ancient spell books, some in English and some in Hebrew. Antoinette needed to climb up on a chair to manage the heaviest down from the top, and she took them down carefully one by one, and breathed them in deeply and held them against her body.

"All Scripture is breathed out by God and profitable for teaching, for reproof, for correction, and for training in righteousness, that the man of God may be competent, equipped for every good work," she said.

Antoinette was equipping herself for the fight with the Devil. The crowd was shouting, and the gun had gone off upstairs. Amelia could have shot that girl. This couldn't wait any longer. Determined, but with a delicacy that frightened her, Antoinette took down God's books one by one and placed them neatly around Simon in the Pack 'n Play. Finally, a way to swaddle the boy in God. She'd found it. She hadn't realized how tense she'd been. She was able to begin to relax.

She'd save both herself and Simon. She'd protect the baby and prove to God that she was worthy to keep living. He could take Jupiter, and he could take that kid outside. But not her. And not this baby.

She'd been looking for this fight all day, and there it was in the Pack 'n Play. She saw him there. Simon was milky eyed. His body was limp. His eyes were milky and gray. He was slack bodied and gray skinned. She opened up the largest book, over a thousand pages. It was titled *Talmudic Studies: Investigating the Sugya, Variant Readings and Inscriptions and Aggada,* and she placed Simon on top of the open book, then surrounded his body with more and more religious books in Hebrew and English. Simon didn't seem to notice. She sang to Simon: "Oh Devil, God shall defeat you! Oh, you think you know the way, but you don't know, you don't know! Oh you think you know the way, but you haven't met the Lord!"

Antoinette made more and more trips to the bookshelf, returning with more and more books until the baby was surrounded and covered by a mountain of books, his arms and legs pinned down below. He breathed but didn't scream, which confirmed Antoinette's belief that what she did was right.

Daniel watched, horrified, intrigued as Antoinette buried the baby under the mountain of holy books, but as he drew in closer he heard Aaron's voice outside. Now Daniel tried to hear Aaron on the stoop below. Antoinette didn't hear or was too caught up with Simon.

Simon lay there milky eyed. The innocence of a baby. It wasn't fair. So much wasn't fair. It wasn't fair that she was working so far away from everything. So far away from her childhood. It wasn't fair that she worked so hard, every day, that Friday was Mosque, Saturday was church all day, and Sunday was prayer dance, and every minute she wasn't taking care of someone else's baby, she was taking care of her own. She was an adult now and no longer a girl, and then a nice man was there with her and showed motions toward wanting to take care of her, and after only a few months spending a handful of hours together he was taken away from her.

Had she loved Jupiter?

She had loved Jupiter.

She had—

"... Oh, you think you know the way, but you don't know, you don't know!" she hummed. "Oh, you think you know the way, but you haven't met the Lord!"

She had loved him as much as she had loved any man her entire life. Antoinette, seeing Jupiter's goodness in Simon, focused back on Simon, surrounded by hard covers under a tent of the lighter ones bound in cheap paper and twine. She was jealous of Simon, covered in all that spiritual knowledge and guidance. She wished she was small enough to get in there with him. She could rustle around between the holy pages, feel them all over her body.

Antoinette sneezed, which scattered some papers. One softly landed on Simon's nose.

It tickled his face and he batted it away.

"*You,*" Antoinette commanded, "*will be trampled underfoot by the devils. Prepare yourself, my son, the Demon at my orders will be the one that will add the last touch to my plan that I will accomplish in you, that is, your sanctification.*"

She had loved Jupiter as much as she had loved any man her entire life since Billy. She couldn't have Billy. She couldn't have Jupiter.

But she could have the Lord. She'd make sure Teddy was

protected. Because the alternative was to wallow in self-pity, and that would hurt Teddy as much as it would hurt her.

"So fight!" Antoinette told Simon. "Fight with the Lord!"

Again, Simon batted at his nose.

"You like that, do you?" Antoinette said. "Fight alongside me, baby Simon! We can't let anyone come in and tell us what our lives are. We decide! Simon says! We decide!"

The baby perked up some, claiming his muscles for himself. This was something.

Antoinette liked taking care of Simon. She had the touch. She was too humble to say she had God's touch, but others had said it to her. Pastor V had said it. Her aunt had said it. Teddy's father had said it long ago. She could beat the Devil back, sometimes.

"Devil be gone!" she whispered into Simon.

She could beat him back. Maybe not all the time. And maybe not in her own life. But in other people's life. For other people. For baby Simon. And for her son. Teddy would become something. He was smart. He was conservative. Other kids looked up to him. The right ones at least. He studied hard. He would be a lawyer, probably. Or a dentist. A judge.

"We decide!" she whispered. "Simon says! We decide!"

Teddy would make money. He would buy a house like this one. He would be Muslim. In a community that looked after one another even if the whole world was against them. He would make money and be safe. He would have a mother who loved him and be safe with his God. She would take care of him. That was her strength.

"We decide our own lives, Simon," Antoinette whispered into Simon's ear, perking Simon into himself. Slowly his gray skin pinkened.

"There you go, baby boy. There you go. It's just you and me right now, baby boy. Simon says. Simon Simon says. We're in charge! We give our lives to God!"

Simon revved up like a car and barked a laugh. Antoinette dug the boy out of his grave of books and ran him into the kitchen where a bottle was waiting. "We're in charge!"

Simon guffawed and waved his arms.

"We're in charge!"

Simon was laughing now in anticipation of laughing more.

"In charge! In charge! In charge!"

Simon leaped at the bottle and sucked it down.

Chapter 45

On the subway, Aaron had been thinking of bartering with God. Now he wanted to tell the story of Abraham. He had wanted to be Abraham. But that was impossible. Abraham had been the truest believer. Abraham had had such unquestioning faith in God he'd been willing to kill his son. Aaron couldn't cast himself as Abraham. But he was stuck in that story of Sodom. He looked around and saw the angry mob, smelled his neighborhood burning. Sodom was the story for this moment.

"I've been thinking about the story of Sodom and Gomorrah," Aaron began. He spoke from within his chest, but quietly at first, and he commanded a deeper attention than when he had been out on the street as part of the crowd. "In order to understand the story of Sodom, you have to understand that there are two equally important halves of this story: that of Abraham and that of Lot. In the Abraham half, Abraham tries to save Lot's life." Aaron raised his voice slightly here. It was a technique he'd developed as a first-year rabbi. Start quiet and then increase volume. Now he did it without thinking: "And in the Lot half, Lot's family is overrun by an angry mob." Aaron let that phrase linger. He let the crowd hear itself be compared to the mob of Sodomites.

But then Aaron said, "You, my friends, are like Abraham."

This hooked them. Enough of them knew their Bible. Aaron would save his own life, and the lives of Simon and Amelia. If they were okay inside. They had to be okay. For anything to ever make sense again.

Aaron looked out at the lake of bobbing faces spilling over the sidewalk, into the street, onto the far sidewalk and up on the steps of the mansion across the way. The sun was raw. The sun was yellow. The yellow sun lit the street, empty of passing traffic. Some kids climbed up and listened to him from on top of parked cars. Aaron's gut seized up on him, as if he'd been starved and the food was just uncovered. He spoke louder. He'd define this moment for them, define their role in it.

"Lot's half of the story starts with angels. A group of them. They show up at Sodom, which is the kind of city where, when strangers show up at your door, you get nervous. And it's late at night. Lot has no idea they're angels because they're all dressed as men, but he welcomes them into his home, welcomes them inside, with his wife and daughters. This is a gamble. The calculation Lot is making here is that though these men could be criminals who might hurt his family, they could also be good men, innocent travelers, who might fall victim to the Sodomites if Lot doesn't let them in. So Lot, a good man, does the noble thing and takes a risk that these travelers are also good. He takes the gamble of hurting his family over letting these strangers get hurt."

"Fuck you, you a preacher or something?" someone yelled from the crowd, to laughter among the teenagers. No laughter from the kid with the gun, Aaron checked, but from others. The kid with the gun wore a bright yellow shirt, but because of the gun Aaron hadn't noticed it before.

"Shoot the preacher," someone said.

"He ain't no preacher, he's a Jew!"

"Cap the Jew!" another said, seriously, Aaron thought, but many others laughed.

"The Jew cap! That little hat they wear!"

"Let him talk," a female voice called out.

"It's his house," a man said firmly, and Aaron continued. "And after these angels—who Lot thinks are regular visitors in his city—after these angels are bathed and fed in Lot's home and in bed for the night—after these angels settle in and Lot thinks he and they are safe, suddenly every single man in Sodom shows up at Lot's house and starts banging at his door. That's what the Bible says: 'Every single man in Sodom.' It doesn't say how many. But I wouldn't be surprised if it's a few hundred. If it's a crowd about your size. And they demand the angels' heads."

"That's right!" someone shouted from the crowd. A woman. An older woman. "That's right!" a few of her friends join her.

This was good.

"The crowd," Aaron said, "had heard that Lot was housing fresh meat, fresh money, and flesh, and so they called out to Lot, 'Where are the men who came to you tonight? Bring them out to us, that we may know them.'"

A siren a few blocks away alerted everyone there to how long it had been without sirens, without gunfire. The part of Aaron that spoke was separate from and yet the same as the part that thought into the future of what he was going to say next, and he savored this duality of self. He had his audience listening. That was what mattered.

"Lot has put his whole family at risk, and he has put the angels at risk. Lot makes his family vulnerable. But then Lot does something courageous. He goes outside to the mob and locks the door and says, 'I'm here. Take me. Don't take those men. Take me.' And right when the mob is about to storm Lot's house, the angels punish the crowd with blindness and lead Lot and his family to safety."

Aaron took a deep breath. They were listening to him. They wanted to know how Abraham fit in. How the city burned. And how it related to them and their city. Or maybe they just liked the show Aaron was putting on. But either way, they were leaning toward Aaron, eager to hear what would happen next.

Chapter 46

And so were Sara and Amelia, on the other side of the bulletproof door. Amelia had never heard Aaron like this. She'd imagined it, but she'd never been present for it. His voice was confident but gentle. It confirmed what Amelia had hoped. That Aaron had a gift. That he was meant to lead. That she loved him fully and not just in comparison to someone else.

Amelia held the gun to Sara's waist, but their affairs with each other were over. The gun was unnecessary, and they both knew it. It was embarrassing in comparison to Jupiter's body on the floor. Amelia had shrieked when she'd seen the body again as she came down the stairs. Now they tried to ignore it and listen to Aaron.

So did Daniel, begrudgingly. Daniel hated how assured he was.

Only Antoinette didn't listen. She heard the sound of the voice. She heard the cadence, and she let it buoy her up. Simon was smiling in her care, under the balm of her strength and his father's voice.

Chapter 47

"So that's the Lot half. Lot takes in the angels and is saved from the flesh-hungry crowd. But what about the Abraham half?"

Silence before him as they waited.

"If you remember, before God sends his angels to Sodom, Abraham approaches God for a conversation. People remember this conversation as a debate or negotiation. Actually, I was just remembering it like that on the way over here. But it couldn't have been like that. God wasn't arguing with Abraham. God is God. God knows everything. But that doesn't mean he is thinking about everything all the time. Men have to show God, direct God, be a model for God as he was their model on creation."

"Amen!"

Aaron felt this woman's energy. He started speaking faster and breaking between sentences to let the crowd react.

"Just by talking to God," Aaron said, "Abraham made God see that there were in fact good people in Sodom."

"That's right!"

"In the beginning, God was going to kill the entire town," Aaron said. "He saw Sodom as a single mass of people. But then Abraham initiated the conversation. He acted. Just as you are acting today. He broke up the mass into individuals. Abraham got God to focus on his people. On the individuals. First fifty, then twenty, then ten. Which made God realize there was a good man. There was Lot and his family." Aaron paused. Looked as many of these people in the eye as he was able to from up on his stoop. "You are doing the right thing here," he said. "You are drawing attention to yourself. You are making people see you as individuals."

"That's right!"

"Making people see your families. Because when Abraham acted, God saw Abraham's family. God saw Lot. And Lot was saved. Being seen is enough sometimes. And you're making sure you've been seen here today."

Aaron had been building up to this. He wasn't sure he would get here, but:

"The thing is, that's only one part of the lesson. The other part is that you must not become the mob. Thus far, you've been Abraham, saying, 'Look at me. Look at my cousins.' You've brought attention to the right grievances, and New York—the United States and the world—will take notice. Things will change now. Police will think twice before shooting. But don't become the mob. Don't become the Sodomites when you've done such a wonderful job being Abraham. Stop now. You've done your job. Don't hurt the women and the children. Don't go too far and go from the hero of this story to its villain."

"Amen!" shouted one woman from the crowd.

"Because Abraham's love for Lot," Aaron said. "It was real love."

Here Aaron was accomplishing something real.

"God's love!" someone shouted

"Love of family," Aaron said.

Aaron was using his training for good. To reach his family.

"I understand the desire to burn this city down," Aaron said. "I understand the desire to riot. To show the Godless, ruleless, compassionless murderers that the cop cars and mayor's offices and high-rises and brownstones deserve to go up in flames. But be Abraham—be those who remind the mayor and God that you exist, that your mothers and fathers and children and cousins exist and are individuals—as opposed to a mob. Don't be the Sodomites who reach out to punish the children and wives."

A kid yelled out, "Don't you tell us how to—"

The bulletproof outer door crashed opened behind Aaron.

Aaron saw Amelia and grabbed her and held her tight in his arms. They hugged out there in front of the crowd.

Aaron didn't want to cry, but he cried, which was as fitting an end to all of this as he could have invented with words or violence or planning ahead.

The mob applauded. It broke out in cheers.

Some shushed or cursed the applauders, but most, carried away with the real live moment or maybe with the story of Abraham and Lot—the love between them—yelped and clapped.

And they were doubly happy for the black girl to walk out behind the couple. They whooped and cheered.

"You all right?" they called to Sara.

"They treat you all right?"

"Her arm! They busted her arm!"

"They mistreat her in there? Are those handcuffs?"

But Amelia was inside again, closing the door behind her, pushing Sara out, grabbing Aaron and dragging him in, too. He wanted to be there for the end of it—to see the end of the story out there—but Amelia had pulled him into safety.

"No," he heard Sara saying. "It's all right. They're good enough for me, at least."

"Then who killed this boy."

"Another one."

"In there."

"Yeah, in—"

. . .

But something had already passed among them. They'd found their faith. So many of them, that those who hadn't couldn't fight the crowd. Some prayed over Damien's corpse, while others went home to be with family. Soon the cops would come, and ambulances, and garbage men, and newscasters; and the members of what had constituted the crowd, having murdered a man, lost one of their own, vented their anger, and had their release, turned into individuals again.

Chapter 48

Of the forty-five hundred inhabitants of the Marcy houses, Police Commissioner Bill Bratton was looking at a thousand or so out front in tents that had been set up by black cops. Black cops from the city, from neighboring cities, from Jersey. The mayor must have called everyone he and his wife knew. Crown Heights had been calm. There'd been no policing to be done. But he was here now, and that was important.

What he'd liked as a child was staying in the back room at home, where it didn't smell as much like coal or kerosene, and toying with clay. Now the Marcy Projects smelled like a fire that had recently been put out. Bratton stood on top of the black police car. People were starting to gather. Cops, mostly. The buildings looked like they were rising up from underground. Giant gray behemoths, rising, rising. Like space buildings for black people who'd never be educated out of them. He'd been walking the tightrope, the tightrope snapped, and he'd still been walking for years. The police commissioner? He needed an education department, a parks department, teachers' salaries doubled, cops' salaries tripled, triple the number of cops. Especially black cops. Look at all these black men wearing blue. Here was a start. Right this moment.

He'd built figurines as a child. It began with Dr. Seuss. He'd loved those books, the characters, and he re-created in clay what was in the books. He'd built whole worlds. It'd started with the fish. The red fish and blue fish, even though he'd only had one color of clay. Gray-green clay. He could do one fish and two fish. Then Cat in the Hat. Then the one about the boy who lived among all those roads. And when he'd gotten older, Hopalong Cassidy, Wild Bill Hickok, Zorro, Davy Crockett. Whomever kids were talking about.

People were hugging one another, and black cops were hugging the people. The only white people Bratton could see were members of the press. Giant cameras and trucks and lights, so Bratton told a deputy to get their attention. The Marcy Project buildings looked like giant plus signs made of bricks and concrete rising up out of concrete. What a backdrop.

And when he'd brought his clay figures into school, his teacher was so impressed she sent him to the principal, who assigned him to be the King Keeper of Flag Day celebrations.

He'd stood on the field—just like he was standing now up on his car—in front of the whole school in his Boy Scout uniform, and he'd sung the school anthem in front of the big brass band.

His father, only five foot six, slapped him on the back.

The end of those celebrations felt something like this. People were tired after a long day.

He graduated with honors and passed the exams to get into the most prestigious public school in all of Boston.

Now Bratton started calling over cops and reporters. Cops called over more cops. Bratton straightened his tie. Smoke rose up off the building behind him, and though it was only the afternoon, the sky was dark.

A radio played somewhere. WFAN—Mike Francesa—a guilty pleasure. "New Yorkers hurting New Yorkers? New Yorkers hurting New Yorkers! This is not my New York. Not *the* New Yorkers I know. Not even Mets fans hurting Yankees fans. I've worked here every day for thirty years, and now you're telling me New Yorkers are hurting cops? This isn't Rodney King. It's worse. This isn't Crown Heights. This isn't Attica or Selma or the march on Washington. This is—"

He didn't know where it was coming from. Most residents were crying and hugging, as though they weren't the ones who had just been fighting the police. Bratton's father would have called the inhabitants street monkeys, but Bratton's father was dead, and Bratton made sure never to judge a Jew or an African American by anything other than his actions. Bratton judged a man by what that man could control, and a man could not control his thoughts, and a man could not control the color of his skin or the religion he was born into. His last day at Sunday school, Bratton had taken one look at that priest, humored him, and said, "Yes, sir," and he had never gone back to that church again.

Bratton thought about what he wanted to say. He thought about the best medicine. The medical perspective. Tests. Stabilize the situation. A medical approach to dealing with crime. Cops on the dots. Used to gather stats twice a year to send them off to the federal government. Now it's every day. Used to be a million times a year you'd dial 911, like a doctor giving you placebos. Now it's real medicine.

Cops were everywhere, mostly black, but a few white ones and Asian ones, too. He was their leader. He would lead them into the future. Fires were mostly out. People were hugging. TV cameras panned, pointed at him, and waited. The afternoon grew even darker.

When Bratton had been a boy, he had been protective of his sister. She got in a fight with Gene Stanley, a neighborhood tough. Gene pushed Bratton's sister into a puddle of mud. It was a cold day in March, and Bratton's sister came running into the house with a torn skirt and her shirt pressed wet and cold against her slick white skin. Well, Gene was out in the street, not hiding or anything, and Bratton grabbed him by his collar, the front of his collar, and he punched him in the face and blood poured out of Gene's mouth and was all over Bratton's shirt, and all over Gene, and Bratton punched Gene again, and Bratton's father ran out of the house, and Bratton's sister was crying, and Bratton was crying and yelling at Gene and ordering him to make things right, saying, "apologize, apologize, apologize."

"It's all over," Bratton began. "The streets are once again calm. And I won't apologize for keeping New York safe."

Part 2: Days of Awe

Chapter 49

"What?" Amelia said.

"What?"

"Gentle," Amelia said.

"I'll let go in a minute."

"Okay," Amelia said.

Amelia was on her back at 2 a.m., her arm draped over his body, Aaron's body wrapped around hers.

Simon whimpered in the next room. Aaron rolled away from her for his iPhone, opened the baby app. Light pooled out of the phone into the room. On the illuminated screen, Simon banged his little first on his mattress. But weakly. He feebly banged and banged. Aaron showed Amelia, who started to tear up.

"It's okay, Ames. He's just a baby. I've read that babies' memories recycle every two weeks. What he saw is the same as burning his finger. The circumcision. Don't read your fear into him. We've been over this."

"It was horrible, before you came home."

"Tell me about it."

"I already have."

"Then tell me again. What about it was horrible?"

"Thinking I'd lose him, lose you. Not knowing what to do."

"You'll never lose me," he said.

She started to cry, he asked her why, she cried harder, but the baby wasn't crying anymore.

He held her gently, then hard, then harder to the point where he wondered if he was hurting her, but she seemed to like being held like that. He could tell by the way she was tightening her muscles in the same pattern he was squeezing his.

They were two people in a big house in a never-ending city, and he was holding her as tightly as he could. The streets were calm. Politicians had apologized, but four more cops had been shot. The police had taken her statement, their fingerprints. Daniel downstairs was out on bail. Aaron wanted to kick the murderer out of his house. If Daniel hadn't shot the kid, his friends would have moved on. There wouldn't have been a mob. Unless Daniel had saved Amelia's life by shooting that boy.

Aaron's grip had loosened, so he tightened it. Aaron feared it was all over and lost. That he had lost Amelia. He feared something had happened to her, to them, and the possibility of this exact emotion was why she hadn't wanted to marry. His grip had loosened again, so again he tightened it. He felt her strain to breathe. But what, then, about Simon? Simon was more important than marriage. And what she'd said was that her fear was that she'd lose him. Lose Aaron. And she hadn't lost him.

They should spend the rest of their life rejoicing.

"We should spend every day for the rest of our lives celebrating what we have. That we almost lost each other but we didn't. That we made it through."

She kissed his forehead. He was the vine. She was the tree. Their bodies.

"That sense of what could have been taken away," he began in a whisper, his voice filling out as he spoke. "I'm not saying always think about it, but maybe it's not the worst thing to hang on to it and remind yourself that you could have lost us. But that you made the right decisions and we're still here. Because you were able to protect Simon. And now for the rest of your life you are able to live with the rewards of your good actions."

"With Simon," she said.

"And me," he said.

Perhaps hearing his parents' voices, Simon yelped.

Aaron and Amelia were silent.

"I love you," she said.

"You, too," he said.

Chapter 50

"Soy milk?" she said the next morning at breakfast.

"I'm good," he said.

"For me," she said.

He had taken half or full days off that week. This was the first day Antoinette was going to come back to work after her week off, and they were all three downstairs eating. Simon was drinking formula in Aaron's lap. Neither of them had fasted the day before. Amelia had never fasted. Aaron hadn't for years.

"Berries? FreshDirect, I ordered them for you."

"Please!" Amelia said.

Antoinette rang the bell. Amelia was excited. This was the first step back to normalcy. Antoinette would come back. Amelia could write, figure out what it meant that as soon as Sara cashed the check Amelia would be poor. Figure out how to tell Aaron. Or call the bank and cancel the check. Sara Hall—Amelia had asked if it was "all" or "ahl" to write the check—still hadn't cashed it. When Amelia wrote that check, she'd wanted to be good. She could still picture her hand quivering over the checkbook. She'd steadied it. She'd done the right thing. The right thing to protect her son, and the good thing to give Sara Hall the money for her brother.

"Bring the boy!" Amelia said. "Let's all greet Antoinette together."

Aaron carried Simon to the interior decorative door, which had already been fixed by the construction guys. But the intricate carvings had needed to be replaced by a blank board. They had fixed that first, and were now working on the office. There had been more damage than Amelia had thought. The office's entire back exterior wall had to be redone, the window replaced. Then they'd deal with the front of the house. The damage done by all the thrown concrete.

"Good morning!" Amelia said, opening the door. The air was cold. The temperature had dropped in a week to feel like autumn. Antoinette was wearing jeans, a white blouse, and a gray hijab. Even so, seeing her would be good for Simon. Amelia could admit now that Simon was never as happy as when he was in Antoinette's arms.

"Now I don't want to come in, but I'm just happy you brought my Simon Simon to the door. How's he doing, Simon? Simon says? My big boy eating okay? Is he drinking okay? Simon, Simon? Simon says. Look how big he is!" Antoinette collected herself. "I can't work here anymore. I see you've got it all cleaned up. But I can't work here anymore. I just wanted to say goodbye to Simon says if that's okay."

"Come in. Please come in," Amelia said. "It's all cleaned up. Of course. Of course it is." The idea of Mr. Jupiter's body still in the foyer horrified Amelia.

Behind Antoinette, men and women walked to work. Mostly black people, but white people, too. The two mansions and the church behind Antoinette looked brown and tall behind the trees that were still clinging to the last of their leaves.

"I can't enter this house again," Antoinette said. "I've made my decision."

Antoinette, in her gray hijab, was trying to deliver rehearsed lines. Amelia stood where Jupiter had been, Antoinette where they'd banged on the door.

"Are you sure?" Amelia said.

"I'm sure."

"We can try to give you a raise."

"It's not about that," Antoinette said. "It's not a healthy place. That's all."

Amelia was offended—even if she understood—but she was desperate. "Take another week to think it over? For Simon?" Amelia said, while Aaron stood by dumbly with the baby.

"Goodbye Simon Simon. I love you. I love you," Antoinette said. "I'll never forget you, Simon says. Remember who's in charge! Simon says! Antoinette loves you. You grow up healthy and strong."

Simon cried. He reached out to Antoinette. His mouth opened up and twisted, and tears poured down his eyes.

"Goodbye, Simon Simon. Don't you ever forget me."

And then they were alone.

Amelia was crying.

"They were close, I guess, Antoinette and Jupiter. And he died here," Aaron said. "It makes sense."

Amelia was crying, harder now.

"For her, she can get another job that pays the same amount, and she doesn't need to work here every day. It makes sense for her."

"What about for us?" Amelia said.

"You were complaining about her before all this happened. We can find another nanny. Or you can take some time off from work to spend with Simon. This could be a blessing."

"You think I should?"

"I think we shouldn't make any decisions today. This morning. I think we should both take some time off and spend it as a family."

"Yeah?"

"I love you."

"I love you, too."

Chapter 51

Sara went first to the Chase on Fulton near Nostrand. There was a Citibank close by in case she didn't like the feeling of the Chase, but the Chase was nice inside. It had a hand-sanitizer machine up front and a little table with coffee and a tissue box and a water machine that anyone could use even before you checked in or whatever, so they weren't pressuring you not to use it if you didn't have business there.

Sara had never been in a bank before, but she wasn't an idiot, so she knew that she couldn't just put the check in one of the machines and take money out. Her brother had a credit card and a bank account, and her mother got food stamps and had a card for that but Sara had never had any of that. Still, watching her brother, she figured out that a credit card and a check were entirely different.

When her brother had given her cash recently, and when her mother had given her cash growing up, or when she'd been paid cash doing some of the jobs she sometimes did like when she waitressed at the restaurant two summers ago, she'd had money. It wasn't like she'd never had money. It was just she'd never dealt with checks or banks before. But she made sure when it was her turn next in line to tuck the handcuff bracelets under her sweatshirt sleeves and to be quiet and respectful.

At her mother's place the night before, Sara had tried to pry and then smash her left handcuff bracelet off with her mother's big hammer, but she couldn't even dent it. She'd really wanted to get these fuckers off. Her wrists were chafed and starting to bleed.

She'd imagined that with the right tools she could get them off, but she didn't know what the right tools were. A power drill? A pocketknife? She'd edged one cuff into the drawer of the kitchen table and tried again to pry the back of the hammer into it between her wrist and the cuff, but the stronger she'd twisted the hammer the more her wrist had hurt, and the cuff hadn't even bent. She couldn't twist any harder without snapping her wrist. She'd twisted a little bit harder—as hard as she could endure the pain—and the drawer had snapped off the kitchen table. A shard of cheap wood had splintered out and cut her arm. She'd howled. With pain and misery. Her mother was going to kill her. If her mother ever got out of jail. And the cuffs were still on.

"Can I help you, miss?" the man asked. The man was Indian. Dot not feather. He was respectful. Used to working with blacks.

"I'd like cash from a check," Sara said through the bulletproof glass.

"Swipe your card, please," the man said.

"I don't have a credit card."

"You're not a Chase cardholder?"

"No."

"Then, I'm sorry, miss, I can't help you."

"Oh," Sara said, disappointed but happy she wasn't in trouble.

She hadn't shown anyone the check. No one knew how big it was, or where she'd gotten it. No one had taken it away from her. She knew this was going to be hard, and though she didn't get her money, she didn't get the check taken away, which meant she still had a chance of giving the money to her mother.

Next Sara went to the Pay-O-Matic on Fulton off Marcus Garvey. There was a Pay-O-Matic just half a block from the Chase and Citibank, but she wanted to walk the three extra blocks to clear her head. She knew these places better. They were everywhere. She'd been in them with her brother and uncle before and you didn't need to have any account with them. They just took their cut and gave you the cash. Though she didn't want to give up the 10 percent or whatever it was to Mr. Pay-O-Matic that could have gone to her brother's bills, she'd be happy to have forty-five thousand dollars.

She hadn't eaten since wings the night before for dinner. Her mom had called from jail while she was eating and yelled at her for not being there with Andy that whole week. Sara so badly had wanted to tell her about the check, but couldn't until she was sure the money was real. Sara so badly wanted to have the money for bail, for the hospital bills. Then she could visit her brother. Sara had just kept saying, "It will be okay," and her mom kept saying, harping on the money along with the loss, "How will it be okay? Andy's all messed up, I can't be there for him, you refuse to, they don't know how bad he is, they don't know when he'll wake up, and he's still under arrest for attacking cops. If, *if* he gets out, Medicaid or the government or whatever will pay for the hospital, but not the therapy, the physical therapy. The occupational therapy his doc told Janet he'll need. We can't afford that. He's all messed up, Sara. Everything that was supposed to be his can't be now. You get that, right? He was supposed to take care of all of us, and now we've got to take care of him. It's all messed up. We are dead now. All the talk about books and futures that went on in our apartment. It's all dead now."

When it was Sara's turn at the Pay-O-Matic windows, the lady asked: "Can I help you?" She was black.

"I'd like to get cash for a check," Sara said through bulletproof glass. But everything was smaller than the bank, so Sara minded the glass now. The ceilings were lower and the lights were brighter. The place was like the combination of a car repair shop and a bank. It had bricks up and down the side with big glass windows and giant blue and yellow signs.

"Check and ID, please."

Sara, trying to breathe deeply, removed the check, smoothed it on her sweatpants, and handed it over along with her old school ID.

The teller didn't even look at the check. "This ID won't do. Unless—this check from your school?"

"No."

"No—" The woman barely heard Sara. She was forty, overweight and overconfident. Clearly good at her job, rude, glancing at the line behind Sara. "I can see that. This ID doesn't even have the right sticker. And this is a personal check. No personal checks no matter what. Following customer."

Sara was scared now. But she walked the block and a half down to Atlantic to Checks & More. The place was on the corner of a strip mall between a mom-and-pop drugstore and a Golden Krust. Sara knew about Checks & More because in eighth grade she used to come to the Golden Krust on Fridays after school with friends and eat the jerk chicken patties. Now, there was no one inside Checks & More. It was dark. There was no bulletproof glass, just a middle-aged white man behind a waist-high counter.

"Can I help you, young lady?" he said. He smiled. He had just opened a Snapple.

Sara hated him. She hated him because he called her young

lady and because he wasn't going to give her the money. It was her money. She wasn't trying to trick anyone.

"I'd like to cash a check," Sara said.

"Sure thing! Nice day, isn't it? Things quieted down around here. Strange how the riots were here but the cops are being shot in nicer neighborhoods. Nice to have things back to normal around here at least, though I feel awful for those cops. Even though cops have never done me any favors. They don't deserve to be shot. And their families. Jesus fuck, am I right? How scared must their wives and kids be right now? But right. Sorry. It's nice to get back to business. Chaos around here means no business for me. No business means no money," he said, rubbing two fingers together. "Check and ID, please."

Sara, steadying her breath, removed the check, smoothed it on her sweatpants, and handed it over along with her old school ID.

The man looked at the check, whistled. "Well looks like you had a good day the day everyone else's life went to shit. Good for you! It's nice to know someone did. And I'll be thrilled to take my three percent of that. But I'll need a driver's license or non-driver's state ID, and a social security card. Two pieces of state ID, honey, okay?"

"My mom has the New York State Benefit card. And my brother has a credit card, checkbook, and all that."

"I'm sorry. The check is made out to you. It's under your name. And a check that big you can't sign over, either. Looks too suspicious. I'll get audited for it."

"But I'm not doing anything wrong. This check was made out to me. This is my money. It was a gift to me."

"Do you have a social security card?"

"I don't know. Maybe."

"You're nowhere, girl." He sipped his Snapple. "You're not even close. You're as close to that money as if you were holding an IOU. Ha! I wish I could help you, but wait until I tell Gerard. A girl with busted handcuffs on her wrists walks into the store with a fifty-thousand-dollar check that looks completely legitimate and no way to cash it. Jesus fucking Christ. And they tell me gentrification isn't changing the neighborhood! Why don't you go home and see if you have a social security card. That would be a start. And if you can find it, you can apply for a nondriver's state ID. Doesn't take more than a few weeks. I know it seems like a long time to you, but six to eight weeks? If I were sitting on fifty grand, I'd wait six to eight weeks."

"What if I don't have a social security card?"

"You were born here, right? In this country?"

"I can't ask my mother. She won't know. I don't know."

"I'm sorry. Who wrote you that check anyhow?"

Chapter 52

"I'm going to take Simon today," Aaron said the afternoon Antoinette told them she wouldn't be back. "He's been inside too many days in a row. We'll be careful. You try to write."

"Yeah?" Amelia said.

"It's safe," Aaron said. "As long as you're not a cop, the city's safe."

"You sure?"

She hadn't been away from Simon for more than an hour since the day.

"I'll take him to the Children's Museum," he said.

Amelia wanted to write. To get her thoughts down before they got away from her, and to figure out whether she had the beginning of something. She had to find the beginning of something. This couldn't have all been for nothing. For suffering. Hers and Simon's.

She had to marry Aaron now that she had no money. Or she could come clean and apologize for doing what she'd always fear he'd do—frivolously losing their money. Though it hadn't been frivolous, giving that check to Sara. It had been necessary.

When she wrote a book that sold, she could replace the money. The money! Even if a book sold, which it wouldn't, it would take years! She called the 1-800 number on the back of her credit card.

"Yes!" she said when she finally got a live person. "I'm calling to cancel a check."

"Check number?" Amelia told it to the woman, who wasn't in India. The woman had a midwestern accent. "Okay," she said. "I'll find it."

"Yes," Amelia said, "for fifty-thousand dollars."

"No," Amelia said, "the check wasn't stolen."

"No," Amelia said, "the goods or services were not misrepresented."

Sara had said she'd leave and Amelia had said she'd pay, and Sara had left, and Amelia was safe, and so was Simon, and now Amelia was reneging on her end of the deal. Amelia had moved into this neighborhood and taken everything, and everything was hers.

The demand Sara had made was reasonable in its way.

"Never mind," Amelia said. "Forget it."

Amelia hung up the phone and breathed. She could always call back later.

She had time now that Aaron was taking Simon out. The Brooklyn Children's Museum in Crown Heights had reopened the day before. The extended neighborhood of Jews (not the religious ones because it had been Yom Kippur) and Muslims, blacks and whites had lined up—highlighted by local news outlets looking for positive stories—to demonstrate solidarity. Amelia and Aaron had watched together on TV, and now Aaron would get a kick out of carrying Simon around in the Ergobaby and mixing in. He could share his story about racing home to be with his family. Others could sympathize. He could tell stories and make friends, maybe invite other parents with young babies over for drinks.

Since the day, Aaron had been eager to show himself. He'd wanted to have opinions on aspects of the day that were difficult to have opinions about. He'd planned on working full days but had come home before lunch. To supervise the repairs. To hold Simon because, with Antoinette gone, he wanted to share the burden of child care. Or just because he wanted to hold Simon. But Simon had been catatonic. Simon had been replaced by a doll Simon who barely ate, hardly slept, but didn't cry, just lay there in his crib and waited for morning to come.

So let Aaron mingle with other parents, Amelia thought. Counsel other parents. Give speeches to them. Let Simon be around other babies. Be read to in the infant area. Aaron could read him *I Am a Bunny* five hundred times as she had the last time they'd gone. *I am a bunny. My name is Nicholas. I live in a hollow tree.* They could watch the older children play in the water area. It might liven Simon a bit to be around other children. She'd be eager to find out.

.   .   .

Forty-five minutes later Aaron removed Simon and the diaper bag from an Uber on the Upper East Side in front of the synagogue where Aaron had spent six years working as an assistant rabbi.

Simon had just finally fallen asleep after staring backward, eerily silent, for most of the ride. Aaron scanned through his phone after that. Facebook was dominated by people all over the world expressing unity with the citizens of New York. Twitter was full of hot takes about how the unity was misguided because either the police or the looters were to blame. Aaron couldn't empathize with either side, so he checked LinkedIn and connected with a few people he didn't know. He checked Snapchat for the first time in days and saw the ten-second photo Amelia had sent him of Jupiter's dead body lying in his entryway. He was in the back of the cab so there was nothing he could do. By the time he could focus on the photo, it was gone. And he couldn't get it back. By the time he understood what he was looking at, there was no record of it. The dead man's legs had been closest to him. To Amelia, when she'd taken the photo. When he'd been at the track. Now it was the ghost of an image. A ghost that Amelia and Simon had lived with for those two hours while he'd been at the track, then racing home, then delivering a sermon out on the stoop. His wife and baby had been alone with the dead body that had been shot four times and was bleeding into the wood. He'd covered the stain with the Turkish carpet from the office. Eventually he cleaned up his books from the Pack 'n Play.

Simon wore overalls and slept heavily in a bucket Snap-N-Go car seat that Aaron carried in his right hand. The diaper bag slung over Aaron's right shoulder and bounced against his left hip. Aaron wore jeans, a brown button-down, heavy cotton shirt, and a gray hooded sweatshirt.

This was the first time Aaron had been back to Rohr Shalom since the senior rabbi had fired him. He walked in though the heavy wooden front doors. The front of the building was covered in its familiar milky crimson marble. The familiar bronze handle on the door was being polished by an African American maintenance man who nodded to him. The man was new. Aaron had avoided this block for the past six years. He had worked here for six years then avoided the block for six years. Aaron didn't know whether to walk straight to the synagogue or turn left up to the offices to say hello to the temple president and rabbis, assuming the same people worked here. The senior rabbi would be the same. The others, Aaron wasn't sure. A freestanding black sign with white letters listed

Rohr Shalom Bible & Bagels 8:15 a.m.–9:00 a.m.
Volunteers at Head Start 10:00 a.m.–11:30 a.m.
Weekly Torah Study noon–1:15 p.m.
TSBP noon–2:00 p.m.
Book of Samuel: The Road to Kingship 1:30 p.m.–2:30 p.m.

It was after three, so congregants would be gone for the day. Aaron walked straight past the forty rows of pews to the bimah and took a seat in the front row with Simon in his car seat beside him on the bench. The diaper bag lay by Aaron's ankles. Aaron suppressed simultaneous urges to vomit and reminisce. His voice had echoed off these walls. The synagogue was empty except for two maintenance men, one who'd worked there the entire time Aaron had but who was pretending not to recognize Aaron; the other, who had been polishing the doors and was new. The Torah ark was majestic, the tapestries behind it surreal with swirls of purple and yellow. Fresh-cut flowers bloomed on the bimah and in front of it; the podiums were thick and sturdy, one with a closed siddur resting on top of it. Aaron couldn't help himself.

He left Simon on the bench buckled into the car seat and circled around the side to climb onstage. The bimah creaked. The maintenance men looked up. Aaron waved.

"Rabbi," the one he knew saluted.

"Max," Aaron said, just at that moment remembering his name.

He looked out at the synagogue from the bimah, and the size of the place was overwhelming. It was mostly made from light wood, though the pews in the mezzanine on top were dark wood, and the chandeliers were metal. The stained glass was purple and white. The balcony and the pillars that helped hold it up were white and copper. This had never been Aaron's place. He had never held High Holiday services in this, the main synagogue, but he studied here, sometimes was on the bimah for Shabbat, led prayers occasionally, felt the power of the room repeat after him. The lamps—dimmed now—when fully lit, shined bright and combined with the voices echoing off the wooden pews to come close to the feeling of God. The effect of the voices in song did something similar. As close as anything had until—Aaron looked down at his son—the feeling of talking to the angry crowd on his stoop.

"Modeh ani lifanecha, melech chai vikayam, she-he-chezarta bi nishmati be-chemla – raba emunatecha!" Aaron whispered, not knowing where he was going with this. The mic wasn't on. No one was there except for the maintenance men. Aaron was going to begin daily ritual prayers of gratitude. He was thanking God for the day, for returning his soul to him with compassion.

Simon stirred.

Steps echoed down the main corridor. From their rhythm, Aaron knew the senior rabbi had been radioed.

Aaron looked to find Max, but Max's head was down, sweeping.

"Aaron," the senior rabbi said, still twenty paces away.

"Rabbi," Aaron said.

"And who do we have here?" the senior rabbi said.

Aaron put his finger to his lips. He whispered, "Simon."

"Sorry," the senior rabbi whispered.

The senior rabbi wore a suit. Aaron had never seen him in anything else. He was in his late sixties. He was casual, beardless, and friendly. Always had been, but Aaron hadn't seen him in more than six years, and he'd lost weight, was a little bit crooked now. He'd always been serious when he led services. But was gregarious and warm in his offices. Offered the other rabbis a drink of good wine after 6 p.m.

Now he joined Aaron on the bimah. He hugged Aaron very hard. The senior rabbi seemed to have lost some of his vanity along with the weight. He wouldn't have hugged Aaron a decade ago when they had been working together. Maybe he wouldn't have hugged Aaron because they had been working together? Or maybe because his suits had always been just so. Aaron, midhug, realized that much of his—Aaron's—recent vanity had been borrowed from the senior rabbi. Aaron had only over the last year been able to afford the kind of suits the senior rabbi wore, and he'd been keeping them pressed as the senior rabbi had done, wearing pocket squares in the style of the senior rabbi. Today, the senior rabbi wore a charcoal-gray three-piece suit with a white shirt and a white pocket square. The senior rabbi had a full head of gray hair, and the vest beneath the suit filled him out. The suit was very soft against Aaron's cheek.

"It's wonderful. It's so wonderful to see you, Rabbi," the senior rabbi said. Aaron remembered the senior rabbi's affectation to always call the other rabbis "rabbi." "And that's your son? It's so wonderful to see you and to meet your son. We've missed you around here," he said. "It's so wonderful to see you. And your wife? You're married?"

"Of course," Aaron said.

"And she's Jewish?" the senior rabbi said.

"Of course," Aaron said.

The senior rabbi took a step back to look at Aaron in the manner of a doting mother. He never would have expressed this kind of pride when Aaron had worked there. Aaron was buoyed up by it. He was full of gratitude and pride for his own son and new life. The senior rabbi stepped forward and hugged Aaron again.

When they separated, the senior rabbi said, "You're a man now. You left us younger. Unformed. Look at you! It's astonishing. You filled out. You're a man now. And you're married with a son. And the look in your eye. It's wisdom. I can tell. It's real wisdom."

"Thank you," Aaron said, tearing up. "Thank you."

"And you've come to visit?"

"Something like that," Aaron said.

"Well why have you come?"

"I've come to consecrate my son to the Lord," Aaron said, thrilled to feel empowered when he said it as opposed to silly.

"What?" the senior rabbi said. "I don't understand. What are you talking about? He didn't have a bris?"

"No, I mean. He didn't, but that's not what I mean. I mean. He was circumcised. At the hospital. It just seemed more sanitary. But that's not what I mean. I was in the riots. Right in the middle of them. And, like Hannah, I promised that I would consecrate my son to the Lord if he and I and my . . . my wife came out okay. And we did. So here I am."

"What have you been doing? It's awful what happened. And what's happened, with the policemen killed, since. Innocent men, taken in anger. You're not a rabbi anymore, correct?"

"I'm a financial manager. Doing well."

This was when he felt juvenile.

"I see," the senior rabbi said. "Can I tell you? You don't look lost anymore. It's extraordinary. When I think about you, I think about someone who every day was utterly lost. Who didn't know if he was going right or left. Up or down. Who was trying so hard to help people but couldn't help himself. I can't tell you how often I've thought of you since. How badly we treated you here. You weren't equipped to be a rabbi. But we took you in and didn't support you. After you left us, we changed the entire system. We changed our intern rabbinical program. I work much more closely with the new training rabbis. They are not so much on their own now. We have more group study. And social gatherings. We have bowling nights, and we watch Knicks games together. Which this year isn't so great, but you know what I'm saying. I've thought many times about reaching out to you. We could have stood by you. For all you did or tried to do for members of our community. And, though you had strengths and weaknesses, you showed potential. We could have stood by you in your shame. I'm so happy you've come back—"

"I've come," Aaron said, cutting him off, "to read Simon the story of Hannah, and bring Simon here and dedicate him to God. That's the reason I've come."

Aaron didn't want to be pitied. He didn't want to be a source of a second layer of shame from the people who once respected him. First he'd committed the crime, and then they weren't able to tolerate their memories of him. He wanted to read his son the story of a woman who'd made a promise to Adonai and then kept her promise.

But equipped to be a rabbi? Aaron hadn't come here to be told that even when he was leading services and serving the community, meeting with families, leading prayer groups, teaching Torah, he wasn't equipped? Every day for six years that was his job. And he did it. He did his job, and he did it well.

"Yes. I see," the senior rabbi said. "So bring him here. Let's do it. Come on."

"Do what?" Aaron asked.

"Let me pray over him. Let me dedicate him to God. So that

he will no longer be yours, is what you are saying. Correct? You are saying that Simon will no longer be yours. He will be God's. That you would like him, like Hannah's son, to be God's."

Aaron had planned on reading the verses himself, but maybe they would be more powerful coming from the senior rabbi. The senior rabbi waited for an answer, so Aaron nodded. "Yes. I want him to be God's, not mine. That was what I promised."

The rabbi gestured down toward Simon. Aaron hopped off the bimah and returned with his son in the bucket car seat. Simon was awake, wide-eyed. Aaron held Simon up to the senior rabbi as the older man read the verses in Hebrew, which Aaron knew well, having focused on them every Rosh Hashanah. They translated to: "Please, Adonai, as you live, Adonai, I am the woman who stood here beside you and prayed to Adonai. It was this boy I prayed for; and Adonai has granted me what I asked of Adonai. I, in turn, hereby lend him to Adonai. For as long as he lives he is lent to Adonai." Simon remained silent as Aaron placed him at his feet.

"You understand?" the senior rabbi asked. "You want to change his name, too? Does he have a Hebrew name?"

"No," Aaron said.

"So call him Samuel from now on."

"I will," Aaron said, feeling a rush of pleasure.

"And have your wife—his mother—call him Samuel. She knows you are here?"

Aaron looked at the rabbi, at his face attempting to understand, and at the radiant synagogue behind him.

"No," Aaron said. He wanted to be honest.

"What's wrong?" the senior rabbi said.

"I shouldn't be here."

"Do you want to be here?

"Yes," Aaron said. He could be honest, and it could be okay.

"Then what do you mean you shouldn't be here?"

"I have a new life," Aaron said. "With a son and a new house and a new job. I've moved on. I've spent the last six years moving on."

"Does it feel successful? That you want to move on? That you are happy with your life as a successful financial manager and you don't want to be here anymore?"

"Happy? Is that what I should want to be?"

The senior rabbi looked at Aaron and believed he understood.

"You are a rabbi."

"You fired me," Aaron said.

"Then apply for work elsewhere. See if you get hired. It's a saturated market, but I'll write you a good recommendation from me, from here—that will go far."

"I have a job."

"I feel terrible for how we treated you. We never tried to help you, only told you we didn't have a place for you here anymore. Do you like—are you satisfied by your new job? It pays well, you said?"

"I don't believe in Judaism. It's all pretend. None of it is true. There's no God. It's founded on a lie."

"Come now, Rabbi. You know it isn't as simple as that."

Simon was awake and screaming, but to Aaron it was wonderful to hear him scream, and to the senior rabbi it didn't matter that Simon screamed, because the synagogue was empty except for the baby and two men. Even the maintenance team had left. Aaron looked to his son and looked to the senior rabbi.

"All the rituals, the traditions, every time I try to help people. It's all based on a lie, or at the very least, on something that I know to be untrue. There is no supreme being that operates outside the laws of science. There was no Adam and Eve. You know that. You must.

And yet we still teach it as though it's all true? If I want to help people I should be a psychologist or a judge. A stand-up comedian, maybe. How can I return to this without faith? How do you do it?"

"Aaron. No one has absolute faith."

"So you don't believe."

"Of course I believe. I trust in Adonai. Not in an anthropomorphic God of Genesis, perhaps, who strolls in the Garden, but an Adonai who exists in parallel with the comprehensible, who is part of and apart from science. Asking for a simple understanding will leave you without faith—you know Moshe ben Maimon's teachings as well as I do."

"And suffering? The Holocaust? What would Maimonides have said about Hitler?"

"No one has any convincing answers about Hitler, Aaron. But you are as good a man as anyone to help ask the questions. Stop looking for easy answers. That's for the Christians and atheists. Keep asking questions."

"Stop it. You're not listening to me, Rabbi. I don't believe."

"Maimonides taught that evil exists where good is absent. God didn't create Hitler. He allowed Hitler to push aside good. And it is our job as rabbis to fill in those vacuums."

Teachings were coming back to Aaron, but he pushed them away. "Why is that our job? Why isn't it your God's? You're still not listening to me. I don't believe in him."

"I am listening to you, Aaron. And more importantly, I am seeing you. Here."

Both men looked out at the empty synagogue, then down at the baby by Aaron's feet.

"Shall we dedicate your Samuel to the Lord?" the senior rabbi said.

"Yes, please," Aaron said, and they offered up Simon together.

Chapter 53

t was the first time she'd been alone in a week. The construction crew was in her office, but she had the bedroom and parlor floors to herself. Aaron and Simon were out at the Children's Museum. Antoinette was gone forever. No more detectives or police. She couldn't hear Daniel or Thela over the sound of the workers upstairs. And she had energy. She didn't want to nap. She wanted to write, but more than that, she wanted to think, conclude, make sense of that day without needing to color it for someone else's feelings. What had happened over the last week?

She wanted to mother her child as opposed to pay someone else to.

And now she could.

She wanted to spend her life with Aaron. If it was safe to. She'd heard him out on the stoop talking about what love could accomplish. He'd been talking about her. And he really seemed to mean it. It was unlucky that he was damaged. She loved him, but he was damaged, and she didn't know what to do.

Except that she wanted to work. No more celebrities. No more witty phrases about strangers' bodies.

And now she could work. The article she'd published a week before about Bed-Stuy's history and architecture had been a right step forward, but it had been superficial. It was just words about a place. It had nothing to do with living there. It wasn't the experience of living there. Now she had her story. She knew Antoinette. She'd met Sara. She'd borne witness to Mr. Jupiter. She understood the situation better. And herself. Now she understood herself. She had a story. Though just because she had a story—a unique, potentially career-making story—should she tell it? It *was* hers. It had happened in her home. It had changed her life forever. But, really, it belonged to Sara. And to Jupiter's family. Amelia would be the appropriator. But even as she was going back and forth, she sensed the lack of sincerity in her prevarication. She knew there was something not fully decent about telling this story, but she equally knew she was going to tell it. This was exactly what she'd been looking for. It wasn't an assignment. It wasn't entertainment. It mattered, and even if it didn't belong entirely to her, it was enough hers that she wouldn't be able to let it go. She just had to figure out how to get the story right. And how to convince the *Times* or *The New Yorker* to let her be the one to tell it.

Chapter 54

Amelia had two pages written when she heard the doorbell buzz. Timing was about right. She figured that Aaron was carrying the diaper bag in one hand and the car seat in the other and didn't have the spare finger to fish out his keys. Time had compressed in front of the keyboard. She was reliving just the single moment of Jupiter talking to the kids on the other side of the doorway. She thought that could be a hook into the piece. Make the whole thing less about race than chaos and generation. *Gentrification and Generation.* But then she wondered if maybe that was wrong. If it *was* more about race than generation. Or if chaos and race were the culprits, and she hadn't yet gotten a handle on why those kids killed Jupiter. Why had they? She still didn't understand it. Would she ever?

The doorbell buzzed again, and she was excited to see if the museum had animated Simon. She saved the document, spun the computer off her lap, and skipped down the stairs to greet them. It wasn't until the new interior wooden door was open and her hand was on the outer metal door that she realized what she was looking at. She was looking at the girl again. The girl she'd just been thinking about. She had so many questions for her. She was energized to see her. Amelia had a million questions to fill in the blanks of the week before. To help her start writing an article that made sense. A book.

Sara had been living in Amelia's mind. But now to see her again could undo all the success of getting her out of the house the first time.

"Come in," Amelia said.

"Really?"

"Do you have a gun?" Amelia said.

"No."

"Then come in," Amelia said. "Neither do I."

"Really?" Sara said, tugging her sleeves over her wrists.

"Yes."

"Come in," Amelia said.

Sara stepped inside.

"Nice house," Sara said.

"Thanks," Amelia said.

They looked at each other. Sara looked even younger than she had looked a week ago up in the office.

Amelia hugged Sara.

She hadn't planned on it, but Sara was so thin and vulnerable, and they had gone through so much together. Amelia had just been thinking about Sara, and then there she was. But Sara stood stiff in Amelia's arms.

"Can I get you something? A Diet Coke?" Amelia said.

"Okay," Sara said.

"Come in," Amelia said.

"Nice house," Sara said.

"Thanks," Amelia said. "Some guys are upstairs, construction guys from when you . . . last week."

"Yeah," Sara said. "That's why I'm here."

Sara was wearing black jeans and a long-sleeved black T-shirt, and her face was like Simon's after he's been crying. Amelia was ashamed she'd shot at this girl. It was the worst thing she'd ever done. And she'd been so proud of it just minutes before. A link of chain was visible by her thumb.

"Why? To apologize?" Amelia said. "Can I get you anything to eat?"

"No," Sara said. She was tapping her foot, sipping Diet Coke from a glass. Maybe, Amelia thought, it was a mistake to give her caffeine.

Amelia looked around the dining room at the inlaid mahogany china cabinet, at the decorative ceiling plasterwork, at the reclaimed wood table and art deco lamps and Jonathan Adler pendant light.

"Fifty thousand dollars isn't anything to you," Sara said.

"Excuse me?"

"I mean, I'm here because I can't cash that check. I don't have ID except school ID that's expired, and I can't cash that check, so I need cash. So I've come to say, can I please have the money you gave me in cash?"

Fury wasn't the right word for what quickly and forcefully came over Amelia, but neither was the need to buy time. It was something between the two if they could be on the same spectrum. Knowing she had the right to be furious. Righteous indignation. Something like when the gun has been on you in the movie, but now you've got it and you're pointing it at the other guy.

"Why would I do that?" Amelia said.

Sara looked up from her glass of Diet Coke.

"You just hugged me," she said in a voice that seemed to Amelia to be sincerely confused.

"Get out of my house," Amelia said, feeling like she'd only felt before twice in her life—when she'd found Kevin's gun under the bed as she'd realized he'd been cheating on her, and when she'd been up in that office with Sara the week before.

"You promised," Sara said, like the little girl she was.

It hadn't been part of the plan—Sara's inability to cash it. Amelia hadn't thought about that. Amelia had made a mistake but was weighing now if she should be angry at herself for that mistake or congratulate herself for her subconscious foresight.

"I can't," Amelia said. "I can't just go into a bank and ask for fifty thousand dollars."

"Why not?" Sara said, revving up. "I did and they told me I needed ID. You have ID, right?"

"Okay: I don't want to," Amelia said. "I just gave you that so you'd leave my house. I didn't have a choice. Now I do."

"So you're a liar?"

"To protect my family, sure."

"What if I trash this place?" Sara said, working herself up, looking around.

Now Amelia had fully transformed into the version of herself from a week ago: "Go for it," she said. "You couldn't do close to fifty thousand dollars' damage. There's not five thousand dollars of damage here. And you already did your best upstairs, and insurance is paying for all the repairs. Just leave. You're making a fool of yourself. I thought you were okay, that you were better than they were, and you didn't want to be stuck with those kids, that you didn't want to get in trouble with Jupiter's son, but it's been a week now. Get out of here."

"No. Not without my money. I need it for my brother."

"Your brother," Amelia meant to say dismissively, but it came out curious.

"I told you. The police beat him. He's all fucked up. He had a good job at Barnes & Noble's. But now he's all fucked up and under arrest and you swore you'd pay me."

Amelia's horizons widened.

"What's his name?" she asked.

A change in perspective and scope. Sara had a brother who'd been working a good job. Sara had been trying to earn money for her brother. Her mother was in jail. Her brother was in the hospital. Her friend had killed Mr. Jupiter. Inside Amelia's own home.

Amelia hadn't known how to tell such a scattered and all-encompassing story. But she now saw that Sara was the way in. They could both benefit. Amelia could admit it wasn't her own story. It was Sara's, and she—Amelia—was merely in the right place to document it. Gentrification. Poverty. The riots. A smart, undereducated young black girl who never got a break.

"His name is—"

"What if instead of giving you cash, I gave you a job?" Amelia said.

"You already owe it to me in cash," Sara said, breathing hard. "You fucking swore it."

Amelia saw, though, that Sara was considering it, and she saw that this was going to make everything possible.

"You can be my research assistant," Amelia said. "I'll pay you well. Twenty dollars an hour. That's the offer. I'm not going to pay you the check in cash. It's not going to happen. But I can pay you to work. It'll be a good job. For your résumé, too. To show me your neighborhood. Your life. I'll write about it. Make you famous.

Everyone will know your name. All of Manhattan will know your story and want to take care of you. And I'll teach you research skills."

"Fifty."

"What?"

"Fifty dollars an hour."

"No."

"You don't give a shit," Sara said. "Fifty dollars an hour."

"Okay. Fifty dollars an hour. But no higher. You show me your world. Explain why it's messed up. Introduce me to your brother. And your challenges. Show me where you live. And I take notes. That's all. I write it down and I tell everyone what you're up against. This is a good thing."

"You'll pay for my 'challenges.'"

"It's really that you help me research," Amelia said.

"Fifty dollars an hour, ten hours a day, is five-hundred dollars a day, right? Five days a week is more than a two thousand a week. In cash?"

"Sure," Amelia said. "Cash." It would be an investment in the neighborhood. In the community. In both of their careers.

Chapter 55

Bratton took the podium, swaggered up there nose first, smiling, waving, cameras flashing and recording, but Derek only really heard the beginning:

"I'm going to make this quick," he shouted at the microphones. "I know you have questions, but I want to say a few things quickly. People died. It's a tragedy. It's dozens of tragedies. But not as many as could have died, and the city, we're working through the aftermaths, and there will be changes. There will be arrests of the perpetrators. We will locate police officers in at-risk areas. We're going to let the little stuff go and start fresh on day zero."

. . . and then the bit about his father:

"And for Derek Jupiter. His son, Derek Jr., is here today, too. Mr. Jupiter owned his own small electrician business and was doing well for himself in one of the beautiful brownstones on Stuyvesant Avenue in the Stuyvesant Heights neighborhood of Bedford-Stuyvesant, Brooklyn. Mr. Jupiter—an African American—happened to be looking after a white neighbor's baby son when a gang raided the house and he was murdered trying to protect that boy. Derek Jr., fear not. Your father's death will not be forgotten. He will live on in the minds of all his friends and neighbors as the upstanding citizen he was. The perpetrator of this heinous crime has already been brought to justice. And we will not forget about you."

. . . before zoning out again.

A *New York Post* cover showed the police commissioner standing tall up front while the mayor cowered in his shadow. Or Derek thought that was what he was looking at.

"Derek Jupiter?"

"Yeah?"

Derek wasn't good at guessing white people's ages, but she couldn't have been over twenty-five.

"Thanks for coming! Sorry about your dad. I'd like to offer you my personal condolences."

"They said they'd arrest me if I didn't come," he said.

He'd been on his way to settle what little was left to be settled. He'd finally found Sara late the night before, which had just left him feeling worse. He was only still there at the speech grounds because he wasn't sure he was allowed to leave yet. The speech was over and no one had told him if he could go.

The woman's clothes were all shiny. And so was her face. Glossy. She was the whitest, shiniest woman he'd ever met.

"No way," the woman said. She seemed actually surprised. Like she couldn't believe the people she worked for were capable of threatening arrest. There was a park bench with bird shit all over it, and she motioned for them to sit, but then she saw all the shit, and they both smiled. Cops were everywhere, and construction workers were breaking down the bleachers where'd he'd been seated.

"They knocked on my door, said they'd arrest me if I didn't put on a suit and sit and smile during the speech."

Sara had been scared of him, but he wasn't mad at her. Or he had been, but he wasn't going to do anything about it. He'd asked her who killed Damien. They'd been in Sara's mother's house. Sara had been asleep in bed when he got there.

"You still don't know?" Sara had said. "There was this other fucking redneck in the house. He had guns."

"But who shot my dad?" he'd said.

"Damien did," Sara had said.

"Why?" he'd said.

"Because your dad was in Damien's way I guess," Sara had said. "No reason. He was fucking crazy."

"Then it *is* my fault," he'd said.

"It's a nice suit," the white woman said.

He hadn't been able to help himself from buttoning it. His father was dead and he didn't have any friends, but still he'd checked the mirror before coming over. In a suit in the back of a cop car, he'd hoped the neighbors saw. What would they think? That he was arrested, of course. But let them think it. His father had just been killed. There was nothing left to worry about, in terms of the thoughts of others.

"Perfect for television," the woman said, and smiled.

Was she flirting? She was cute. She was blond and wore glasses and this could be the beginning of turning his back on everything in the entire fucking world that meant anything to him. He could fuck her and murder her and be a real fucking criminal.

"Thanks," he said, and he smiled, too. It might have been the first time he smiled since he'd been arrested that day in the park.

"Sorry about your dad," she said, again. She took off her glasses and did something to fix her hair in the back. She had a slight overbite. She put on her glasses again.

"Yeah," he said. He'd never seen a black girl with an overbite like that. That was the kind of thing that white people didn't mind having. That he bet she thought looked cute on her.

"You did good," she said.

Clouds covered the sun and everything was dark.

"I just sat there," he said. He didn't want to be patronized or humored by this shiny white girl with an overbite.

"It's not easy," she said.

"Thanks," he said. Maybe she wasn't humoring him. Maybe she was just being nice.

"Some people squirm around or sweat or need to stand up and leave. You did good," she said.

"Thanks," he said.

Like five hundred pigeons flew overhead and everyone ducked.

"Did they really say," she said, "they'd arrest you if you didn't come with them? After the week you've been through?"

The crowd was starting to thin out, and Derek didn't know if there was something on the clipboard that meant she was supposed to be talking to him, or if she wanted to be talking to him. Either way, he didn't know what to do exactly, when the conversation ended. He knew what he wanted to do, what he told himself he needed to do, what he'd been on his way to do when the cops had picked him up—but not what he was actually capable of doing. And it seemed like he was free to do it now. The feeling of this conversation was that he wasn't being kept there by force.

"I was at the park where the whole thing started," he said, prolonging their conversation purposely. "I ran after I was arrested. The cops must have known that when they brought me here."

"But your dad died," she said.

Derek looked at her. On second glance, her suit fit like shit.

Her job was to wear a fucking suit, and it was shiny and it fit like shit. And the overbite was strange. He wouldn't even fuck her if he could.

"Sorry," she said.

"It's okay."

"Want cab fare to get home?"

"Naw," he said with a strange accent.

"Why not?" she said. "It's my job to give you cab fare." The breeze blew strong.

"Okay. Eighty bucks?"

"Okay."

"Really?" he said.

"I don't care," she said. "I just have to write it on this list."

"That's tight."

"Who are you going home to?" she said.

"Why do you give a shit?"

"Sorry," she said. "You remind me of my son."

Now the sun was bright again.

"Home," he said. "To my father's home."

Hot dog carts were everywhere.

It was strange how all of a sudden Derek noticed the carts.

"Did my dad say anything?" he'd asked Sara.

"Say anything?" Sara had said.

"Did he say anything about me?" he'd said.

She'd sat on her bed looking down. Finally:

"Yeah, he did say something," Sara had said.

"What?" he'd said. "Did he say how I was a fuckup or anything like that? Tell me the truth."

"He said how you loved to eat his cooking," Sara had said.

"Don't fuck with me," he'd said.

"How would I be fucking with you?" Sara had said. She'd looked so small. Like a kid.

"What'd he say?" he'd said. "Exactly."

"He said that you'd come home at night and eat whatever was in the fridge," Sara had said. "That he'd leave extra food there because he knew you'd eat it. So he'd leave it there for you."

Derek had screamed at Sara's feet like he was dying.

Chapter 56

Amelia saw Sara's apartment. It was a small but nice home inside clean-enough Bed-Stuy housing projects. Smelled of mint. An artificial mint cleaner that Sara must have used before Amelia arrived. Amelia took notes on the broken kitchen table. On the soda bottles and chicken wings in the fridge. She took notes when Sara spoke to her mother on the phone. She took notes on bail, and how it was a system whereby poor people had to spend months in jail. It was a modern-day debtor's prison.

Amelia brought Sara to a garage, where a mechanic took bolt cutters and removed the cuffs without asking any questions. Probably, Amelia thought, because Amelia was white and paying cash.

Amelia was learning, and Sara was earning. That's what Amelia said. Sara just glared. She ate her meatball Parm at the sandwich place. Over lunch, Sara texted on her new phone. They never spoke, except when Amelia addressed her directly or when Sara got frustrated.

"I don't have time for this shit," Sara said, counting her two hundred dollars at the end of a four-hour day. "My mother's never going to make bail like this. My brother's going to need physical therapy money. Two hundred dollars ain't shit."

Three days later: "What are you writing down?" Sara asked Amelia as they entered Interfaith Hospital.

It was the day Amelia told Sara she wouldn't get paid if Amelia couldn't meet her brother. Sara had visibly needed to contain herself from screaming or getting violent. A shot cop had been rushed to Interfaith, so there were television crews and people yelling at each other and homeless people in the waiting room refusing to take their medicine so they were chained to hospital beds, and Sara didn't recognize anyone to ask what room Andy had been moved to.

"Just about what it all looks like. How everyone gets treated. No one gets treated like this in Manhattan hospitals."

"You mean white-people Manhattan hospitals."

"I don't know. I guess," Amelia said.

"Don't write stuff down in the hospital room," Sara said.

"Okay," Amelia said.

But they didn't end up getting in. There'd been a chemical spill on Andy's floor, so visitors weren't allowed.

Sara lost her mind, seemed to blame Amelia.

"This isn't my fault," Amelia said, breathing heavily like her body was trying to make her cry. She wasn't sad, but the place was. Amelia was feeling as though it might be her fault. Every day, it took courage to meet Sara and face her scorn.

"This never happened when you weren't here," Sara said.

"You're being silly," Amelia said.

"You're the one paying five times minimum wage for me to show you that my life is like shit," Sara says. "I'm not the one who—you know what? Fuck this."

Sara walked off with her back straight. She wore her uniform of black sneakers, black pants, the Nets cap pulled low. Amelia hadn't focused on it the last few days, but from behind, in the hospital waiting room, Sara was scary again.

Amelia stayed at the hospital, asked the facilities manager how often spills like this occurred, and was told there'd been no spill. They were just washing the floor. Disinfecting it.

"Chemical spill? What would that even mean? This is a hospital. We are in New York City. Goddamn," the facilities manager said.

Chapter 57

Daniel had worked it all out. He was out on bail, and from what his lawyer had said, he would be okay. He'd been 100 percent honest about everything with Thela and his lawyer and brother. His brother told him that he'd done right. That he—Daniel's brother—would have used the pistol and not the shotgun, but Daniel had probably wanted to be safe. His brother had even come over to visit for the first time. Thela had seduced Daniel for the first time in as long as he'd allowed himself to remember.

All those jobs that he'd been thinking about doing but wasn't qualified for—they hadn't made any sense. A dental office in Philadelphia? Daniel liked New York. He liked Brooklyn. Thela needed to stay because of her career, which, now that they were talking again, seemed to have some momentum behind it. Daniel was going to teach. High school history if he had his way. He had already filled out the paperwork to be a New York City teaching fellow. He had the advanced degrees. All he needed was certification, and he wanted to teach in a Bed-Stuy school. That made more sense. He had killed someone. He wasn't as cavalier about taking a life as his brother was. He knew that some part of him was going to have to live the rest of his life attempting to make up for what he'd done. Give back for what he'd taken.

Daniel was going to travel with Thela to her gigs when he could. Over the weekends for now, and all summer once he became a teacher. He was going to reconnect with her and with the friends who would still give him the time of day. Start as a teacher and maybe become a principal one day. Make a difference in twenty lives, then maybe a division of kids' lives, then a school, a district? That was the problem with these kids, was his guess. No one to really care about them. A bunch of nice people collecting paychecks. But no sustained interaction with sensible white people who would dedicate years to them. He was willing. They were living in a world divided into us and them. Into poor and rich. Black and white. And he was just one overeducated fuckup, but why not? And if he had the confidence to shoot one of them, he should be able to teach them with confidence—confidence that he was sure their other white teachers lacked. That was another problem he was sure existed. The teachers must fear their students. What kind of starting point was that?

Thela wouldn't want him thinking about why Amelia was out of the house all the time now, and it was none of his business anyway, and things seemed calm.

Thela was working with Daniel about overthinking things less. Ruminating she called it. He had to stop always ruminating. Going into vicious cycles. Entropic cycles. Anyway, he had handed in both his guns to the cops as part of his bail agreement, so it wasn't as though if things got violent he could help. Thela didn't even allow steak knives in the house anymore. Like he was a danger to himself or to her. She said until the trial or until they decided there'd be no trial, which was what his lawyer thought more likely. Daniel's brother thought Thela was going to leave Daniel—that once the knives were locked up, trust didn't enter back into a marriage, but what did he know? Daniel's brother's wife was blond and worked at Deutsche Bank.

Daniel was cooking now, going back and forth from the window to the stovetop, because he couldn't let more than ten minutes pass without looking outside. He didn't like to let five minutes pass without looking outside, and he set his alarm to wake him on the hour every hour at night, so at night he could look out his window to make sure things were calm, but during the day, he liked to look out the window every five minutes if he wasn't doing any activities, and, at the very longest stretch, every ten minutes, if he was doing activities, such as now, when he was cooking. The only exception was during the commutes between six and eight in the morning and around seven in the evening, when, no matter what, he had to be at his window nonstop and everything else took second priority. One of his worries was whether the exterior cameras would be up by the time he took his first trip with Thela to see her perform, or if, God forbid, Aaron didn't let him mount the cameras or if cameras would be a Landmarks Violation of the Historic District, but then he would just dip into their savings to get the really small spy cameras, and he could check what was transpiring on the block on his phone.

So every seven or eight minutes while he was letting his sauce reduce, he went to the window to look both ways and up and down the block and snap a few pictures with his phone and upload those pictures to the cloud for permanent safekeeping. Then he went back to cooking dinner.

He was on one of his breaks when he saw Derek Jupiter Jr., marching up the street to the house two doors down. Jupiter's house. He'd been worried about Derek so was relieved when he saw him, and then surprised when ninety seconds later he came out again and passed Aaron's stairs to bang on Daniel's own door.

"One minute, Derek! Come in, come in," Daniel said.

"How do you know my name?" Derek said, reaching into the back of his pants.

"I've spent hours talking with your father," Daniel said.

"You had no fucking right to shoot Damien," Derek said.

Derek was unhinged. He wasn't at all like his father was, but he was like his father described him as being. Jupiter had been worried his son was becoming violent.

"Come in," Daniel said. "I'll have dinner ready soon. I'm so glad you came."

Derek pulled a gun from behind his back. Pointed it at Daniel.

"What are you doing?" Daniel said. "Put that thing away. After what went on last week? Are you crazy? That's the last thing you should be carrying around. After what happened to your father? I'm going to become a schoolteacher."

"You had no right," Derek said.

"Your father and I—we were friends," Daniel said.

"Fuck!" Derek yelled. "Fuck! Fuck! Fuck! Fuck! Fuck!"

"Derek," Daniel said.

"That was *my* job," Derek said. "You took away *my* responsibility."

"I was scared he was going to hurt the baby," Daniel said. "That boy. That kid who hurt your dad. I was scared of him. He pointed his gun at me. I did what anyone would have done."

"Fuck!" Derek yelled. "What the fuck am I supposed to do now?"

Chapter 58

The doorbell rang at 8 a.m., three hours before Amelia was supposed to meet Sara at her mother's apartment. Amelia had been in the kitchen pouring coffee and now greeted Sara by the front door.

"This isn't working," Sara said, once inside. "Pay me my full amount. The amount you promised. You swore. I still have the check. You promised me that money."

"My baby's upstairs," Amelia said. "Let's not talk here."

After the scene at the hospital, Amelia had been expecting something like this. But she wouldn't know how to explain it to Aaron. Why she was spending time with Sara; why she was paying her. Aaron had taken a few vacation days and had been looking after Simon while Amelia was "out reporting." He'd told Amelia he'd been adoring the days, even though Simon had continued with his silence. He'd told Amelia he'd loved being with the other parents, talking to them about the riots. But that mostly he'd loved being with Simon. Aaron was upstairs with Simon now, plying him into his clothes.

"Your baby? What's he got to do with it?" Sara looked up and around Amelia into the house.

Amelia reached to her pocket to call the police. Sara was

jumping up and down as she'd been that first day with Damien and Mike.

Now Sara hugged herself with her thin, bony arms and started to shake. It was strange for her to wear short sleeves. The cuffs had been gone almost a week.

Amelia hesitated.

The stairs creaked, Simon yelped, Aaron brought him down.

Sara stood taller. Amelia scuttled between Sara and her family. "We have a visitor," Amelia said.

"I see that," Aaron said. "Whom do I have the pleasure?"

Aaron wore gym shorts and a T-shirt, the baby against his chest. "Who is this?" Aaron asked Amelia, again, about Sara in front of Sara.

"I'm Sara," Sara said.

Simon looked at Sara and started screaming, making noise as he hadn't done for two weeks. Except for at the synagogue, he'd been nearly silent since the day.

Now Simon exploded. It was a high-pitch hyperventilating shriek, and Amelia couldn't stand it. This was the first real sign of life in her son in a week, and it was antilife. Simon went glassy-eyed. It was the look a serial killer has as a baby, blank and in pain. He only stopped screaming to gather breath and scream more.

Simon's face was bright red and his hands were white. His turtle pajamas were rumpled and stretched. Amelia feared he was going to burst a blood vessel or worse.

"Baby," Aaron said. "Baby, baby," but it wasn't going to end, and they both knew it, and it was exactly at the frequency meant to break a parent's sanity, so when Sara said, "What's wrong with your kid?" Amelia said, "Get out of my house," as though she meant it—as though she'd never meant anything as much as she meant that, but the baby was still screaming, and this was clearly the chaos that Sara was looking for or felt comfortable in because Sara took this moment to make a stand and said, "Not until I get my money. This deal of yours was fucked from the beginning. And you know it. It's too slow. And I'm no kind of assistant. As soon as I get my cash, I'll leave," and though Aaron was stroking his screaming baby's face, and Simon's tears were pouring from his eyes and into his tiny mouth so now he was choking as well as screaming and gasping for air, Aaron said, "Is this the same girl from . . . What money?" and Amelia said, "Nothing, no money, she was just leaving," but Sara repeated, "As soon as I get my money," and Aaron said, "Get her away from Simon, and Simon will stop crying. Here," handing Simon to Amelia and shooing them both upstairs, and he was right.

Amelia took Simon up to her bedroom and sat with him on her bed.

"Who-oo's my ba-by," Amelia sang. "You're my ba-by—you're my baby, baby. You're my ba-by—you're my baby, baby. You're my ba-by—you're my baby, baby. You're my ba-by—you're my baby, baby. Who's my baby? You're my baby—You are."

Amelia removed Simon's pajamas so Simon was just wearing his diaper and then she crossed her room into his and removed his diaper and tossed it into the diaper bin so he was naked.

She removed her own shirt and bra, and Simon was shivering but not from cold she didn't think but the postcrying shiver of trying to regulate his system and catch his breath. His little fingers were in little fists and his tiny ears were his father's. He was yawning now, relaxing from the physical trauma of howling and choking, and his eyes were waking up.

295

Chapter 59

Three hours later, Aaron opened the bedroom door to see Amelia asleep with her arms around their son. She was delicate and strong. Aaron slipped under the covers behind her. Simon was naked and seemed to have peed a little bit, or maybe it was sweat. Amelia was wearing just her underwear bottoms, so Aaron took off his shirt and pants, and the three of them were in bed together safe.

· · ·

When Amelia woke up, she diapered Simon and brought him back into bed. It was around eight o'clock at night and she was hungry. But Simon yawned and Aaron was still in bed, so she joined them.

Aaron opened his eyes and smiled, which made her smile.

"What happened?" she said.

"It's taken care of," he whispered.

"What happened?" she whispered.

Simon was between them nearly asleep again. He'd need a bottle soon, but he seemed happy for the warmth of his parents.

"Do you think he'll be okay?" he whispered. "Do you think he's going to get over this?" The room was big, but so was the bed, and the shutters were closed. Amelia felt close to Aaron and the baby.

"He was laughing earlier," she whispered, smiling. "Before we fell asleep. It was the most wonderful thing. He looked just like you. And then he was laughing."

"He was laughing?" Aaron whispered, smiling himself.

"What *happened*?" Amelia whispered.

"We went to a bank," Aaron whispered, "and I tore up the check and paid her cash. Fifty grand in cash from my account. More than that, actually. She told me about her brother. Told me about working for you. I think that's great. Great that you're doing serious work. But we have to talk. I have to talk to you. I came home as fast as I could. It's awful what happened to her brother. I wanted to give it to her so she could take care of him. But we need to talk. About me first."

Amelia sat up under the sheet and turned on her bedside lamp. Simon was fully awake now. He looked at his mother. Suddenly Simon was able to look at her like he knew who she was.

"About you? Are you okay? That wasn't yours to do," she said, no longer whispering.

"She told me what happened here, too, that day," he said.

"And you believed her?"

"I want to live better from now on," he said. "I want to live right. I didn't want that money I made. I wanted to give it all to her. I gave it all to her. I don't want it anym—"

"You believed her." Amelia was scared. She'd been caught. She should have told him about the check. "What did she say happened here?"

"She showed me the check. It was your handwriting. And it was something you would do. I think it was wonderful that you did it. I love you. But she can't cash a check like that."

"I know."

"Did you know it at the time?" Aaron said.

"No," Amelia said.

"You made her a promise. It ends it this way. It ends it morally. I love you so much. I think you did wonderfully to pay her to leave," Aaron said. "To protect Simon. It's just money. I wouldn't have thought of that. I would have done something self-defeating or rash. But you did the good thing."

Aaron seemed to understand. Not just to pretend to. But still:

"She blackmailed us." Amelia said. "You shouldn't have paid her."

"It's my money I gave her. You still have the last of your family's money this way. My money was dishonest money. Gambling money. I don't want it anymore. It's money I would have spent at the track."

She deflated. There was more to this, but she didn't know what yet. "Aaron?" she said. He had done something far worse, and he would have forgiven her for anything.

"I gave her the rest of it," he said. "More than just the fifty. I gave her everything. A hundred thirty thousand dollars. I gave her all of it. It was the—"

Far, far worse.

Her intellectual comprehension of what she'd been told didn't match up to her emotional understanding of the man.

She rushed to put on her shirt.

This might be it. This might be the end of everything. She'd thought she was the one who'd done wrong, but it had been him the whole time. Everything she'd known had been going on had actually been going on. Everything she'd feared.

"It was the best feeling," he said. "It was terrific. It felt great. I feel great. I love you so much. But wait. I have to tell you everything. You already know. I know you know. But I have to tell you."

"There's no way you gave away one hundred thirty thousand dollars! And to Sara!" she said. But she wanted to hear the truth, at least. If it was true, she wanted to hear the nonhysterical truth. She didn't want to cry. If her life was over, she wanted to understand why.

The baby. She held the baby. She and Simon were alone now. In the woods, in the city. In Bed-Stuy, New York. She was a pioneer woman crossing the plains in a covered wagon and she was dying. Could she hunt? Would she remember where she'd set the traps? Simon, Simon, Simon, Simon . . .

"That's where I was during the riots," he said. "Not at work. I was at the track. I couldn't help myself. I am sick. It's an addiction. Gambling. Not the risk stuff. Maybe that, too. I don't know."

Aaron reached for her, but she wouldn't go to him. He'd been lying to her forever. For the entire time. She could leave him still. If she wanted to. What if she had never gotten together with him in the first place? If she was still with Kevin. If Simon was Kevin's. Kevin as a father. He would have never gone for the name Simon. He would have demanded Kevin Jr. On weekends, in the park, the three of them. Kevin cooked eggs for the three of them. Rosé for the two of them. The park full of children. Water in Junior's shoes. Kevin wasn't there. Kevin was off having fun. At Balthazar. In Europe. Telling stories just to hear himself laugh. Stories that didn't include her, that didn't include their son.

"But the gambling," he said. "That's real. Lying to you was the worst part. Every day it made me sick. But it's over now. I've already started a program. In Cobble Hill. That's where I've been over the last week, when you've been with Sara. They let me bring Simon. I've started Gamblers Anonymous. I'm going to get better. I want to get married. To combine our money. To combine our lives. I'm going to beat this thing. Because of you. With your help. And the program. A real program. Because you love me. I can do it. My life is mine, my responsibility. That's what I've learned. But I can't do it alone."

Aaron, standing now, turned away toward the stairwell, not to ignore her but to prove that he was speaking to a higher power.

"Stop it," she said.

"And I'm going to be a rabbi again," he said. "Work is just another manifestation of it. My job, I mean. Of gambling. I have to quit. Today. I gave away the money because it was unhealthy money. We're going to start over. Here. In Bed-Stuy."

"Stop! Aaron. Stop talking," she said. "I watched our neighbor die."

Simon, startled, started to cry, but not loudly. Amelia held him with one hand and put the other one over her face.

"I, I—" Aaron said.

"You've gambled," Amelia interrupted. "Okay. You gambled. I saw our neighbor killed. You still think this is all about you. That you can come in here and tell me that your life has been so hard. I know that. It's made my life impossible! You think every day I haven't feared you'd come home and tell me we're penniless? At a certain point, this stops being about you!"

"I gave her the money for us to get married," he said. "For me to get healthy."

"Married?" she said. "Married! We're not getting married. *I* had Simon. *I* was in labor. He lived inside *me* for forty weeks. His body was inside *my* fucking body. *I'm* the one who fed him from my body. *I'm* the one who shot at that fucking girl. I . . . I paid her to leave. I'm taking the chances. I've been paying her to be my source. I've been building up to something. I'm getting closer. Now you want to tell me how you've been thinking, and you have a plan, and it's all going to be different now? This isn't about you. It was never about you. Get over yourself. My life isn't about you. Be there for it, if you can. But my life isn't about you."

Aaron had that look again. Like this was too much for him—like he'd been prepared for anything but this.

"I'm on the cusp of something," Amelia continued. "But Jesus fucking Christ don't tell me you've figured out how I am supposed to be happy. How I'm going to be happy is with Simon. He's safe. And I'm getting my name out there. I'm doing real work now. And," she looked at him.

"You saved us," Aaron said. "I couldn't, and you did. But I don't want you to do it alone anymore. That's what I realized. I can help myself. That will take a burden off you. The important thing is that we survived." He looked at her. They were so close to each other. "Maybe divine providence . . . I can let it exist. Lying to you has been hell. That part of my life is over. I've never felt as good as I felt today after giving away that money. And now, telling you the truth. I feel like I'm floating. Because of you. You've saved me."

She comforted the baby. Their son. Aaron was an asshole. They were the only ones who understood each other.

"I'm going to be a rabbi again. And the program will get me healthy. With you and Simon, and honesty, I can do it."

"Then you shouldn't have given away all your money," she said.

"I can make it work," he said.

"You shouldn't have given away all your money," she said, laughing despite herself. It took all her power not to stroke Aaron's head in the same way they were both stroking Simon's.

"Yes, I should. I did. I am going to be a rabbi again. We're going to get married. I've already joined a program. I'm going to get better. We are going to be so happy."

"You don't even believe in God. Fuck! How did you join a program? How are you going to be a rabbi!" Amelia said, but she was smiling. She thought about her experience in the stairwell on the way up to Sara, and that maybe Aaron was turning toward a truth. Maybe it was the right thing for Aaron to do. Maybe Aaron could feel that truth. Maybe she could, too.

Their life could be about truth. Honesty with each other, and a greater honesty where she could try to begin to better understand the trajectory of her own life. A new life of repentance after shooting at Sara, refusing to cash her check, and paying her to be a source. Amelia could start over just as Aaron could. "Who's going to hire you?" she said.

"Someone will."

"And you'll stick with it? How much does a rabbi make?"

"Enough," Aaron said. "I love you."

"I love you, too," Amelia said. "But all that money you gave away?"

"Does that mean yes?"

"Simon is hungry," Amelia said, smiling.

"Marry me."

"Aaron," she said.

"Marry me," he said.

They were looking at each other now, and instead of always before having seen Aaron in Simon's face, Amelia now saw Simon in Aaron's.

"Amelia, will you marry me?" he said. "Please."

"I don't know. No. No!"

"You don't know? You don't know! Does that mean yes!" Aaron was shaking with joy, which made her shake, too.

"I don't know," she said.

"Will you marry me?" he said, shaking.

"Yes," she said.

"You will?"

Chapter 60

Derek's aunt greeted him at his front door. She was a short woman who'd looked even shorter since the funeral. The gun at the back of his jeans made them too tight.

"Where'd you go?" she said.

He walked past her up to his room. The lights in the house were all off except in the kitchen at the back of the parlor floor. Derek wouldn't go down south to live with her and her fat-man husband in their dark house.

She'd been sleeping in his father's bed.

After ten, fifteen minutes she called up to him, "What do you want for dinner?" He'd hidden the gun, paced around his room, wished he'd gone to the bodega for Heineken instead of coming straight home.

"I'll get it for myself," he called down. He didn't want her touching his food.

He took out books and tried to read but couldn't focus. *Autobiography of Malcolm X* and even *Watchmen* took too much focus. If he did go down south, he would take the gun with him.

"I'll heat up anything!" his aunt shouted from the base of the stairs. "Casserole! Ribs! Chinese! We need to make room in the fridge!"

He could start the grill himself. His father wasn't the only one who could light a grill.

"We need to talk, Derek!" she called. "Over dinner? Chinese food? You like that, right?"

"I'm tired," he said, probably too quietly for her to hear.

Then there she was, at his door. He had put the gun away, thankfully. If she'd seen it she wouldn't even let him live with her.

"Uncle Rick and I talked," she said. One Christmas when Derek was ten, Rick gave him fireworks for New Year's but he wasn't allowed to keep them. "Your dad put you in a good position. We're going to try to rent the house. Maybe even earn money off it. For you. This neighborhood is hot now with all the whites moving in. We were impressed by the funeral. The deputy mayor, the neighbors. That was nice. The house will be here when you come back after you graduate. High school or college. It will be yours."

"Let's talk at dinner," Derek managed.

His aunt went back downstairs. When he heard her back in the kitchen, Derek covered his mouth with his orange pillow, lay facedown in his bed, and screamed. He screamed like a little boy. He screamed like he was vomiting. He screamed so hard into the pillow that his old aunt ran upstairs and found him still screaming and got down over him and hugged his back and stroked his hair.

Derek stopped screaming when he felt her body on his back. He'd hold on to this feeling and use it.

"It's all right, sweet boy. We'll make it through together."

Chapter 61

There's a brown girl in the ring
Tra la la la la
There's a brown girl in the ring
Tra la la la la la
Brown girl in the ring
Tra la la la la
She looks like a sugar in a plum
Plum plum
Show me your motion
Tra la la la la
Come on show me your motion
Tra la la la la la
Show me your motion
Tra la la la la
She looks like a sugar in a plum
Plum plum
Skip across the ocean
Tra la la la la
Skip across the ocean
Tra la la la la la
Skip across the ocean

Tra la la la la
She looks like a sugar in a plum
Plum plum.

I'm too old for those old songs, Mom," Teddy said.

"You don't even like it a little bit? Not even a little bit when I sing those old songs around the house?" Antoinette said. "You can't fool me. I don't believe you. You've been doing your homework and smiling."

Teddy made a show of burying his head deeper into his math textbook, and he put on a serious face. He was sitting at the kitchen fold-up table while Antoinette made chicken Parmesan for their dinner.

"I know you're getting tired of me here in the afternoons," she said, "while you're doing your homework. I'll get another job soon. But I like being home. And the last family I worked with were nice people. It's not right what happened to them, and they deserved better. They are going to suffer for what happened there. And I don't want to bring that suffering into this house. But they were good people, which is why I've told you to pray for them. They sent me a couple weeks' pay even though I was the one who quit them."

"I like when you're home. I'm just saying that I'm too old for those songs you sing to the babies at work."

When Teddy was finished with the problem set, he took off his glasses and rubbed his eyes. He put his glasses back on and closed the textbook, then the notebook, and he made a neat pile and deposited both books into his backpack.

Dinner wasn't for another couple of hours.

He went to the refrigerator, took an apple from the crisper

drawer, and placed the apple on the counter. He wiped down a cutting board, set it beside the apple, removed a knife from the knife block, and wiped the knife down with the same dish towel he'd used to wipe the cutting board, but he'd forgotten to clean the apple, so he laid the knife down on the cutting board, turned the tap on cold, rinsed the apple, wiped it down with a paper towel, held it stem-up on the cutting board, cut it in half, retrieved plastic wrap from the cabinet, wrapped half the apple and returned it to the crisper drawer in the refrigerator, got a small blue plate from the cabinet, and placed the apple skin-side down on the plate. He cored the apple and adjusted the glasses on his face. He returned to the cabinet—the same one with the plastic wrap—reached for a jar of peanut butter, used the same knife he'd cut the apple with to scoop out a chunk of peanut butter and smear it onto the apple on the plate, at which point he used the same paper towel he dried the apple with to scrape the knife clean of excess peanut butter. Teddy threw out the dirty paper towel, rinsed the knife with soap and water, put it in the rack to dry, tore off a second piece of paper towel, which he placed under his plate, and he took the apple on the plate with the paper towel to the kitchen fold-up table and began to eat.

"I'm standing right here in this kitchen," Antoinette said. "I could have made you a snack."

"I'm twelve years old, Mom," Teddy said. "I can do things like that for myself."

Antoinette couldn't help herself. She went to her son and kissed him and hugged him tightly in her arms.

Chapter 62

Everyone sat in a cramped Bronx gymnasium with high school kids sweating in the bleachers. A few beat reporters asked for information relating to the recently murdered police, and then Bratton's press guy called on a few faces he didn't recognize to round off the conference:

"Ta-Nehisi Coates, with *The Atlantic*. A question about how to make police more approachable. There are young black people whom folks on TV are dismissing as thugs and all sorts of other words. These young people live lives of incomprehensible violence. They are regularly jumped by older kids in the neighborhood and beaten by adults. I know this. This is not theory here. I'm telling you about what my daily routine was like when I was growing up in Baltimore. And no one dreams of calling the cops. Because they're scared of police, too. Violence is a product of violence. But people won't tell authorities anything because they think it will lead to more violence. So my question for you, Commissioner Bratton, is how you plan on changing things so kids aren't scared to call adults—in your case, the police—who have the ability to stem the tide of the violence in their lives."

The high school kids politely applauded. Amelia was going

to ask a comparable question and would get her answer now, even if she wasn't called on.

"Well that's perception more than reality," Bratton said. His chest was thick, but he spoke through his nose. "In New York City, the abusive cop is an exception, and we make it our priority to root him out. Come tell us about these attacks you're referring to. We'll book the perpetrators with assault. Put a cop there to make sure it doesn't happen again."

Amelia's hand shot up along with the others.

"Yes, you?" the press guy said, revealing a lake of sweat beneath his armpit.

"Amelia Lehmann, *New York Times*. It's not just violence. Daily public embarrassment is why they don't call the cops. Broken-window policing is why the riots happened. Why a kid murdered my neighbor in my house."

"In your house?" Bratton was in a gray suit, looking a decade younger than his midsixties.

"Yes. The victim's name was Derek Jupiter," Amelia said. "You mentioned him in a speech a few months ago. You met his son. The father was murdered in my house right in front of me. The reason people don't call the police is because they get shamed by the same police officers on a daily basis. The broken-window policing you've staked your reputation on makes it so people endure violence on a daily basis and have nowhere to turn."

"That's not a question," the press guy said.

"Then," Amelia asked the commissioner, "why do you think these riots occurred?"

"Oh—you're the one who wrote that series in the *Times*, aren't you?" Bratton said.

"I am," Amelia said.

"Well good for you. You did a great service to the city. And to that girl, Sara's her name, if I'm not mistaken."

"Thank you, Commissioner," Amelia said.

"I read she's attending private school now? Thriving?"

"Private donors have been very generous to Ms. Hall since my articles," Amelia said.

"And her brother, too?"

"That's right, sir."

"He attacked police, if I remember correctly."

"Your department dropped all charges."

"Thanks to your excellent work," Bratton said. "You must be proud of yourself."

"I am. I mean, her story—and that of Mr. Jupiter—found its way to me," Amelia said, smiling. She couldn't suppress the smile. She didn't need to.

"You are becoming quite well known as well," Bratton said.

"Thank you, sir," Amelia said. "Now my question, sir. If not because of a culture of embarrassment and fear perpetrated by your department, why do you believe these riots occurred?"

"Because of individuals within the community who chose violence. With all due respect to you, and especially to Mr. Jupiter, who was an upstanding man, an individual decided to take a gun to your house, point it at your neighbor, and shoot him. Maybe that individual did have an interaction with the police that was unsettling. And I agree that training could lessen the tension in those interactions. We're in the process of reimplementing that training. Also, of putting more African-American officers on the street. And we've just received a federal grant for body cameras. But are you insinuating that it wasn't his fault that he picked up an illegal weapon, brought it to your home, and killed an innocent man? You're telling me that is my department's fault?"

"I'm telling you," Amelia said, "that you are focusing so much on punishing people for the way they choose to live their lives—issues regarding drugs, child support, school violations, jumping turnstiles—that they won't report real violence. It wasn't just one individual who acted out after an 'unsettling' interaction with the police. *Thousands* rioted. Their lives are saturated in violence, so when they get angry, they act violently. It's a bad situation that you are making worse."

The high school kids applauded politely again.

"Do you have a question?" the press guy said.

"Yes. Do you feel," Amelia said, "as the top cop in the city, and as someone positioning himself for potential higher office, that you bear some responsibility for all these deaths that came under your watch? That you will revisit the police methodology that makes these kids' lives more violent and antagonistic?"

"To be honest, no, I don't. I feel as though I've saved lives. We've done our best under the circumstances. And I will continue to put the cops on the dots. To make sure we're where we need to be. To foster community relations. To decrease violence. To punish the perpetrators. And to do our best to ensure nothing like this ever happens again."

"Ever happens again?" Amelia said. "Your cops are—"

"That's enough," the press guy said.

"It's fine. Please continue," Bratton said.

"Your cops are getting shot," Amelia said. "Another two this week. Thirty since the riots? It is happening. And as much as I blame that kid who shot Mr. Jupiter. As much as I blame him every night I try to go to sleep, and I fear him—even though he's shot dead, too—I fear *you* more. I fear that you and your tactics are making more and more of him. And that my son will be shot in Bed-Stuy by someone like him. Or that because your officers now believe their lives are in danger in my neighborhood, they won't come when real help is needed. It's your job to keep us safe, and I don't believe you're doing it. Can you tell me that you're changing policing so you're not creating any more angry, disenfranchised kids?"

"We are doing our best to catch the perpetrators and bring them to justice. And we're doing our best to keep Bed-Stuy safe for you and your son from people like him."

"Please tell me that you're not just making them angrier," Amelia said.

"Them? They are individuals, Ms. Lehmann. Individuals who don't need to choose violence. I'm doing everything I can do to keep this city safe."

The high school kids applauded politely.

"You are creating criminals," Amelia said.

The press guy stood and whispered something to the commissioner. Bratton whispered something back.

Bratton leaned into the microphones. "We are protecting the good people of New York City from criminals. I'm like a doctor. I diagnose a problem, and I go through the possible cures. What medicines might treat the disease. In this case, local street policing combined with . . ."

But Amelia had stopped listening. She'd come to get a quotation from the police commissioner for her book, not to win an argument. She'd calm down in time, and she and Aaron were planning on mashing up a banana for Simon that night before bed.

"Ms. Lehmann?"

"Yes?" Amelia said.

"I want to publically invite you to join my advisory commission on police-community relations. As a respected public intellectual, a resident of Bed-Stuy, and a friend of Mr. Jupiter's and Sara's, you'd be an invaluable advisor to the department on these issues. Do you accept?"

The high school kids leaned forward.

Amelia's heat beat faster. She felt the kids behind her, and Commissioner Bratton in front of her, and the real journalists to her side. She knew she shouldn't accept. She wasn't qualified, and Bratton was trying to co-opt her. But her one story had found her. The fact that she was at the center of it—that it had occurred in her home—meant the *Times* hadn't been able to turn it down. But even if her book was successful, she didn't know how she'd ever find another story like this one. Bratton's offer could be a stepping-stone to real power. She didn't want to be the only one who turned down an opportunity. She didn't want to be the sucker who was given a seat at the table and let some impossible-to-articulate principle stand in the way.

"I do," Amelia found herself saying, the world opening up before her. She could come to know the man. Be a voice for her neighbors and her community. It could help her write her book.

"No more questions," the press guy said, wiping his brow. "It's too goddamn hot in here to continue."

The high school kids applauded politely and stood up to stretch out their legs.

Chapter 63

Aaron sat in the office. The molding had been removed, along with the stained-glass window. The contractor said irreparable damage had been done. The mahogany, carved to look like columns holding up a frieze, had been cracked when the girl had swung the glider into the window. The upper corners, into which had been carved little torches surrounded by wreaths, could no longer remain. The windows were now double paned with argon gas inside. They'd keep out more noise and keep in more heat. It was a more practical room now, better for working, Amelia said. She was in the TV room at the moment, singing to Simon.

Aaron was watching them live on the cracked computer screen. He had just finished watching Antoinette with Simon from the month before. He limited himself to one viewing per day. Antoinette burying Simon in a tomb of Scripture—the giant Mishnah below him, various Tanakh on all sides—and Aaron's own voice coming in faintly from the street. Empowering Antoinette to perform her insane ritual. It was the stuff of three thousand years before. Aaron would watch it every day for the rest of his life to understand it. It was the day that changed everything. Maybe it was the power of God on-screen. It was Aaron's voice. He could hear his tone, if not the words, and he was able to follow the emotions. And then Amelia rushing Sara down the stairs. All on the screen. The computer functioned, even though the screen was cracked in half with a few large lines that quaked from the main one, and a dozen cracks splintered out from there. The upper left quarter of the screen was mostly clear. In the present, Simon was on Amelia's lap. Simon's back was to the camera, Amelia was facing forward. The back of Simon's head obscured Amelia's face.

Aaron hadn't spoken to his father in weeks, though his father had called every day and left messages. Aaron hadn't wanted to lie to his father, and he hadn't wanted to worry him with the truth. He also wanted to show Amelia that his life was his own. Even if it made his father suffer, he would wait a week, each week, to respond to his calls. Though Aaron planned, at the end of this week, to call his father and tell him about the engagement and the wedding that they all would plan together. It would be small, only what they could afford.

On the computer screen in front of Aaron, Simon was crying, but like a normal baby cries. And when Amelia rocked Simon, Simon quieted. It was funny how eating and sleeping and all the things that mattered in a baby had nothing to do with kindness, intelligence, hard work, and everything else that defined an adult.

Aaron watched his beautiful, famous fiancée and his healthy baby boy on the cracked computer screen while he tinkered with his rabbinical résumé. Life wasn't perfect, but they had started sleeping together again. And with a new intensity. As if she was showing him he belonged in the house, with her, in this new life. He had a long list of responsibilities ahead of him. He had to find and keep a job as a rabbi; he had to build up some kind of faith or not let the lack of faith ruin him; he had to stay with Gamblers

Anonymous and keep himself away from any kind of gaming (though he had to head back to the track to claim his winnings from the fifth race at Belmont on that awful day); he had to pay the mortgage; and then he and Amelia had to maintain their love for each other forever. But life was good, or at least it felt better now than it had been a month before.

Chapter 64

New York Post
OPINION

POST EXCLUSIVE:

New York Times Pays and Threatens Sources

By Sara Hall

You already know about my life. I'm the girl from last year's
New York Times series on the Bed-Stuy riots. You know
my house smells of mint fresheners, my kitchen table is
broken, I dropped out of high school, and my tenth-grade
teacher said I had potential. You know I drink orange soda
flat because my mother prefers soda like that so she leaves
the caps off the bottles in the refrigerator. You know I wear
black and I'm gay but I haven't had a girlfriend in months
because I don't want to.

What you don't know is that the writer, Amelia Lehmann, paid me to tell her these things. She paid me cash,
so I don't have receipts, but every time she paid me I went
home and had my neighbor take a picture of the cash. One
time, I had my neighbor take a picture of Amelia Lehmann

handing me the cash, which is the photo under this article. This was after Amelia Lehmann wrote me a check for fifty thousand dollars that I couldn't cash. Also, Amelia Lehmann shot at me with a pistol when I was in her house. She tried to kill me. What if she'd hit me? What if she'd killed me? Would she be famous then?

I've wanted to write this since day one, since I saw how easy it is to be a writer. I'm writing this now because Amelia Lehmann can't affect me anymore. People aren't giving me donations anymore, anyway. I'm going to graduate high school next year, and my tuition has already been paid. I'm doing well in school, and they say they won't kick me out no matter what. And my brother is never going to fully recover, no matter how much physical therapy he gets. His life is ruined no matter what.

I get to graduate from private school, and that's good. I'm going to be a lawyer. My new teacher, Mr. Keating, says I'm good at school, and he says law school is just more school, so I'll be good at that, too, after college. But my brother is never going to recover. My mother has been depressed since she spent five months in jail. She got fired and can't get another job. I'm going to need to spend all the donations on a new apartment for her. Mr. Jupiter is dead. And Amelia Lehmann is famous. I see her on TV talking about black people.

When I'm a lawyer I'm going to make sure people like Amelia Lehmann can't get away with the crimes they commit. My brother and mother got punished for hitting cops. I get that. Amelia Lehmann should get punished, too, for shooting at me and paying me to be a source for her story.

It hasn't been fair that everyone knew everything about me, and no one knew anything about Amelia Lehmann. They're not good people, her and her husband. They use people. They care about themselves and nobody else.

Chapter 65

Amelia looked out the parlor window. Snow had been plowed into giant blackening hills divided by stomped-out pedestrian valleys of newspapers and ice.

She'd cried when she'd first seen the article.

"I just heard," Aaron said. "I just saw the op-ed, I mean. I came home right away. Why didn't you call me?"

Aaron paid Sara one hundred thirty grand and she condemned him in the tabloids.

"You gave that speech," Amelia said, nodding to the stoop. She meant she'd fallen in love with him again that day.

"Uh-oh!" Simon said, "Uh-oh!" A mess of blocks scattered around him. The nanny heated chicken nuggets in the kitchen. She had dressed Simon head to toe in Brooklyn Nets gear. Socks, shorts, shirt, two wristbands.

Ice thickened the iron bars between the windows and street. Her editor at the *Times* had left a message.

What I keep coming back to—and Joan was practically hissing here—*is why didn't you tell me you* paid *your source?*

Amelia had felt her cheeks go hot with shame as she listened to the voice mail. But come on—if she had disclosed paying Sara, the *Times* would never have run the piece, and Amelia wouldn't have gotten the book deal. She had no authority to write about Bed-Stuy without Sara as the hook.

And the book itself was everything Amelia had dreamed it could be. It was about Sara, sure, but it was also about her brother and mother, and case studies of almost a hundred years of police violence, from the waning days of Tammany Hall through the present. It was about how Bed-Stuy residents reacted again and again to reassert their own authority and stand up to those in power. The book gave shape to what had previously been formless to Amelia, and it did so through the stories of individual lives. She'd done research, conducted interviews, spoke to cops and her neighbors, and, along the way, she illuminated the inequities of redlining, bail, stop and frisk, and gentrification, which she illustrated through her own family's arrival in Bed-Stuy. She was proud of what she'd written, and she'd made friends in the process. In the six months since finalizing the manuscript, she'd had dozens of neighbors over. Simon had played with the children of police officers and sanitation workers, and Amelia had established herself as a regular on NPR and MSNBC. So yes: she'd paid one source in the beginning. But who hadn't bent the rules? She'd gotten here. No matter the censure, she finally felt like she belonged.

Still, she couldn't—

"Amelia," Aaron said. "It will be okay."

"Do you feel his body here sometimes?" Amelia said. "Because I don't. I can remember it. But the feel of it is completely gone. I'm trying to make myself remember the feel of it. But I can't. I can picture what he looked like, but not what it felt like." Her career had been made on the man murdered in her foyer. She owed it to him to remember what it felt like. That bothered her.

And maybe she hadn't needed to shoot at Sara. She sometimes wished that away.

Aaron hugged her. He'd been staying late at funerals, at bar mitzvahs, at Torah study. He was counseling grieving family members and giving Amelia time to prepare for media spots and Bratton meetings.

"*The New York Post*," he said "won't be enough to tarnish the reputation you've built over this last year and a half."

Did Joan think it would it have been better for Sara if Amelia hadn't paid her? At least this way Sara benefited, too. If Amelia hadn't paid, would the information have been more valuable to the readers? Would it have been more accurate?

"Uh-oh!" Simon said. "Uh-oh!"

She—they—could have another baby. A brother or sister for Simon. Amelia's roots would grow deeper still, take hold in the cement beneath her.

"Ames?" Aaron said. "Did you hear me? This isn't enough to destroy everything."

"I spoke to my agent"—Amelia swallowed—"who says we couldn't have planned it better if I'd written Sara's article myself. The book will be out in a few weeks, and this will be all the publicity we need. I'm going to be everywhere."

The wind battered the windows.

"Wait—" Aaron said. "What about the allegations? Or not allegations—you did shoot at her, right? Will there be charges? Have you spoken to Bratton's people yet?"

Bratton had left her a message, too. The commissioner himself. He wanted her to respond aggressively to the article. *For all you've done for her. You shot at her because she invaded your home. And she's* blaming *you for paying her. She isn't making sense. She should be thanking you the rest of her life. You and Aaron gave her everything she has. We'll call a press conference. Just say the word.* Amelia was powerful now. But Bratton's tone made her feel more shame than the message from her editor at the *Times* had.

"He wants me to respond," Amelia said, "but as long as he's not too close to me on this it doesn't matter to him. I'm not going to say anything. I'll let the book speak for itself."

But her book could never tell the real story. With Simon paralyzed downstairs and Amelia uncertain she'd ever see Aaron again. It was just her and Sara in that room, and Amelia telling herself she could do it, *she had to do it,* she had to do whatever was necessary. She had to take care of her baby and herself. So she did. When Sara started to swing that metal rod at her, she shot. Sara was going to hurt her. Sara would have killed her. So Amelia reacted. She was the hero of the story. Even if nothing was clean or easy or perfectly comprehensible, Amelia was the hero of this story, and she couldn't let herself forget it.

"Well I'll be here with you," Aaron said.

Amelia smiled. She leaned forward and let the wind try to unmoor her. She dared it to.

Acknowledgments

Thank you to Mom and Dad for raising me in the most loving, caring, life-affirming way. Thank you to Jamie for being the best sister and friend.

Thank you to Trena Keating, America's best agent. Without your editorial guidance, publishing-industry wisdom, and all-purpose kindness, I'd be lost. And thank you to everyone at Atria, especially my editor, Sarah Cantin. That someone so brilliant, gracious, and skilled exists in one person is a miracle.

Thank you to John Paul Carillo for improving every sentence in this novel, to Andrew Palmer for adding a few of his own, and to Rafael Yglesias for generously inducting me into the life of the writer.

Thank you to Rod Keating and all my teachers at Grace Church School for instilling in me the love of books, and doubly thank you for welcoming me back and providing such wonderful students and colleagues. Thank you to Lisa Stifler, Catherine Gillot, and my other inspiring teachers at Dalton; to the English and writing departments at Columbia; and to Alice McDermott, Jean McGarry, and all my brilliant teachers and classmates at the Johns Hopkins Writing Seminars. Thank you to everyone at Lake Owego. And thank you to my friends and neighbors in Bed-Stuy for everything.

ACKNOWLEDGMENTS

Thank you to Eli. My house—and life—would fall apart without you.

And of course, to Alex, the best thing ever to happen to me. And to Owen and Sam, more than the best. I love you three the world.